Bully Boy

This book is a work of fiction. Any resemblance to actual events or persons, living or dead, is entirely coincidental.

"Bully Boy," by Tom Wade. ISBN 978-1-63868-020-8 (softcover); 978-1-63868-021-5 (hardcover); 978-1-63868-022-2 (electronic).

Published 2021 by Virtualbookworm.com Publishing Inc., P.O. Box 9949, College Station, TX 77842, US.

This is for the good kids

PART ONE

THE SCHOOL BUILDING OF BRICK AND GLASS STOOD WAITING as the morning arrived bright, blue and warm, and seemingly safe. Henry Wilton viewed this scene uneasily from the window of his bus as it rumbled to a stop, and anxiousness gripped him like it usually did on the first day of school. Henry shook his head, as he pondered another long school year. He felt alone in his own desperation. A kid bumped him. "C'mon, Wilty, let's go." As Henry stepped onto the sidewalk, the doors slammed shut on his heels and the bus roared away, as if, he thought, it wanted to get out of there and leave him to his fate.

"Yeah, let's go," he said to himself, and he stepped through the doors along with everyone else.

Okay now, watch where they are, he thought.

Henry scanned the bustling hallways, light gleaming off the newly polished floors. He made his way through the maze of students and all the spirited chatting and the clanging of blue and grey lockers that lined the walls as far as he could see. Hearing so many conversations, as various as backpack shapes and colors, he bristled at everyone so happy and energetic, which he could not be. From his locker, he perused the animated scene with the jaundiced eye of a fifteen-year-old.

"Chloe," Sharonda called out. "We gotta get to the aud. C'mon."

"I'm coming. I'm coming."

"What's in the auditorium?" Henry stopped to ask Sharonda.

"Soccer meeting," she replied.

"Uh-huh. Have a good summer?"

She shrugged. "Kinda boring." She pulled her large, black equipment bag onto her shoulder.

Chloe walked up to them.

"Yeah, same here," Henry said. "Okay, soccer girls. Have fun."

"Thanks, non-athlete," Chloe said.

Henry smiled. "And happy to be one."

The girls left him and Henry checked the hall again for kids he didn't particularly want to see. He, and kids like him, the oppressed in his mind, weren't usually bothered too much by enemies during the first week. He figured kids were generally in a good mood and kept to themselves.

But he followed protocol anyway and skillfully evaded and avoided those who pestered him, hustling up to a group of other kids to hide behind or slinking around a corner to disappear. That was his first rule: Always look down the hallway to see where they are. He hated doing it. Just to keep the peace, he had told himself, at least for now. He had heard about the mouse that learns early in life that everything is its enemy and scurries to hide. He swore over the summer that mouse would die.

In his classes, avoidance was pointless, so Henry obeyed his other rule to never enter a classroom without the teacher already there. He impatiently loitered in the corridor next to the door, staring into his phone.

By Friday, relieved that nothing nasty had happened, Henry wondered if all the years of ignoring and avoiding his enemies so they'd go away had paid off. Maybe this was the year, he thought. Wishful thinking came easy to him, always hoping things would "get better," stringing him along mercilessly day after day.

Then he caught Billy eyeing him after leaving class. Instantly, he slowed down and futilely searched for escape.

"Shit," he said, berating himself for being stupidly upbeat and relaxed, violating his first rule.

"Hey, Wilty," Billy said, stepping in front of him.

Henry's anxious heart quickened.

"How was summer?"

Henry sighed, not looking up into Billy's eyes. "Good. Yours?"

"Not bad. We never hung out."

Henry knew Billy cared nothing about him or his summer. He tried to get around, but Billy side-stepped to stop him.

"What's the rush, buddy?" Billy said, looking Henry up and down. Billy stood lanky and lean, with stringy black hair and a thin, angular face. Bulging veins snaked through his sinewy arms. Henry, shorter, had a slimmer build that intimidated no one and no veins showing at all.

Henry blinked with impatience. *C'mon, idiot, do something.*

"I gotta go. Out of the way."

Frank sauntered up to them.

"Wilton giving you a problem again?" he asked.

"I think he is."

"C'mon, Billy. You were told last year not to do this."

"Mmm...I don't remember that."

"Outta the way."

Billy stepped forward and pressed his hands against the lockers, stiff arms on both sides of Henry, as a boy would do to a girl.

"Say please."

Henry drew back from Billy's sour breath.

"Say the magic word."

Henry stood uncontrollably petrified. *Just go ahead and do it this time.*

"Alright. Please."

"There you go. Finally showing some respect. You gonna behave better now? You got us into trouble last year. Don't do it again."

Billy moved aside, allowing Henry to go along, and then pushed his leg out. Henry tripped and fell to his knees, his backpack slinging against his head as his face puckered in pain.

"Oops," Billy said, turning to walk off with Frank.

"Jerk," Henry said rashly under his breath, standing up.

"What did you call me?"

"Nothing," Henry said. He felt his heart skip a few beats.

Billy peered around him and placed his arm on Henry's shoulder.

"You were told last year not to call kids names. I'll let it slide one last time." Billy rubbed the curve of Henry's ear. "Since you're not much of a man, you don't want to get hurt."

Frank, shorter and beefier than Billy and with a large, protruding stomach, calmly leaned against the lockers next to Henry with a faint smile.

A crowd had gathered, like on a sidewalk. A few of the kids smiled, while others walked away shaking their heads, as if they had seen this show before.

"C'mon, Wilton, do something," someone said.

"What are you gonna do?" Billy said. "Here's another chance for ya."

"Teacher," Frank said.

Billy pulled back and stood easy. "Keep your mouth shut, Wilton."

"Alright, what's going on?" Mr. Johnson demanded, pushing his stocky frame between the boys.

"Nothing," Billy said.

Johnson, head football coach and history teacher, checked both kids for injuries.

"Alright, move out," he told Billy.

"I didn't do anything. I just had a word with him," he said, lifting and rolling his shoulders and walking away with Frank.

Henry let out a nervous breath.

"What happened?" the teacher asked.

"He got in my way again," Henry said, petulantly. "Then he tripped me."

"I did not," Billy called back. "He's lying. He always lies."

Everyone else walked away silently.

"I brought this up last year."

"I'll talk to him," Mr. Johnson said. "Just try to avoid him."

"I do. He comes after me. You can ask these kids."

"Okay. I'll look into this for you."

Johnson slipped away, as though he had more pressing concerns, Henry thought.

Other kids walked by, not looking at Henry. At his locker, laden with embarrassment, he wanted to cry—or die—as he placed some books and his phone inside the dark space.

With a suddenness that shocked him, his face scraped across the steel edges of the open locker. He dropped back as Jeremy smiled at him, hurrying away. Henry quickly turned to see who else might attack him, dabbing at his face for blood that wasn't there.

Two girls passed by. "Wilty," one of them said with a little smile, "you okay?"

He gathered himself for a moment and finally got to class, checking his burning red cheeks again for blood as he sat down. He heard laughing behind him.

"Hi, Wilty," one of them said with a curling smile.

"Wilty," another added, cackling at the name.

Henry glared.

"Don't look at me that way, Wilton."

Henry turned back and huddled in his seat. He seethed with an anger he could not release.

At home that night, after dinner with his parents, and lying about how his day went, Henry lay on his bed with his hands behind his head. All summer he had planned what to do if one more kid messed with him. Now that it had happened, the choice of doing something or not was gone.

You've done everything you were told to do. You've given everyone every chance in the world to do better. Be better.

7

But they won't. You know they won't. All the lies and meanness.

"I will not live like this anymore," he said aloud.

Something had to change fast, he knew. But he had told himself that over and over for years, trying to convince himself. His mouth quivered as he again faced the awful truth: He was the only one who could put an end to the pain and shame of his weakness.

You have to now, moron. You're hiding days are over.

He sat up.

"How are you gonna do it?" he whispered. "You're too scared. You can't move. You can't think. You just stood there and let Billy do what he wanted." He shook his head. "You can't do that anymore, or you may as well give up and die."

His cat jumped up next to him, as was her habit. She sniffed at his face and pressed her paws into him as though testing how comfortable he would be. Her claws pierced the skin under his jeans, but he didn't mind. She finally settled for a space next to him. Henry moved onto his side and playfully pushed her and she swatted back.

"It's...it's crazy. I just can't stop this...this fear. It just totally freezes me. What am I going to do, cat?" He sighed tiredly, then laid his face in his hands.

Henry spent the weekend sequestered in his room, pushing through homework and playing games on his computer. His father, John, pulled him out to help put summer furniture back into the shed, then had him mow the lawn. His sullen silence prompted Elaine, his mother, to ask him what was wrong. He replied with the usual "Nothing." He always kept silent about his school issues, believing he had to handle them himself. He couldn't expose his shameful weakness to her.

On Sunday evening, anxiety tightened in the pit of his stomach like it always had, every day since the fifth grade, when he first remembered being scared. He sat on the edge of the bed with arms folded across his stomach, rocking

8

himself. Later, he could not sleep. His heart thumped as he dreaded the week ahead and what he had to do. He wiped his eyes. His lower lip drooped and he shook his head slowly, his sign of futility.

What're you gonna do? Think.

When he thought about stopping these kids, fighting back, anxiousness welled up. Henry hated that awful feeling, a foreboding sensation of failure he could not stop.

"Either do it or die. But, in the end, that's what you want. You want to die. You want peace."

After lying quietly for a while, Henry pulled open the drawer of his bedside table and took out a small, spiral-bound notebook. He opened the cover and flipped through several pages until he came to a blank page and wrote in it everything that had occurred that day. He looked down into the drawer at other past notebooks. Since the seventh grade, he had written down all the incidents, all the abuse, that had happened to him in school. As he recorded them, a corner of his mouth turned up in a rueful smile. He knew he was right all along—that nothing the adults had told him to do to avoid the bullies worked.

He closed his eyes and imagined everyone reading them.

"Without this, you have no proof. Especially if you die."

Henry dropped the notebook into the drawer and shut off the light. He turned over onto his side and huddled as if against the cold, and finally fell asleep.

On Monday, Henry walked into school. Other kids quickly passed by him and around him, as though he walked in slow motion. He hated the awful sensation of being out of step with his classmates, separate from them, insignificant, as though he walked among them invisible, in another dimension, yet there with them. Meandering through the crowded, noisy hallway, conversations flew around him but never included him.

In first block, the teacher's desk stood vacant, so he reluctantly waited by the door.

You can't do this anymore, guy.

Mrs. Tomkins passed him with her typical wide gait, her long brown hair bouncing behind her.

"Alright, everyone, find your seats," she said breathlessly, dropping papers and briefcase on her desk. "Let's go."

Henry sat down in one of the seven rows of arm desks. Windows lined a side wall, offering a view of the back of the school. Leafy trees swayed in a stiff, late summer breeze, depressing Henry over the waning season and the challenging school year ahead. He listened to morning announcements from the vice principal.

Later in science class, Mr. Bronner stepped out for a moment, leaving the class open to mischief. Henry perked up at the possible danger. He could leave the room until Bronner got back, which he had done several times before. But this time, he decided not to and quietly read.

"Wilton, give me a piece of paper," Derrick said, sidling up to him.

"Leave me alone, Derrick."

"Fuckin' just give me one, will ya?" Derrick said as he looked back at his friends.

Henry sighed and shook his head, opened his notebook and handed him the paper. Derrick put it down on the desk, grabbed Henry's pen, wrote "you suck" on it and put it in front of Henry. Then he walked back to his friends.

"Mature," Henry said with habitual resignation.

A moment after Henry closed his notebook, a blow to the back of his head stunned him. He lolled forward onto a forearm as though his head had loosened on his neck. He took a long minute as the shock wore off. He heard nothing in the classroom.

C'mon, get up. Get up.

Dazed, Henry lifted himself up and he blinked quickly as his senses returned. The blunt thud got everyone's attention. Derrick casually threw a book onto the desk next to him.

The kid sitting there, Jose, took the book and slid it into his backpack.

"Welcome back to school, Wilty," Derrick said.

While some of the kids frowned and turned away, others sickened Henry with their grins.

"You okay, buddy? You don't look too good."

Derrick stood a few inches taller than Henry. He had short, brown hair and dark eyes. Henry now faced up to another test, but felt like passing out instead. He attempted toughness, flushed with a mix of fear and rage.

"Don't…. don't hit me again," Henry forced out.

"Ooooo. Listen to this," Derrick replied. "Grow a pair over the summer?"

"He doesn't have a pair of anything," Pam chuckled, prompting a few laughs.

Bronner walked back in. "Okay, let's get started. What's going on here? Problem?"

Henry, relieved the teacher had come back in, sat down first and said nothing.

Class went on slowly for Henry. He rubbed the back of his head that now throbbed, trying hard not to cry, while Derrick sat at ease. At the end of class, the kids started filing out of the room.

C'mon, this is it. You can't let this go.

Henry showed Bronner the paper.

"This is what Derrick wrote," Henry said, his voice hoarse, fearful of his own boldness. "He hit me in the head with a book. They all saw it."

Bronner read it and frowned.

"Derrick, come over here."

Derrick sauntered over.

"Did you hit him?" he asked.

Derrick growled. "No."

Bronner sighed impatiently. "No more of this, you understand?" he demanded of both kids.

"Hey, this isn't my doing," Henry replied with a rising voice. His body slightly shook. "Forget the paper. He attacked me. And…and I want something done about it."

Henry noticed surprise on Bronner's face at his sudden demand. Derrick's as well.

"Alright, I'll talk to these kids in private. I'll let you know."

"Oh, you know Wilton always lies," Derrick said. "I would never do something like that anyway."

Henry sighed. Derrick walked out.

"Why would I make this up?" Henry said.

"I didn't see it, so I can't comment," Bronner said. "If you think it's necessary, you can report it to the Office," Bronner said. "When I go down there today, I'll report your accusation."

Bronner handed the paper back to Henry.

"Please tell Derrick never to come near me again."

He stared at Bronner.

"Alright, I'll tell him," Bronner replied, but not very convincingly, Henry felt.

Henry stomped out.

In the hallway, Donny called out to Henry.

"Hey, Wilty, you suck." Laughter.

Mrs. Hernandez stood at her door. She glanced at Donny and then at Henry as he walked by.

She stepped forward. "Boys, no more of that talk," she called out.

In his next class, Henry rubbed the back of his head, wondering why his eyes didn't pop out when he was struck. His insides quivered like jelly, and he hated that the class would see his red-hot face.

"Hey, Wilton."

"How's your head?"

"It hurts," Henry murmured.

"What happened now?" asked Robin, who sat near Henry in the next aisle.

"Derrick wound up and slammed him with a book," Tom said.

"What do you expect from the home run king?" another kid added.

Everyone chuckled. Robin shook her head pathetically. "Wilton, your head does look like a baseball."

"Going to take it to the Office?" Jose asked.

"Why don't both of you tell Bronner you saw it?" Henry asked.

"Hey, it's your problem, not ours," Jose said.

"You know the Office will slap him on the wrist and let him go," Tom added.

Henry bit the inside of his lip until he tasted blood, and he tolerated a slight headache for the rest of the day.

That evening, he sat on his bed reading history with his arms folded tightly to his chest, analyzing the day. He believed he could be proud of standing up to Derrick and demanding that the teacher do something, more than he would have done just a year ago. The moment frightened him and he withstood it, a big step forward. But, in the end, it wasn't enough. His attacker won.

They always win.

Henry obsessively relived what had happened after a bad day, why it had happened, and what he could have done better. Only then, in the comfort and confinement of his room, did new scenarios flash through his mind, and he always got angry at his inability to think of them at the time. The fear paralyzed him, turning his conscious mind to stone. He groaned at all the missed chances of the past.

"You should have watched Derrick, for Christ sake. You know what he is. You can't keep your back to him."

Rage surged inside and he slapped the textbook off his lap, the pages rattling in flight.

"C'mon, idiot," he whispered fiercely, "you have to start thinking." His fingers curled in frustration. "You're never going to stop them if you can't think. Or you're going to be a meek forever."

But the thought of hitting someone, actual fighting, nauseated Henry, and he couldn't bring himself to do it. So he learned to keep his mouth shut or his backtalk would get him in trouble, and he quashed the boiling temper inside, weakening the shaky pride he desperately needed to keep.

He let out another heavy sigh and rested his head against the wall. "Ouch." He softly rubbed the bump that had blossomed, one of many he received over the years, and wondered if he had a fractured skull. There was no headache. He poked a finger in his ear to check for blood that wasn't there and picked the textbook off the floor.

Henry awoke groggy and tense the next day, his stomach gurgling. In school, he passed Johnson standing at his door.

"I was wondering if you spoke to Billy."

"No, I haven't seen him."

"You haven't seen him?" Henry said nervously.

"That's correct, Wilton," Johnson said sternly, as if trying halt any further questions.

"Can you just tell him to stay away from me, please? He's in school today."

"I can't guarantee that he'll do that, but I'll try."

"You have to guarantee it," Henry blurted.

What are you doing?

Johnson looked at him, surprised.

"I don't have to do anything, Wilton."

"Just tell him to stay away from me. That shouldn't be hard for him to do."

Johnson grimaced. "I don't think that's the best way to handle the problem. It would help if you talk to him yourself and apologize for calling him a name."

"Shouldn't he apologize for attacking me?"

"Well, he didn't quite attack you, Wilton."

"Please tell him to steer clear of me," he said.

"I will. But this is something you should do yourself. Be respectful to him and he will likely back off. Okay?"

"Sure," Henry answered, again having to push a teacher to do something.

Nothing changes. Making me do everything.

At lunch, he got himself a tray of food and settled himself among his friends.

"You know what's going on in gym today?" Henry asked.

George shrugged. "I think its hoops."

Henry shook his head. "I miss dodgeball."

Kam smiled. "Too dangerous for us."

Henry nodded. "Yeah, more than football."

They laughed. George finished eating quickly.

"Still hungry?" Henry asked him.

"Starving."

"I'm not, so have mine." Henry handed the tray to George, who took it gladly.

"All that lacrosse and workouts," Kam said.

George shook his head. "I can't eat enough."

"Got chess today?" Henry asked Kam.

"Tomorrow night," Kam said. "Got a school council meeting tonight."

"Who you playing?"

"This senior kid. He's really good."

"Let's play again sometime," Henry said. "I think I can beat you."

Kam snorted. "In your dreams."

Kids milled around their table as lively conversations bounced off the walls of bright, multi-colored tiles arranged in mosaics of school scenes and happy kids. Three one-word signs hung from the ceiling: Respect, Diversity, Knowledge. The first sign amused Henry, since he didn't see much of it in his school. Through the large windows at one end of the room, cars moved around the parking lot bordered by green lawn and a stand of hourglass fir trees.

"Did you get into trouble with Bronner?" Sharonda asked, while applying some lipstick.

"No. He just said he'd check into it."

"Got whacked, I hear," George said.

"Yeah," Henry answered feeling the back of his head. "He really nailed me. Thought my skull cracked. But nothing happened to him."

"Nothing ever will," Kam said as he scooped food into his mouth.

"We have to do something," Henry muttered. "We can't let this go on anymore. These kids just keep smacking us around."

"Smacking you," Chloe said.

"I need your help, guys," Henry added, and blushed.

Kam's brow furrowed. "What do you mean?"

"We got to stop them."

"How?" George asked. "That'll just cause more problems."

"They're too good at hiding what they do and the Office doesn't like expelling kids anyway," Kam added.

"I just talked to Johnson. He never talked to Billy about attacking me last week. I don't think he even reported it. I mean, he's supposed to. I'll go to the Office and report him."

"You can," Caleb said, rummaging through his backpack, "but they won't do anything to Johnson."

"Yeah, he has too much football power," George added with too much food in his mouth.

Sharonda and Chloe ate as if they didn't hear, or, Henry thought, didn't want to. That irritated him. He was hoping to get their help with his issues, since they involved both boys and girls, especially from Sharonda, who was a steadying influence in the group and among the girls in general, both kind and direct. She was slightly heavy-set, but agile, and always leaned forward confidently, as she walked the hallways. Along with Chloe, she was respected for being a good athlete. Since grade school she had been friends with Chloe, who was taller and slimmer, and kept her brown hair wavy and short, easier, she said, for running around the soccer field. Chloe also had a sensible attitude when it came to problems in the school. Henry knew they saw harassment happening, but felt this was one issue they may not want to deal with.

They all went silent. Henry regretted bringing up the problem. He believed their reticence reflected how sorry they were for him and how little they were willing to help. He stood up. "Yeah, well, let's get to gym."

Typical middlings. They don't really care. And why should they? They're never picked on. No one bothers them. But it's your problem, anyway.

In gym class, Henry waited patiently for the teacher along with other boys in tee shirts and shorts. Some scurried around shooting hoops while others worked out on the mats. His anxiety level automatically jumped in a class that condemned the un-athletic. In this class, the anxiety for him could be as strong as the odors of sweat and rubber. Henry had failed there too many times to enjoy it. He knew the kids saw his nervousness, his insecurity, and they played to it. Balls had caromed off his hands in the wrong direction, shots rarely swished through the hoop and he beat no one in a race. He didn't care to be an athlete, considering how many of those so-called athletes treated him. He lost count of how many basketballs were thrown at his head.

And gym teacher Robert Roach didn't make it any easier. Henry always had the impression that Roach loathed kids like him. Roach even smiled occasionally when the kids joked at Henry's bumbles. Henry seethed when Roach did that. Hating to make mistakes for fear of looking ridiculous, Henry ended up loathing himself for his incompetence He just didn't have the heart to compete—at anything, actually. His mouth clenched. He had to change gym class, too.

Mr. Roach walked into the gym with a basketball under his arm. He always appeared to Henry as a would-be bodybuilder, with his wide, stocky frame, probably compensating for his short stature. But Roach intimidated his students with glares and tough talk.

Henry waited uneasily for what else Roach had planned, unable to stop the growing cramps in his gut.

"Huddle up," Roach said. The boys encircled him. A few rose a head above him. "We'll have a scrimmage today. Let's do a workout first, loosen up, then we'll climb the ropes."

The frickin' ropes.

His gut usually took the brunt of his anxiousness. The past week of problems and the prospect of gym failure stressed him out and the discomfort worsened. He asked to be excused. Roach used his black, beady eyes to keep Henry in place for as long as possible, as if not believing him or just messing with him, Henry thought. But Henry winced from the dire need to get to the toilet and finally Roach let him go.

He hurried to the locker room and into the bathroom stall. He dropped his forehead onto his knees as the knife-like pain pierced his abdomen.

In what seemed only a few moments later, Henry heard someone moaning. His eyes opened, and it took a moment to understand what he saw—the bottom of the stall door just above him and the ceiling beyond that. He realized that the echoing moan came from him as he found himself on the floor in front of the toilet. He sat up. His mouth hung open and he rubbed a smarting pain on the side of his head. He got up on one knee, took a deep breath, then stood up. He stepped gingerly out of the stall, went to the sink and threw water on his bloodless face before looking in the mirror. He couldn't believe he had passed out and couldn't tell for how long. He walked slowly to a bench in front of the lockers and sat down.

After about ten minutes, all the kids started coming in, talking and joking.

"You all right?" one of the kids asked.

Henry breathed out, "Yeah, terrific."

He rubbed his face and changed into his clothes. He figured he must have been out for probably a half hour.

That night in his room, he lay prone on his bed, exhausted, hopeless. Passing out scared him.

Gee, maybe you won't be able to do this. It's too much for you. You're too weak. You're just too frickin' scared.

"You can't stop it. Since the fifth grade. You're so scared of everything. Christ!"

He rolled over on his back and put his arm across his eyes to stop himself from crying. His despair signified, once again, the inevitability of his failure.

"No," he whispered, sitting up, "if you give up, you'll die. You've got to find a way. You're not doing this just for yourself." He closed his eyes and let hot tears roll down his cheeks. He wrapped his arms under his knees and rocked his body back and forth to ease the fear. His heart pumped hard against his chest. "C'mon, calm down. Calm. Calm." After a few minutes, he rubbed his eyes dry, walked over to his desk and, with a sniffle, grimly started his homework.

Life was quiet for Henry for the next week. He wasn't surprised Billy or Derrick didn't get into it again. That's how it usually went. After a run-in of any kind, the enemy would lay low, ignore him, maybe give him a menacing glare. Eventually, they would come after him again. That randomness kept Henry on edge and suspicious.

"Hey," Henry said coming up on Caleb, a close, long-time friend who was just as harassed as Henry was. "Let's get to math."

"Anything happen with the Office?"

"I haven't gone there yet. I'm giving Bronner and Johnson one more chance. I was hoping things would be different this year, but no. Billy and Derrick. What do they get out of it?"

"Exercise."

"Well, I'm three knocks ahead of you."

"Three?"

"Yeah, Jeremy pushed my face into the locker."

Caleb shook his head. "Mine will come. Just a matter of when."

They stopped at the class door.

"If it does, tell the teacher to make them stay away from you. That's what I told Johnson and Bronner."

"Ha. You think that will work?"

"It's worth a try. It's time they started doing what they're supposed to do."

They entered math class, where Mr. Davis and a full class were waiting.

As Henry sat in class, episodes of his own past humiliations flipped through his mind, the teacher's voice only a murmur. His mouth clamped shut, remembering. His face reddened from embarrassment. He berated himself for not handling things better. Fifth grade, sixth, seventh. He didn't know how to do better then, and still didn't. All the kids were miles ahead of him in thought and action. He avoided them back then, too, ignored them as the good kid was told to do. He came out of his remembrance, gave a side-glance to the other kids in the classroom and sneered at them—they were happy and free of persecution, while he wallowed in his pain.

Was it the way he looked? he wondered. How he walked or talked? He had examined his face in the mirror multiple times. What was wrong with it? he had asked himself. Forehead not too high, light brown hair, dark brown eyes, thin lips, slight cheekbones, smooth skin and no angles at all. Decent-looking, in his opinion, unblemished by violence, and he wanted to keep it that way. But, attached to a rather slender body, the whole package hardly commanded respect.

Yeah, they can see it. Soft and weak. Inviting. Time to hit the weights.

He certainly lacked the square, angular, menacing features of Billy or Derrick. Neither did Kam or George, but each of them had a stronger, more confident appearance and stride through the hall, which he lacked and fretted he may never have. Now in the tenth grade, his place was firmly woven into the fabric of school life. His eyes froze in distress as he realized an inescapable fate of being the victim

20

forever. He suddenly clutched the edge of his chair and gave out a moan.

Two kids turned to him.

"Hey," one of them whispered.

Henry's eyes slowly moved to gaze at him. He blinked a few times and his breathing eased. His lips clamped and he stared with the horrible thought of a future no different from the past. He shook his head.

No. No. It's not going to happen. You can't let it happen. You can't die a coward.

Henry hurriedly got to his locker and then catch his bus.

The next morning, while Henry waited impatiently by the open classroom for a teacher to arrive, he heard a small group of boys and girls laugh out loud while watching one girl, Carla, walk stiffly past him into the classroom.

"Your mother let you out looking like that?" Robin called out.

He heard the word "weirdo" from them and thought he heard "lesbo" from Laurie, but it was spoken too softly to be sure.

Robin and Laurie had called out Carla and other girls in the halls before, but Henry had ignored it. Carla rose a head above most of the girls in the class, darker-skinned, short, curly black hair and black-rimmed glasses. She always wore a unique blend of clothing and colors to match, making her look sometimes gypsy-ish. She had arrived a few years before. Henry had spoken to her only a few times in class. At first, she smiled and was talkative, but slowly she withdrew and sat more by herself. As the months went on, the smile was gone. Henry couldn't figure out why until he heard the kids make fun of her.

A few days later, Henry found Carla in the library alone, writing, books open in front of her. Other kids sat around talking quietly at other tables. A round receptionist's desk manned by a student filled the middle of the large, square room. High metal bookcases stood like sentinels against the walls.

He observed Carla for a moment. Maybe, he wondered, he could get to know her.

All you have to do is talk a little. Nothing big.

He exhaled sharply, as if he were about to jump off a cliff, and went to her table.

Hi," Henry said.

Hello," Carla said flatly.

"Mind if I sit here?"

She shrugged. "I suppose."

Henry opened a book to start homework.

"So, how you doing?" he said, smiling.

She looked at him suspiciously, but his smile pulled a smaller one from her.

"I'm doing alright."

"How did you do on that history quiz?"

"Fine."

C'mon. Is that all you can say? Think.

Laurie passed by and looked at both of them, whispered something to Meaghan and giggled about it.

"There goes Laurie, laughing again," Henry said to Carla.

Carla glanced at the two girls as they left the room.

"I've noticed that she's one of the girls bugging you. Saying nasty things."

"What?"

Henry tensed up.

"They always seem to say nasty things to you?"

Carla's eyes narrowed. "What do you mean?"

Henry looked past Carla to Laurie and Meaghan at the door. Laurie punched her thumbs into her phone. Meaghan smiled at what she was typing and glanced at Carla. Then Carla's phone pinged. She picked it up, frowned, and went back to her book.

"Was that from Laurie? She's cybering you, isn't she?"

"What?" she said.

"She's cyberbullying you, isn't she?"

Carla stared a moment, as though figuring out an answer.

"I think you should just mind your own business."

Henry reddened. "Well, maybe instead of taking their crap, you should give some back. Actually, maybe we can help each other with this. We're both having problems."

Her eyes bulged.

"I'm not having any problems."

"I have an idea. You should call them the vultures."

"What? Who?"

"Laurie, Robin, Meaghan, Pam. Say something back to them. Don't just let them get away with it. Haven't you had enough of them?"

"I don't want to talk about it," she said pointedly. "I'm busy. Now leave."

"Well, we may be in the same boat. Let's talk about this."

"I need to study. Goodbye."

Henry stiffened a moment and closed his book.

"Okay. But you can report them anytime, you know."

He returned the book to his backpack and left. As he glanced back at Carla, he shook his head disappointedly.

He passed Laurie and her friends at Robin's locker, where they usually met.

"Hey, vultures," he said to them as he passed.

Henry went on to gym class with Caleb. He felt good this time. Running and a workout first, then more basketball. Roach yelled at them for getting soft over the summer. Henry actually kept with the pace, running faster, concentrating, but not good enough. Two teammates, Ervin and Jermaine, who played for the school, berated his passing (his passes were intercepted, some by Caleb no less) and his shots (he missed all of them).

Henry slammed the ball against the floor, and it ricocheted way up in the air. (The sound of the ball hitting the court reminded him of his own head getting smacked with a book.) He told them to stuff it and stomped off to sit in the stands.

"Wilton," Roach said. "What are you doing?"

"I'm sick of their crap," Henry said, his face flushed and sweaty. "They're on the basketball team so they think they can put down everyone else."

Jermaine and Ervin smiled at each other as another classmate took Henry's place.

"Is that right?" Roach said. "Well, maybe they're helping you play better."

"Yeah, right."

"Alright. Go over to the mats and give me fifty sit-ups and thirty push-ups."

"Why?"

"Because I told you to," Roach demanded.

"Hey, I'm not the cause of this."

"I don't care."

"As usual." Henry stomped off the stands.

"That's enough."

Henry could barely do thirty sit-ups and only fourteen push-ups. He panted on the mat, his chest heaving as Roach came over to him.

"That's...all I can do."

"You'll have to do better than that," Roach remarked.

Henry chuckled. "Whatever."

Roach called everyone together to end the class.

In the locker room, Henry stood in front of the wooden bench after showering and had started pulling his pants on when Wyatt and Gray arrived on both sides of him.

"Hi, Wilty."

They began pushing Henry back and forth between them like they were exercising.

Gray, strong and stocky, was a lineman on the football team, and Wyatt, the best athlete, the future starting quarterback. Both grinned as they played with Henry.

Henry had been attacked like this before and remembered how to defend himself if it happened again, which he knew it would. Now he had to cross the scary line between dreaming and doing.

"Hey, we're next," Todd called out, with chuckles around the room. He pointed his phone toward the action.

Roach passed by. Just as Henry looked at him, Roach turned away with a little smile on his face.

Enraged, Henry dropped to the floor. Wyatt fell forward, pushing nothing but air. Henry put his shoulder into him and both went over the bench. The quarterback landed on the floor with Henry on top of him. Wyatt yelped in pain. Henry put his hand on Wyatt's head, got up, and went after Gray, mouth open, cheeks crimson. Gray's eyes widened and Henry threw his arms out to push him. Gray waved off Henry's arms and got in a few jackhammer pushes. Henry came back with several attempts. Some landed and some didn't.

"Wilton!"

Henry attempted a few more pushes and stopped. He returned to his clothes and finished dressing as though nothing had happened. Wyatt got up cautiously, holding his back. He groaned.

"What are you doing?" Roach asked him.

Henry returned to his clothes.

"You okay?" Roach asked Wyatt.

"My back. Shit."

Roach pressed Wyatt's lower back.

"Alright, go down to the nurse and get it checked out."

Wyatt walked stiffly out of the room. He put his hand against the lockers and then the door jamb.

"What happened?"

"Wilton pushed him over the bench," Gray said.

"Why?"

"Because they were pushing me," Henry answered while putting on his shirt. "And you saw it."

Gray shook his head at Roach.

"Oh, we were just joking with him," Gray sneered. "Then he turned on us."

Roach sighed. "Wilton, come into my office."

Henry feigned surprise. "Why?"

"Because I said so," Roach demanded, holding his arm out. "Let's go."

"I'm not going anywhere but to class."

"You either come into my office or we go down to the other office."

"Don't think so," Henry said in weak defiance. "I'm tired of you teachers blaming me for what these clowns do."

"I'm not going to tell you again."

The locker room hushed.

Roach walked slowly to Henry, who stood up.

"You're going way over the line."

"I'm not. They are," Henry said, pulling his backpack onto his shoulder.

Henry started to pass Roach, but Roach stepped in front of him. Henry chuckled.

"Just like these tough guys. Always getting in my way."

"Let's stop the routine, Wilton. Let's go down to the Office and we'll talk about it there."

Henry shrugged. "Fine. Lead the way."

They both started walking out of the room.

"See ya, Wilty," Gray said.

A few minutes later, Henry waited in front of the tall counter of the administration office. He sat patiently on one of the five chairs against the large glass-paneled wall. The Office was adjacent to the spacious main entrance to the school. Sunlight streamed through the upper windows and brightened the area, and strings of sparkling red and blue beads hung from the lofted ceiling. A curving staircase led to the second floor of more offices, lockers and classrooms, and a sitting area in front of a wall of large windows, one of which had the word "READ" pasted across it in large letters.

Mary, the secretary, a spindle of a woman with short, auburn hair and small eyes, busily moved in quick, short steps behind the counter.

Henry's anxiety rose by the minute. *Alright. Steady. You knew you were gonna end up here eventually. Did the right thing there, telling them off.*

26

Roach opened the door and motioned to Henry, who walked in with a show of fake bravado, yet both anxious and angry. Roach stood off to the side, his muscular arms crossed over his chest.

Behind her polished wooden desk, Vice Principal Jane Peterson sat erect with a stern appearance, her shoulder-length dark brown hair hanging professionally around her face. She wore all dark blue, a dress covered by a neatly cut jacket. She was writing something and finally turned her attention up to Henry.

"Mr. Roach tells me you were in a tussle and someone got hurt."

Henry remained silent.

"What happened?"

Henry let out a breath.

"I was attacked again," he replied.

She settled back into her black leather chair.

"And in response you hurt one of them." '

Henry shrugged. "It was self-defense. They hurt me."

"Wyatt is seeing the nurse. Are you?"

"Well, that's his fault. He and his buddy pushed me back and forth like I was beach ball."

"Doesn't look like it did you any harm."

Henry froze. He stared at Peterson, who lowered her eyes.

"Didn't do me any harm," Henry repeated. "He saw what was happening and he did nothing about."

"Mr. Roach to you. And I didn't see a thing."

"I saw you look at us while they were pushing me. He saw it happen and did nothing."

Peterson glanced at Roach.

"Alright, that's enough," Peterson demanded.

"This…this whole thing is their fault."

"You took it way too far," Peterson insisted.

Henry gave Peterson a slow head shake. Her face reddened.

"You owe Mr. Roach an apology."

"For what?"

"For arguing with him and defying his orders."

"Well, I did nothing wrong, and he was blaming me."

"You retaliated and someone got hurt. Then you disrespected Mr. Roach. You owe him an apology now."

Henry couldn't take the chance of any punishment. He gritted his teeth and turned to Roach.

"I apologize."

"And you owe Wyatt an apology as well. He may not be able play Friday night because of this."

She casually moved some papers aside and re-positioned her computer.

"Now you continue to have issues with your classmates, since last year. I don't know why, but you'll have to find a way to get along better. I would advise you to be more careful going forward."

Don't stop. Keep going.

"Once again, they attacked me."

"I don't consider what they did an attack. A little pushing and shoving can happen." She placed her pen onto the desk and sat back. "You know, it might be wise for you to get a better sense of humor. Something like that can go a long way."

"But these kids were talked to last year about this stuff, and they're still doing it."

She straightened up and placed her arms on the desk.

"Apparently they didn't get the message. We will make sure they do this time."

"What if it happens again?"

"If there is an incident, run off quickly and get a teacher," Peterson said impatiently. "It's a lot better to do that than have it escalate."

"So, you will talk to Wyatt and Gray?"

"Yes, Henry. We will have a word with them."

"Did Mr. Johnson report that Billy attacked me as well?"

Peterson furrowed her brow. "And when did this happen?"

"First week of school."

"I was not made aware of this. I'll look into it."

"And Jeremy pushed my face into my locker. I'm reporting that now."

"Alright," Peterson said hesitantly. "We will speak to him as well."

"And Derrick hit me in the head with a book. Mr. Bronner said he would report my complaint."

Peterson sat silently a moment. "It's possible he did. I'll look into it. But why are these things happening, Henry? What are you doing that attracts these incidents?"

"Nothing. They come after me."

"Look at your behavior. It's possible you may be doing something without knowing it."

"But you will talk to these kids?"

"Of course we will."

"Thank you."

Roach stood quietly as Henry walked out the side door. He inhaled deeply to relax the nerves. He shook his head—different day, same old results.

Later, Henry went up to Gray, who was talking easily with Charles and Todd.

"How was your trip to the Office?" Gray said with a haughty smile befitting someone speaking to an underling.

"I'm supposed to apologize to Wyatt."

"And you should, asshole. Look what you did."

"Wilton, what makes you so violent?" Charles said.

"Has Peterson talked to you yet?"

"About what?"

"Attacking me."

"No. We didn't attack you. Just having some fun with you. And as usual, you got pissed."

"Well, get ready," Henry said in a burst of anger. "My fun's coming."

That night in his room, Henry plopped down on his bed and rubbed his face, wondering when that "fun" would actually start. He pictured the typical smugness on everyone's faces as he lost again. He could write whatever he wanted to in his little notebook, rage quietly all he wanted at the injustice, but how to beat them? He worriedly paced his room, rubbing the back of his neck.

They have a lock on it. They can do whatever they want. But at least you did something. That's the key. No matter how scared you are, keep doing something.

He wondered anxiously how he could overcome powerlessness and the terrifying thought that he actually was trapped in his position in the school—indeed, in the universe—from which there was no escape. The battles had to come because he knew his enemies would never let him go. They liked him there. They needed him there. They needed someone to pick on.

For the next several days, Henry stuck to his rules, avoiding and evading, keeping life stable. He asked Gray and Wyatt if Peterson ever talked to them. They laughed and said no.

Of course, Henry fumed. Football immunity.

Damn it. What is wrong with these people? You're gonna have to go back there again. You can't let it go.

But he hesitated returning to the Office to face Peterson. He gave in to his fear again and let another week pass. He fell into a routine of supper, doing homework and then back to school the next day. His rattled mind relaxed a bit. He was not harassed, mainly because he'd reverted to his mousy self. He wanted to get together with friends and do something. The football game Friday night was likely the best place to do that. He found Caleb, in his baggy pants and jacket, and Kam, always in straight-cut shirt and jeans, at Kam's locker.

"You guys going to the game?"

"I guess so," Caleb answered.

"Yeah, I might go," Kam said.

"Good. I'll meet you there. George is going so I was wondering if you were."

On Friday night, Henry walked to the game. The park that included many of the town's sports fields was down the street from his house. The lights over the football field shone brightly against the black sky as the stands on both sides of the field filled up. Cars lined up on the street as they slowly made their way into the huge parking lot. Henry walked along the sidewalk in the cool, windless evening with several other fans and eventually met Kam, Caleb and George at the entrance.

He and his friends dawdled through the entrance toward the stands. The bright-green football field to their right centered a six-lane dirt track bordered by a high stone wall all the way around. Attached at the top of the home stands was the press booth filled with local radio announcers and sports writers. It amused Henry that adults took covering a high school football game so seriously.

The boys stopped at a few food vendors for giant pretzels and hot dogs and, later, in the restroom in a small, flat-topped, white-washed building. People milled about the main runway.

Everyone hung out at the games, including several kids from the neighborhood. As the night went on, Henry relaxed and joked with his friends and actually made them laugh a few times.

"Hey, there's Wyatt," Henry said of the quarterback who waited among teammates. "Think he's gonna play?"

George smiled. "Why don't you go ask him?"

Henry burst into laughter and settled into an unusual contentment that went deep. Take advantage of it while you got it, he thought. He felt a part of the hundreds of people there, not separate from them. The boys sat in the packed stands, analyzed their team's problems, and rated each one of the cheerleaders as they jumped and split on the sideline. Part-way through the second half, with the wrong team winning, the boys got up to stretch.

They ambled through the shadows behind the stands.

"Hey, Wilton." Jeremy stepped out with Todd.

Shit.

Frightened, Henry kept walking but his friends stopped and turned.

"C'mon," Henry exhorted, angry they halted at a bully's call.

Criss-crossing shadows from the stands covered Jeremy's thin face, darkening his left cheek and eye.

"How's it goin'?" Henry said lightly.

"Good. Yourself?" Jeremy answered.

Henry kept walking, followed quickly by his friends.

"You're not in school now, Wilton. No one can protect ya."

"Ha. No one protects me in there either." He waved. "Have a good night."

Henry pinched his lips impatiently at his friends, who walked too slowly.

He heard running footsteps on the gravel behind him.

Alright, here we go. Fuck.

Jeremy stopped him. Todd came up from behind.

"Get outta the way," Henry exclaimed, putting up another bold front. "Why don't you two take the night off? We're all having a good time here, so let's keep it that way."

Jeremy shrugged. "I'm having a good time." He turned to Todd. "Are you having a good time?"

"I'm having a great time."

"Great. See you later then," Henry said and kept walking.

"But not until I get a piece of you, bitch," Jeremy said in a low, intense voice. He grabbed the lapel of Henry's jacket. "You narced on me, asshole."

"Over what?"

"Pushing your ugly face into the locker."

"Not me. Maybe some other kids did."

"Henry," Kam said. "C'mon."

Todd positioned himself between Henry and his friends.

"You guys take off. Wilton's busy."

Henry's eyes widened at being manipulated. Jeremy peered over at two police officers strolling nearby.

"What are you gonna do now?" Henry smiled. "See ya."

Henry walked away a free man. He found his friends standing near the wall with several other people engrossed in their team making a late-game drive to the goal line.

"Where's Caleb?"

"He left," Kam answered.

"Everything done with?" George asked.

Henry mumbled. He breathed slowly to ease his throbbing pulse. "They never quit. But two cops showed up."

"You seem to be popular with them," Kam said

"What do you mean?"

Kam gave a quick shrug.

"What should I do, Kam? Run? I have to stand up to 'em."

Kam sighed. "This stuff always happens to you."

"Yeah. I don't like it either," Henry said angrily. "You could have helped me back there. We all have to stand up to this."

He looked at George. "How about you?"

George shrugged.

"It won't do any good," he said. "They're like vampires. Take down some, others take their place."

"If we all get together, we can stop it."

The team scored but eventually lost. The three boys walked away from the field with everyone else at game's end.

"Hey," Henry called out. "I'll see you Monday."

"Okay," George said.

"See ya," Kam waved.

Henry slowly walked across the baseball field to an opened corner in the fence, snipped by someone a long time ago to create a short-cut. He stopped and leaned against a stone pillar to which the fence had once been attached. Fans slowly left the park, cars lining up at the exit. He exhaled sharply. Once again, he thought, always two or more bullies accosting him. Fear was their weapon, instilled in Henry all his life. Even Kam and George had it.

"Amazing. They have it just the way they want it. Just amazing. I...I don't think I can end this."

He thought about that worriedly until the light vanished. The huge bulbs dimmed to an amber glow. Just about everyone had gone. Henry stepped through the fence and headed home.

On Monday, he took the chance at confronting Jeremy.

"Well, have a good time at the game?"

"You're lucky the cops came along," Jeremy said.

"No, you are. But the way you're goin', that's not, uh, the last time you'll be seeing them." He walked off, not giving Jeremy a chance to respond. He gave Todd a nod. "Hey." But Todd said nothing.

Now you really better watch your back.

Caleb came his way.

"Hey."

"Hey."

"How come you left the game?"

"I didn't want to deal with it."

"We have to go up against them together, you know."

"I don't know, Henry. Just stay away from them."

"There were four of us and two of them. We could have made a point for once."

"What point? This school doesn't care about any point. You think that's gonna change? I'm just trying to survive. Two more years."

In class, Henry and Caleb took out their books and computers.

"We could have scared them," he continued.

"Two of them equals four of us."

"We blew a perfect opportunity."

Caleb threw up his hands.

"We let them do what they want," Henry said

"I know, Henry."

"If we do it once, they'll back off."

"Maybe not."

"How are we gonna know if we don't try it?"

Caleb opened his notebook.

"I still can't believe they tried to shove you into a locker. What's this, the 1980s?"

"Forget it," Caleb said.

"You know it'll happen again. Trust me. Look what happened to Bradley and Josh last week, and uh…the new kid, what's-his-name."

"Oh, Freedman."

"Yeah, they got shoved around." Henry rubbed his forehead. "They use us for sport. It just keeps going and going with no change."

"Let's just walk down the hall together more, okay?" Caleb said.

"In the end, we just can't break through. And the teachers could care less."

Henry peered around worriedly

"Have you ever written down the times you were attacked?"

"What?"

"You know, all the times you were attacked, bullied. Have you written them down?"

"No, why?" Caleb asked.

"For proof, I guess. Go ahead and do it. We may need the evidence."

"Evidence? What will that do?"

"I don't know. It's something, I guess. I've already written mine down. Date, time and place."

Caleb chuckled.

"Alright, I'll try to do it."

"You have a game today?" Henry asked.

"After school."

Henry slowly headed to next class deep in thought, trying not to bump into anyone. He knew his old friend was just as scared to break the bondage, but didn't have the same urgency. Mainly, Henry thought, because Caleb was not as much of a target. He had a more open personality, he laughed more, spoke well, played on the basketball team. He could take the abuse better, as though it didn't bother him at all. Henry envied that, grudgingly admired it. Caleb let the humiliation slide off him. Henry absorbed it. But Henry also thought Caleb accepted the abuse too easily, like he had no pride, no shame.

For days after, Henry paced his room each evening, always anxious about the next day, avoiding and evading in the halls. He continued studying hard, or what he thought was studying hard. First exams came and went, and his grades were the same as always—just average. He was a C-plus, B-minus kid and never did any better than that.

He sat on his bed, face in hands, thinking, always thinking. And had no idea what to do.

It's six weeks in and nothing's changed. You have to make something happen.

The next day, Henry and George watched a gym class play volleyball for a while. George had his computer on his lap, playing some video game. Later, they walked together to their next class, but Henry broke off to go to the lab.

Around the corner strode Billy and Frank, walking in tandem with a military swagger. Henry stiffened. He had no escape.

Damn. He prayed they would just pass by without doing anything. *Why does this always happen to me? Ignore me. Just go by and ignore me for once.*

His face looked like a frightened cat. As they passed, Billy eyed him.

"Wilton, you faggot."

Henry slowed down. *C'mon. Just walk away. Walk away. No!*

"Right back atcha," Henry said over his shoulder.

"What?"

Henry kept walking. "You heard me."

"Hey, get back here."

"Screw you."

Alright, here you go.

Billy trotted up and stopped Henry short. Frank slowly walked behind him. Fear swelled in Henry's chest.

"Pretty rude, boy," Billy said, standing close to Henry. "Still a wise-ass. Fuckin' apologize."

Henry forced outer calm while his insides twitched.

Billy leaned forward slightly. "I'm not gonna tell you again."

"Excuse me." Henry moved forward, starting to get angry.

"Whoa, don't walk away when I'm talking to you, young man."

"He never learns," Frank added.

Henry turned to make sure Frank wasn't approaching him. Frank just stood waiting, wearing his bully smile—close-lipped, patronizing, cornering a weakling. He had a lot of belly fat, a hard layer that only the strongest punch could harm.

"Move."

"Make me."

Henry let out a loud sigh. "You might not want to do this after what you did the first week of school."

"This time you're gonna keep your mouth shut."

"Why are you always doing this? Why don't you just leave us alone?"

Billy smiled. "Makes going to school more fun."

"Do I look like I'm having fun?"

"No." Billy smiled.

Henry bristled. "Screw you."

Billy's fast hands pushed Henry hard against Frank, who pushed him back saying, "Hey, watch it."

Already planning on this attack, Henry skipped away.

"That's it?" Henry said to Billy. "You push like a girl." Henry grinned, surprised by another bold and reckless remark.

Be careful.

He trotted up the steps.

"Catch me now, turkey."

Henry did not run and Billy caught up to him and pushed him into the wall. Then he threw a few quick jabs. Henry raised his arms to protect his face. He suddenly moved forward and threw his own but missed. Billy pulled back quickly.

Good. Keep it going. Keep your strength. His heart thumped so fast; his breathing labored in sheer fright.

"Oh, you think you're tough now?"

"Come and get me," Henry ventured. He had his fists out in front ready for more, but he weakened him fast. Nausea quickly gurgled. Then his arms were yanked back and held tightly.

"Hey."

Henry struggled as Frank held him in a vice grip.

"Let go of me."

Billy came up quick, throwing fists at Henry's face, striking near the mouth and on the cheekbone, missing the eye. Henry kicked Billy, who buckled in pain. Realizing that Frank held him tight enough for some leverage, Henry raised his knees high and slammed his heels down on Frank's feet. Frank shouted. The grip loosened. Henry pulled one arm free and knocked Frank lightly on the cheekbone with his elbow. Billy swung a leg and it struck Henry powerfully in the hip. Henry stumbled back. Billy came up fast again and Henry just as quickly pranced away.

"C'mon, a-holes."

"Stop it!"

Mr. Lentine, one of the school's security officers, tall and athletic, hustled in with two students behind him. He separated the combatants. Billy hit the teacher's hand off his shirt, infuriating him.

"Stop it, Billy."

"They attacked me," shouted Henry

"He jumped us," Billy retorted.

"Alright. All of you to the Office. Let's go."

Frank limped and winced at the pain in his feet.

"What's wrong?" Lentine asked.

"Wilton broke my foot."

"That's your fault," Henry said.

Billy raised his hand to Henry.

"Alright, enough," Lentine said.

In the Office, the three boys waited. Henry, his heart slowing and his muscles quivering, simmered.

"You know, you two are the biggest freakin' morons. Why didn't you just keep walking and keep your mouths shut? Now look. I have better things to do than to be here."

"This is your fault."

"And...and how's that?"

"You mouthed off," Billy said.

"Sssssoo. What did you say to me?"

"Doesn't matter. You just keep your mouth shut."

Henry chuckled. "You know, I'm like the tenth kid you've attacked in this school." Henry moved closer to Billy. "You're all done. I'm gonna see to it. You, too, pal," Henry said to Frank.

"Won't happen," Billy said.

"We'll see." Billy's smug tone angered Henry even more.

The door opened and Lentine waved in Billy and Frank. Henry sat down and waited. He had a burning fear that he would lose the argument along with the fight, even though he was in the right. What lies were Frank and Billy going to tell them? he wondered.

He closed his eyes a moment and breathed rhythmically to keep down growing anxiety Finally, Frank and Billy were done.

"Go on in, fighter," Billy said.

In Peterson's office, Principal David Ruzzo stood next to the vice-principal's desk with hands on his hips, glaring. Lentine walked out.

Henry sighed loudly.

"Well, Henry?" Peterson said. She raised her hands and dropped them. "For your sake, you better have a good explanation for this."

Henry chuckled. "Would it help?"

"Let's find out," Ruzzo interjected.

Ruzzo stood like a bear. He had a big head, bulbous nose, and black, curly hair thinning at the top. He usually had a scowl or a glare that he used to good effect to unsettle students as he stalked the corridors. He wore dark suits with a red or blue tie.

"What happened?" Peterson asked tiredly.

"I was heading off to the lab and they passed me in the hall. Billy called me a faggot. I said right back atcha, and then they jumped me."

Peterson settled back.

"Look, he said something to me," Henry continued, attempting to speak steadily as his heart pumped hard. "I said something back. We're even. We walk away. Instead, they intimidated me, wouldn't let me get by and attacked me again."

"They told a different story," Ruzzo remarked, folding his arms across his chest.

"I'm sure they did."

"They said you bumped into Billy on purpose and wouldn't apologize," Ruzzo said.

"And you believe that."

"Convince me it's not true."

"Well, you know I don't attack kids. I never have."

"There's always a first time for everything," Ruzzo said.

He looked Ruzzo over. "Well, I didn't. I avoid them, especially those two. But they've attacked me before. So I don't think I have to convince you of anything. My record speaks for itself."

"You've had a few incidents so far this year."

"And none of them were my fault," Henry pleaded. "They bring it to me. I avoid them."

"Maybe you're not doing it right."

Henry kept growing anger at bay. "How am I avoiding them—wrong?"

"That is a conversation for the guidance counselor," Ruzzo continued. "We will ask Miss Stagg to speak with you about getting along better with your classmates. Right now, we have to determine your punishment."

"What punishment?"

"For fighting."

"I wasn't fighting. I was defending myself. There's a difference."

Mrs. Peterson sat forward. "We don't have time to make a differentiation. Officer Lentine saw you fighting. So, you have five nights detention beginning tonight."

"But I didn't even touch them. They touched me. Look at my lip and cheek here. And how many times have they attacked kids in this rathole of a school?"

As soon as he hurled it, Henry knew he'd gone a bit too far. That led to a moment of silence.

"Wilton," Ruzzo said, stepping toward him. "You continue to have these temperament issues. Now you're insulting us and your own school."

Henry held up his hands. "I was minding my own business—again—and they stopped me and insulted me again. They're the problem, not me. Mr. Johnson and Mr. Bronner reported the other attacks on me, right?"

"We located Mr. Johnson's report," Peterson said. "I haven't seen Mr. Bronner's."

"Billy attacked me the first Friday of school and Derrick slammed me in the back of the head with a book. And then Jeremy shoved my face into my locker."

Ruzzo glanced at Peterson. "We will speak to them. But, Henry, look, if someone calls you a name, just let it go. Talking back to them started the problem. I don't know how many times we have to tell you kids this."

"You made things worse again, Wilton," Peterson chimed in.

Henry rubbed his face. His gut tightened.

"You're saying that I shouldn't have said anything back to them a...after they called me a name, correct?"

"Correct."

"In that case," Henry continued, "when I said something back to them, they shouldn't have let that bother them. Correct?"

Henry puckered his lips impatiently.

"It doesn't matter, Wilton," Ruzzo said. "You retaliated, just like against Wyatt. We thought you learned something from that, but unfortunately not."

Retaliation, Henry thought.

"So...so it's all about retaliation," Henry mused.

"Yes," Peterson said, "that's what we're trying to teach you, and all you kids. We can't have that. It escalates matters."

"So, the person who retaliates gets punished."

Ruzzo nodded. "Exactly."

"But didn't they retaliate against me?"

Ruzzo thought a moment.

"Your retaliation caused the problem," Ruzzo replied. "You should have kept quiet and kept walking."

Henry's pulse pounded in his ears, and he felt his cheeks grow hot, more from frustration than fear.

Ruzzo sat down on the corner of the desk. "Look, Wilton, we count on you to be the better person. See, we don't want you to get hurt. Antagonizing these boys, getting them mad, could lead to a physical altercation so quickly, we can't be there to stop it. You have to understand that. Remember, you're not as strong as some of these kids, so you have to watch yourself. You got away with it this time. But maybe not next time. So just laugh off whatever they say and walk away."

"Well, some of it is humiliating."

"It's only humiliating if you let it be. So help us out and just let it go. Pretty soon they'll stop."

Henry thought a moment.

"What are we going to do, Henry?" Peterson demanded. Henry saw a little smile, a bully smile, form on her lips, as though, Henry thought, she preyed on his confusion. He knew she enjoyed having a student standing in front of her weak and frightened.

"But I'm the victim here," Henry began softly, happy he said 'victim'. Rarely had just the right word come out of him. "They're the bullies."

"We don't like that word."

"What?" Henry said. "Victim?"

"No. Bully."

"Why not? If the shoe fits…"

"We don't label kids here."

"Really. Is 'faggot' okay?"

Peterson sat back and glanced up at Ruzzo.

"Of course not," the principal snapped.

"Then give them detention for saying that to me."

"We'll take care of that," Ruzzo said. He stood. "You have your own detention. Now go."

"But I haven't done anything wrong."

"Billy and Frank have their detention as well. This ends the discussion, Wilton. Remember, you're only the victim if you let yourself be one. Now go to see the nurse and then to class."

"Speak with Mr. Johnson and Mr. Bronner. They were supposed to help me."

"You can go now, Wilton."

"I…I have to go to the bathroom."

Ruzzo started talking to Peterson about something else as Henry closed the door.

He sped to the boys' room. In the bathroom stall, he rested his elbows on his knees and rubbed his face. His body quivered as his nerves, and nausea, settled down. While he had a rare feeling of pride for what he had said in there—he'd actually been able to think and talk at the same time—he could not have gone any further. A sharp pain in his gut moved through him, and now he really had to use the toilet.

His bowels finally emptied, he washed his hands and cupped water into his mouth. He inhaled deeply. Some boys walked in, talking and joking to each other.

"Oh, man," one of the boys said, "who died in here?"

"Yeah, Wilton, what were you doin'?"

"Hey, when ya gotta go, ya gotta go," Henry said, embarrassed, and he left.

A few seconds later, the two boys stumbled out of the bathroom coughing and gagging. Henry smiled.

Kam and Caleb came up to him.

"Dude, what happened to ya now?" Kam asked.

"Yeah, looks like you met a door," Caleb said.

"Met Frank and Billy." Henry opened his locker. "They jacked me. I fought them off, but they're blaming me for everything."

"That's no surprise," Kam remarked.

"We'll see about that. Oooo." Henry lightly touched his bruised lip. "I'm not letting them get away with it. Not anymore."

"What are you gonna do?" Caleb asked.

Henry grabbed two books and slammed his locker closed.

"Don't know yet. But I have a feeling it's coming."

For the rest of the day, Henry couldn't listen to lectures. His thoughts swirled around finally throwing a punch and an elbow, although very weak ones that didn't land, and the injustice of his punishment. He believed he was in the right, but that wasn't important. Throughout his life, he saw— from television, movies, the news, history books, and from his own experience—that people in the right don't always win. How could he overcome that, he wondered fretfully?

And he didn't go to the nurse or detention.

Henry arrived home and skipped upstairs to avoid his mother.

"Henry," his mother called out. "I got a call from the principal's office. Are you alright?"

"Yes."

In the bathroom mirror, he found a slight bruise on his cheek and a swelling on his lower lip—not something he could hide well. He frowned at the injury. He clenched and unclenched his fingers and wished he had had tagged Billy's jaw. He found the fight so terrifying that he had no conscious feeling while doing it, just put up the fists and see what happens. But he survived, and felt emboldened by it.

Well, it's a good start. Maybe you have an idea how to fight. You'll need it.

He sat in his room wondering if he was moving along too fast. His head swam over too many incidents and the enemy strengthened by numbers with too little punishment. And would his meager strength hold out?

"I get five nights. I betcha they got only two or three. Why can't they just get rid of these kids?"

He placed his books and computer on his desk and tried concentrating on homework, but he would drift off to thinking about school skirmishes and what to do about them.

Called down to dinner, Henry walked into the dining room with face down, but his mother eventually lifted his chin.

"So we got a call about a fight you were in," his father said.

"I didn't fight. I defended myself."

"What happened?" his father demanded.

"Two idiots passed me in the hall, and one called me a name."

"And what did you do?"

"I said right back atcha."

"I thought they spoke to these kids last year about this?" his mother said.

"They did, and it doesn't work. It never does. They don't care"

"This is what we've been talking to you about," his father said. "You make things worse by talking back to them. Just pass by and don't say a word."

"Names can't hurt you, honey," his mother added. "Don't let it bother you so much."

"Sticks and stones can break your bones but names can never hurt you?"

"That's right," his mother replied with a pursed smile.

"I see you find that platitude amusing."

"No. It's very true."

"I didn't call them a name."

"We're worried," his father exclaimed, shaking his head. "You can get hurt bad. It's alright to walk away and be the better man."

Henry put his fork down and exhaled sharply. "I got five nights detention for defending myself. I want you to make an appointment with Principal Ruzzo. All three of us can sit down with him and talk about this. I'm done with being attacked in that rathole."

"Did you go to detention?" his father asked.

"No."

"Why?"

"Because I shouldn't have to." He shook his head. "I...I can't give in anymore. I'm not going to."

His father sighed.

"I'll give him a call and talk to him. Go to detention tomorrow."

"No. I want us to meet with him first. Why do I have to sit in some stupid empty classroom staring into space for defending myself?"

"I'll call him," his father said with finality.

"Tell him you're going to sue him if I get attacked again."

"We're not suing anyone."

Henry kept eating, enjoying the food yet angry.

Later, he paced the floor in his room.

"Alright," he said aloud, "think. What are you going to do tomorrow? Everyone is gonna come after you."

He closed his eyes and let his chest rise and fall slowly, hearing the soft whoosh of air through his nose. The longer he closed his eyes, the sleepier he became. He lay down and let his strung-out body go limp. He snoozed for a half hour, but homework awaited. He sat up, rubbed his face and went to his desk.

Henry labored on math for a while, frustrated with problems he couldn't solve. He finally left the desk and threw the history book on the bed. It bounced a few times and fell to the floor with a thud. Enraged, he picked up the book, slammed it down on the bed and began punching it.

"Stay on the bed," he said out loud. With each word, he struck the book. "Stay—on—the—fucking—bed." Henry pummeled the book into submission until a crease formed in the cover, and then he stopped. He stood motionless, breathless, his chin jutting out. His mind sparked with violent impulses to do more—just tear the frickin' thing apart, like he wanted to do to the whole world. His right hand hung hurting at his side as his heart thumped against his chest. He wondered if his parents had heard him.

He finally settled down and re-gained full consciousness. He was surprised at what he had done. He hadn't gone off like that in a while.

"Relax. Relax."

He grew up throwing tantrums and anything else not nailed down. He hit his head against the wall when he couldn't withstand the pressure of fury and frustration. He had controlled himself lately. He wanted to stop. But sometimes the build-up inside made him want to explode.

Henry eventually settled down and read what he could of history before nodding off, he was so tired. Finally crawling into bed and turning out the light, he could only doze. Anger simmered in his mind, as it often did. He found forgetting a terrible day as difficult as not forgetting the humiliations and attacks of the past. And, over the years, they infiltrated his sleep, playing out in his mind, winding him up to the point of exhaustion as he lay under the covers. His own fear and cowardice played over and over again on the projector of his mind, like that time in the seventh grade while he sat waiting in the auditorium for a teacher to arrive. A kid he didn't know grabbed him from behind in a vicious headlock, lifting him out of his seat. The arm hold was so tight it practically cut off his breathing. In his dream, Henry pulled the kid over the seat and down to the floor between the rows and pounded away at the kid's face, one satisfying punch after another on flesh and bone. He clutched his throat until a blue tint appeared on the kid's lips. Other kids had to pull him off. It played over and over in his mind until Henry opened his eyes to stop the combat, his body hard with tension.

In reality, the kid who attacked Henry finally let him go as abruptly as he had grabbed him when the teacher walked in. Henry had done nothing to stop him, sat and silently sobbed, too afraid to turn around to see who it was. But he did remember that sitting next to the kid was Frank.

"Why didn't you do something?" he whispered. "Anybody else would have."

The next morning, Henry limped slowly to the bathroom, his hip aching from Billy's leg strike. The mirror revealed a slight bluish lump under his left eye. Another bruise appeared under his temple and his lower lip had swelled enough to be noticeable. He dabbed the lump and shrugged. "Not too bad," he whispered. "Get used to it."

In school, the kids buzzed about Henry's fight with Billy and Frank. He kind of liked the attention—maybe he'd get some respect out of it. Then, again, maybe not. He waited anxiously for the call. After math class, Mr. Davis told him to go to the Office.

Well, let's see what happens.

He stood in front of Peterson.

"We didn't see you in detention," Peterson said

"I forgot."

Peterson moved her laptop to the side. "I'm not going to belabor the point. I'll give you one last chance or you're suspended."

"My father will be calling Principal Ruzzo about this today."

He stepped closer to the desk and leaned in slightly.

"And please tell Frank and Billy never to come near me again."

"We will speak with them."

"Which means you haven't already?"

"Mr. Ruzzo is handling that."

"I'm sure he has. Did you ever speak to Derrick or Jeremy?"

"Yes. They both denied they did anything to you, and, without witnesses, there's nothing we can do."

"There were plenty of witnesses."

"Mr. Bronner asked several kids and none of them would admit to seeing anything."

"Of course." He threw his arms out. "What's the use?"

Peterson pursed her lips. "You can go back to class."

Later, Henry passed Frank limping in the hallway with one shoe untied.

"How's the foot?"

"You're gonna find out when it's up your ass," Frank replied.

Henry smiled uneasily, and later found Billy casually talking to Donny.

"Well, how's your five-day detention?"

"What five days?" Billy said sharply.

"How many days did you get?"

Billy laughed. "Three. And you got five? You should have been suspended."

"You should have been expelled."

"Boy, you're dumb. I didn't do anything wrong. You mouthed off and I changed your tone. They know that. And they don't like you anyway. Nobody does. So they're not gonna do anything."

"Beat it, Wilty," Donny said.

"Screw you," Henry snapped. "I'm the one who's going to change everybody's tone."

Henry stomped off, but wondered if he could back it up. By the end of the day, he sat stiff and frowning amid an annoying group of energetic classmates, rubbing sore knuckles. He only thought about what he had to do next. He had plenty of time to think while staring at the wall for an hour in detention, quietly seething at being wronged again.

It's coming. Your day is coming.

On the ride home with his mother, as scenes of town life passed by, sadness gripped him like it had so often, and he wondered about his own life. Was it worth all the aggravation? The school menace grew the more aggressive he became. He had expected it, but wished it gone.

"Alright, so what did Ruzzo say?" Henry asked his father at dinner.

"Ruzzo?"

"Yeah, you were going to call him, remember?"

"Yes, I know. It got a little busy today," his father replied.

"Okay."

"I'll do it tomorrow. Did you go to detention?"

"Yes, I did."

"Good. Finish that up and then keep your nose clean."

Henry snorted. "Yeah, okay. Well, set up a meeting with Ruzzo. Or I'll do it myself."

"No, you won't."

"You know, we can look into switching schools," his mother suggested.

"No. Schools are all the same. Kids are the same. Admin's the same. If we all go into his office, we can end this." But he doubted any meeting would do any good.

Henry arrived back at school now more vigilant than before. Fighting off Billy and Frank had helped, but only a little, for he knew it would happen again. Henry played the mouse throughout the day and always looked for someone to walk the hallway with.

That night he waited earnestly for his father to get home to ask if he spoke with Ruzzo. At dinner, he didn't want to show that eagerness.

But his father didn't bring it up.

"Well, did you call Ruzzo?" he finally asked.

"I did, but he was busy."

"Did he call back?"

"No."

"Don't expect him to. The heck with it. I'll go in and see him in the morning. Obviously, you guys can't get it done."

"No, you won't," his father said. "I will talk to him first thing in the morning."

"Don't bother."

"Let your father talk to him."

"That could take days. Ruzzo is supposed to have this open-door policy, so I'll walk through the open door."

"I said don't," his father said. "I'll talk to him."

"No rush. I know you adults are busy."

"That's enough," his father said.

Upstairs, his forehead rested in his palms, his emotions simmering.

Frickin' adults. You have to go the Office yourself. You can't trust them. The thought of going back to the Office scared him, but the alternative to doing nothing was gone. *C'mon, breathe. Breathe easy.* After a few minutes of relaxing, he pushed himself through homework.

Henry was as reluctant to go into the school building the next morning as he was on the first day of school. He went through the first two blocks not listening but weighing what to say to Ruzzo, or Peterson.

Approaching the Office, he rounded his lips to blow out some nerves. He asked Mary if he could see the principal.

"Hold on."

Mary came back and waved him in.

Ruzzo sat at his desk busily writing something down, and finally looked up.

"Yes?"

"I need to talk to you."

"How can I help?"

Henry began quietly, timidly, unable to be as bold as he had planned.

"Are Frank and Billy getting expelled?"

"Why?"

"Well, they attacked me, and all they get is detention. I don't think that's fair."

"I spoke with them. They admitted they were hasty in their reaction to what you said to them."

"But I didn't say anything wrong to them. You know, I don't get it."

Ruzzo sat back a moment and considered Henry.

"You have to find better ways to react to things, Henry. Plus, getting upset with us didn't help your cause. Watch your own behavior, not someone else's. I did speak to your father this morning and we agreed to reduce your punishment. Your detention is completed as of now. The matter is closed."

"What happens if they attack me again?"

"I assure you they won't," Ruzzo said firmly as he picked up his pen.

"Boy, I hope not," Henry boldly said, making it sound like a warning. Ruzzo did not respond.

Henry went slowly to the door, wanting to say something more. He closed the door behind him, knowing that Ruzzo, along with Peterson, always avoided the biggest issue.

Henry headed to his locker thinking about what had happened but was blindsided by a kid who smacked into him. Shocked, he stared at the kid, a junior he vaguely knew.

"Watch where you're goin', Wilton," he said and kept walking.

Henry recovered, knowing the kid did it deliberately and then realized why. He was friends with Frank.

Henry glumly rolled over that issue in his head at lunch.

"What's wrong?" Sharonda asked.

"Just trying to figure things out."

"Good luck with that."

"So you got detention for fighting," Chloe said. "But you weren't fighting."

Henry chuckled. "That's right. There's no difference between fighting and defending yourself in this hell hole."

"Okay, look," George said. "Kam and I will walk with you more often so you're not getting slammed so much."

"I just did by this junior I hardly know. But he knows Frank. So, because he can't come after me for a while, he's getting his buddies to do it for him."

Henry was happy that George became involved. He was Henry's oldest friend, going back to fourth. They had hit it off immediately and went through all grades together, stayed over in each other's rooms, liked the same music and movies, and their parents became friends. But in the last few years, Henry felt they were drifting apart with George more involved with sports and gaining new interests and friends. He also believed his lowly status wore down their connection.

Over the next few weeks, Henry appreciated the help of his two friends, but eventually he saw them more like nannies or big brothers. His humiliation, and anger, mounted. He still avoided and evaded around the halls when he was alone. He watched for Billy or Frank, who roamed the hallways freely, kings in their kingdom, looking like they expected nothing would happen to them. As each night passed, Henry became increasingly depressed, did less home work, and slept more.

At his desk, homework waiting, his head drooped. "I'm so tired. I just can't...do anything. How much longer can you be like this? You're so freaking miserable."

He slept in all weekend, little motivated to do anything else.

On Monday, pushing himself to take down the kings, Henry headed back to the Office to confront Ruzzo and Peterson again. But, as he approached it, his fear inexplicably surged and stopped him.

Alright, you can do this. C'mon. Go. He looked into the Office. *I can't. I can't. Fuck.* And he fled.

Henry sat dejected in his classes all day. He just wished he could talk to someone who would do something besides him. He believed his parents wouldn't do much more, and no teachers would either. He felt everyone was avoiding the real problem.

That night, he wrapped his arms around his legs and rested his forehead on his knees. He rocked himself back and forth and moaned softly.

Just down to you.

His stomach gurgled.

God, you're scared shitless. It's frickin' amazing you can't control this. It has you by the balls.

After resting a while, he took to his notebook and wrote. Then he brushed his teeth, got himself into bed, and turned out the light.

Henry felt stronger and better after first block the next day. He passed Frank talking easily with Derrick and Trevor, enjoying a freedom Henry yearned for. That fueled his anger and he walked into the Office, inexplicably with little fear and no panic.

"I want to see Mrs. Peterson," Henry said to Mary.

"Again?" Mary asked. She went into the vice-principal's office, and came back out and told Henry she was busy.

Henry clenched with impatience.

"I'll wait."

He dropped into a chair and sat stiffly.

After twenty minutes, he went in.

Alright. Be strong.

"Call Mr. Ruzzo in here, please. I need to talk to you both."

Peterson sat back in her chair looking at Henry. "Very well." She placed her pen down. "Henry, nothing will come of this."

Henry held his body steady, forcing his quivering muscles into a stillness he didn't think possible, at once strong and fearful. He moved his hand inside his jacket.

Ruzzo came in and closed the door slowly.

C'mon. Keep pushing. You have to do this.

"I want Frank and Billy removed from the school."

"Wilton, we're not discussing this anymore," Ruzzo said, taking his usual position to the right of Peterson.

"What's the problem?" Henry asked earnestly. "Why is this decision so tough?"

"Don't make it worse for yourself," Peterson said, pulling her computer in front of her. "Now go back to class."

Henry's head tilted as he now understood Peterson's arrogance in dismissing him so lightly.

He suddenly threw his arms out. "Why are you protecting them? They can do whatever they want around here and…and you do nothing about it. They are a danger to this school and everyone in it. I mean what is wrong with you people? Why do you bullies think you can…"

Henry froze, his mouth open forming a circle and his hands in the air and palms up, as if turned to stone.

Ruzzo stepped forward. "Henry. Stay calm. We will make sure they don't do it again."

"Oh, my God," he finally murmured. "You're bullies, too."

The thought horrified him. Then a cold wave moved through his skin. He shook his head slowly.

"Wilton," Peterson said impatiently. "What is wrong with you?"

"How…how could I be so blind?" Henry whispered, not hearing Peterson.

"What are you talking about, Wilton?" Ruzzo said.

And at that moment, Henry realized he was no longer looking at two human beings. He was looking at two human monsters. "Um, I, uh, I have to go. Um, I don't feel well." He backed up, staring at them, reached for the doorknob, opened the door, and slipped out.

Henry struggled through the hallway with eyes glazed over, not blinking, bumping into a few kids. In class, he couldn't listen and he slogged through the day with a lingering sickness in his belly. People talked around him in the cafeteria and classroom, but he couldn't listen.

They're bullies. Adult bullies.

At dinner that night, he sat quietly, peeking at his parents suspiciously. He picked at his food but could not taste it. His parents spoke to each other, but he could not listen. His mind swirled as he stared fixedly at his plate. His mother asked if he felt alright but he said nothing. His father demanded that he answer his mother, but Henry just stared at him. He then announced he wasn't feeling well and went upstairs.

He lay on his bed and stared. Adults aren't supposed to be that way, he thought. But, then, the evidence shone all around and made sense.

"They're bullies," he said out loud. "How could you not see this? They're protecting these kids. Because they're bullies, too."

When he finally got himself over to his desk for homework, he had no energy for it, and his studies slipped even further behind. After a while he gave up, undressed, and crawled into bed. He took out a notebook, wrote about the awful revelation, and then turned out the light. He stared into darkness until somehow sleep took him over.

Henry returned to school with more gutty anxiety and a problem he believed had doubled overnight. The adults in his school became as suspect as the kids, and he had no clue how to deal with it. Half engaged all day, he struggled to stay relaxed and composed. He pushed minimal effort in gym. In the locker room, he came out of the shower and grabbed his towel, keeping to himself.

"Hey, Wilty," Donny called out. "I forgot my towel, so gimme yours."

The boys laughed.

Henry sat slumped over and tired. "What?"

"Give me your towel."

"Oh, get the hell away from me."

Twice before his towel had been taken—by Derrick, and then Frank. Both times he stood around helpless, wet and cold.

"Give it to me, meek," Donny motioned with his fingers. "I gotta get going."

"Go ask Roach for one," Henry said.

"I'd rather have yours. You ask Roach for one."

More snickering.

"Take off."

"Give it to me or I'll whip your bare ass." Donny took a quick step forward to grab the towel, and Henry immediately wiped his behind and crotch with it.

Donny stopped short.

Henry held it out. "Want it now?" He laughed and wiped his crack again.

He hung it up in the locker

Get ready.

An arm zipped around Henry's throat and he was pulled over the bench. He hit the floor hard with Donny on top of him.

"Guys," Donny said breathlessly. "Time to put Wilty outside."

Todd, Kevin and Trevor ran at Henry, all smiling. They grabbed him and dragged him toward the door that opened to the gym. Henry planted his feet on the damp floor, which didn't stop them. He desperately started pulling his arms out of their grasps. He fell to the floor and flailed his legs frantically at them. A hard knock against his head stunned him, along with other kicks to his side and back. He cried out. The boys scrambled away, which meant a teacher was coming. Henry got to his knees.

"Wilton?"

Roach helped Henry up and walked him over to the bench to sit him down. Henry, dazed, put his hands to his head.

Roach called out to Donny. He walked around the corner where the other boys were dressing.

"What happened?" Henry heard Roach demanding.

"Nothin'," Donny replied in a placating voice. "Just having a little fun. We weren't going to throw him out there."

"He jumped me from behind," Henry said hoarsely.

"That's a lie," Donny shouted back over the lockers.

"Enough," Roach bellowed. "I don't know what's going on or why you kids keep doing this, but I want it stopped now."

No one said anything and Roach came back to Henry.

"Your head okay?"

"I'll live, as usual," Henry answered, his face flushed from the fright of it, heart pounding. He stretched his back. "Take them down to the Office and get them suspended, please."

Roach checked Henry's head for blood and told Henry to go to the nurse if he became dizzy or got a headache. Then he walked away, as though he didn't hear what Henry asked.

Bully.

Henry got up slowly and started to dress. Donny appeared around the corner.

"I'm gonna get you for that, narc," he said.

"Get outta here, you idiot."

Donny grunted. He pointed at Henry.

"See ya."

"Moron."

Henry finished dressing as the other boys passed by quietly. In science, he hunkered in his chair and agonized over another assault, a throbbing head and a mind too preoccupied to learn. Instead of paying attention to Mrs. Hernandez and civics, he reassessed the immensity of challenging bully adults and kids.

They're partners. They're doing all this together.

While passing close to the Office later, he wondered if Roach told Ruzzo or Peterson about the locker room attack.

No way he did. I'm a meek. Why would he?

He walked into Roach's office.

"Hi," he said pleasantly. Roach sat at his desk. "Did you report the attack on me to administration yet?"

Roach dropped his eyes. "No. Not yet. I've had classes all day. I'll do it shortly," he said as he went to his filing cabinet,

"Well, I tell you what. I'll meet you down there."

"I'll try to help you. But I didn't actually see it."

"Uh-huh."

Henry strode to the Office and got in to see Peterson.

Okay. Relax. This is easy.

"Yes, Henry. What is it?" she asked as she typed busily on her keyboard.

"I was jumped in the locker room today," he began tepidly.

Peterson stopped. She let out a heavy sigh.

"Donny wanted my towel. I didn't give it to him so he and his friends jumped me and were going to throw me into the gym naked."

Peterson sat silent.

"Alright. We will speak to them."

"Kevin, Todd and Trevor were the others. Mr. Roach will be arriving shortly to report it. I will expect those animals to be expelled."

"Curb your tone, Henry. We will decide that after talking to them."

"I'll let my parents know, too. This is the fourth time I've been attacked. What are you doing?" He raised his voice boldly.

"Alright, Henry. I understand your frustration. We will get to the bottom of this."

"And how can I trust you to do that?"

Peterson's face reddened.

"At this point you'll have to. Now please leave. I have to get on a call."

He stared at her a moment but left without further discussion,

That night, he sat against the wall on his bed, arms folded, homework waiting.

"Please leave. Please leave. You'd like me to leave, wouldn't you?" He sighed audibly. "This whole nightmare," he whispered. "You have to show them who's gonna leave. But, you're too scared and too weak."

He dropped his hands onto his lap, his brow furrowing and cheeks twitching. His lips clamped hard with frustration and anger, two banes wearing him down, and he was unaware of what they were doing to him. He felt like he was always pulling himself out of quicksand

"You're not gonna beat them." He kneaded his forehead. "You're too afraid to push hard enough. This fear," he whispered harshly. "This goddamn fucking, *fucking* fear."

He formed fists.

"Alright. Stop. Stop." He breathed out. "There's got to be a way. I know there is. Get up, idiot. You showed something against Billy. Use that. You're not dead yet."

He pulled out his diary and wrote, then went to his desk and opened one of his textbooks, easing the rage that twisted his mind. Exams started the next week, another issue he agonized over, and he needed to get ready for them.

He told his parents about the locker room attack. Their initial questions seemed to blame him until they realized he was the complete victim. His father called the next day, but Henry could only wait to see any effect.

Once again, another assault led to a quieter next day. Donny, Trevor and Todd all passed him by as if nothing had happened the day before.

Henry shook his head. *Just another day in paradise. That's what they should call this place. Paradise High School.* He burst out laughing, kids stared, and it felt good.

He hadn't heard anything in three days, so he trudged nervously back to the Office.

"Can I see Mrs. Peterson?"

"She won't be available for a while," Mary said.

"Then I need to see the principal."

"Regarding?"

"I was attacked in the locker room."

Mary stared a moment, and then went in to Ruzzo, who agreed to see him.

"Yes, Wilton?"

"You heard I was attacked in the locker room?"

Ruzzo sighed heavily. Henry couldn't tell if that meant Ruzzo was frustrated by him or by another attack on a student. "Yes."

"What's, uh, happening?"

"Well, all four boys you say attacked you denied it. Mr. Roach said he didn't actually see it."

"And you believe them?"

"We need evidence of their involvement."

"I was on the floor practically passed out. Mr. Roach had to pick me up. Donny told him they weren't going to throw him out there. That means they attacked me. And he headlocked me from behind when I didn't give him my towel. What more do you need?"

"They deny it. It's not fair to them, Henry, if we don't have actual proof."

"What about fairness to me? You think I'm making this up?"

"No. We need to get other boys to come forward."

"Are you going to do that?."

"Yes. We'll check on that."

Henry nodded at Ruzzo.

"Yeah, I understand." He walked to the door. "I really understand."

"And what is that?"

"I'll be back tomorrow. Thanks for your time."

He walked out and stood around a while. He hopelessly sat through his classes and confronted Donny later.

"So you couldn't own up to it, could you?" Henry said.

"What?"

"Attacking me in the locker room?"

Donny shrugged. "I don't know what you're talking about. You must have been dreaming."

"They're going to get you eventually, bully. Your days are coming to an end."

Donny laughed. "Wilton, what is your problem? Lighten up."

Henry shook his head and walked away, knowing no one would admit to the truth and no one would be a witness.

He wandered dejectedly the rest of the day. He thought of the paper he had put off, which required a trip to the city library.

Avoiding and evading until the end of the day, Henry found Kam, Caleb and Sharonda at her locker.

"Anyone up for the downtown library?"

"Can't," Kam said.

"Me, too," Caleb replied.

"Oh, c'mon. Don't you have to start your paper?"

"I have to head home," Sharonda said.

Henry grimaced. "Alright. See ya later."

In about an hour, Henry arrived downtown on the metro bus and hustled up the busy sidewalk bordered by storefronts and an endless line of parked cars. He waited for the walk light along with everyone else, their breath steaming in the brisk breeze. He jogged across the street and up the wide, well-worn marble steps of the library that led him through imposing metal and glass doors. He walked into the huge foyer and the warm, slightly musty air.

Henry pushed himself with some forced grittiness to get started on a class paper early for once. After perusing a few books on the second floor, he walked around a corner of bookshelves and stopped short. Carla sat alone in the large hall filled with other tables occupied by silent people. A few books were spread out open in front of her and she wrote on a notepad. Henry had never found her in the city library before and wondered if she thought it safer to come here and hide, as he had done.

"Hi," Henry said softly as he sat down.

"Oh, hello," she said.

"Whatcha up to?" Henry asked.

"School work," Carla said flatly. "What else?"

"Yeah, me too. Just looking at some books for the history paper we have to do. Started yours yet?"

"No," she replied.

"What's your paper going to be on?" he asked.

Carla gave a quick sigh. "I don't know."

"I think I have some ideas for mine."

"Good for you."

Henry gave her a wide smile.

"Something wrong?"

"Are you going to sit here?"

"Uh, yeah, why?"

"I don't have a lot of time to talk."

"Well," Henry said, motioning to her books, "keep going. I won't bother you. You know, Carla, I'm just trying to be friendly, like human beings do? Kinda mean to me last time. Any reason why?"

"I just don't want to talk to anyone right now."

"You can talk to me. I'm not your enemy."

"Alright," she relented. "What do you want to talk about?"

"Uh, I don't know. What do you think about the school? Do you like it?"

"No, not really," she relented. "It was okay at first. But lately it's gotten worse. Is that it?"

Henry nodded. "I agree with you. I just needed corroboration from someone else. Well, I think we can get together and do something. I'm already arguing with Ruzzo and Peterson about that. If we join up, we can cut these bully kids down."

"Bully kids? I'm not doing that, Henry."

"Why not? The thing is, you're a girl. They'll listen to you. I'm a boy. They think I'm supposed to be tough and not let it bother me and blah, blah, blah. But I need someone else to step up, too. You'd be perfect."

"I'm not sure about that."

"You'll let them know who the bully girls are. You know, Robin and Laurie, Meaghan, and they're cybering you. Do you know why are they doing that to you?"

Carla moved her computer aside, appearing suddenly angry. She opened her math text.

"No. And I don't care why. I try to ignore it. Like you should."

Carla's refusal spurred Henry's impatience

"No. That's what they want you to do. All this ignoring does nothing, no matter what these idiot adults tell you." He spoke even louder. "We can get them, Carla. We can get them if we come together, just like the bullies are always together. We can do it, too."

"Shhh."

"Quiet please."

Carla suddenly got her things together.

"Where you going?"

"I can't help you, Henry. It won't make any difference."

She stood up and walked away.

Henry stood up. "Yes, it will, Carla. It will. Trust me. I mean, how much longer can you live with this?"

"Hey, pal, quiet."

Henry darted an angry glance at the man. Carla disappeared among the shelves. Henry dropped back in his chair and rubbed his tired face, believing he would never convince her, or anyone.

She's just as afraid as I am. Well, she won't help you, either. On your own again.

But, Henry left that behind and stacked up books for his paper as the afternoon light faded to dark. This was the earliest he had begun a paper, and he pushed himself into it. He wanted this to be a success to match the seventh-grade science project that almost never was. He slumped a bit remembering it—spending weeks on a replica of a NASA satellite, getting into it, sparking his mind, feeling good about it, his first real accomplishment, going to get an A.

His parents praised him for it, and when he brought it safely to school, even his classmates liked it. After setting it up, he went to the boys' room and when he came back the project was gone. He stood stunned and asked everyone where it was and most shrugged and said they didn't know.

He saw Frank walk in from an unused side corridor that led to the construction of a new school wing and sit down. Outside was a large dumpster. He went out to it, climbed up, and there was his project, broken up among pieces of wood and sheetrock. He could still see the faces staring out at him, including Frank's, which was totally impassive. Frank insisted he didn't do it, no one admitted to anything, and the teacher did little to help him, since no one owned up to it. Henry argued with her that it was Frank who did it and to do more about it. He ended up in the principal's office for his trouble.

He got away with it. And everyone just moves on and forgets it and you're too fucking weak and scared to go after him. Well, not anymore. You can't cry about it forever. You got a good idea now, so sit down and start writing it.

While he moved ahead on his paper over the next week, he still had to deal with exams starting on Monday, and exam anxiety he could not control.

They're just stupid tests. Lighten up.

He studied in the usual way, believed he knew it all well enough, but came out of the week with the same old frustration and the same old grades. He became desperate to find an answer. Now, older and slowly, glacially, trying to understand himself, he fell back to the main problem: a dysfunctional mind, and totally convinced it was.

Why do other kids just let it flow and you can't do shit? Geez. I can't go three more years like this.

At home, Henry placed his elbows on his desk and his hands pressed against his lips, books waiting. He remembered the teachers he had and he couldn't think of one who came up to him and gave him the confidence he needed to do better. He'd read stories of famous people remembering the teachers who inspired them. Not for me, he thought. No teacher ever said, "Hey, Henry, you're a C student. I think you can be an A student. I can help you. You want to try?" He laughed quietly at that impossibility.

"You know, you're already at rock bottom," he mumbled. "Class is totally boring. Maybe it's time to have some fun in class. Hell, do you even know what fun is?"

Then he decided it was time to make the teachers work for him. It was time to make class more interesting. It was time to raise his hand.

You got to do it. You gotta man up. You can't let the material slide and try to figure it out later. That's never worked.

He tried out the new strategy in math the next day. More than any other subject, math exhibited the chasm between the meek and the bold. Henry stood teetering on the windy edge. He chose one homework problem that eluded him, so he hesitantly raised his hand half-way and flushed to a burn. Davis nodded. Henry got himself to say he didn't quite understand the problem and could Davis explain it again. Davis willingly did. He listened and understood the problem a little bit better, though not completely, and left it at that. He had done enough for one class.

As Davis went through homework problems, Henry mused that teachers must know all the kids sitting in front of them don't understand the material. But they go on to other things if a hand isn't raised. *We've let them get off so easily.* Now he wanted to raise his hand, not only for himself, but for the kids who wouldn't. Admit ignorance, take the shame.

C'mon. This is good.

The stressful hand-raising continued, at least once in each class that day and the next few days. However, the more he did it, the more relaxed, and less embarrassed, he became. He discovered how little he actually understood in any of his classes, which worried him. That in itself drove him to raise his hand to the point where, after a full week of it, teachers and classmates began to manifest annoyance.

Davis glanced at Henry.

"Yes," Davis said tiredly.

"Can we go over problem fifteen again? I don't quite understand it. Um…"

"We have to move on, Wilton. If you need further help, we can talk about it after class. There is also tutoring if you need it, which few of you take advantage of. Everyone, turn to page seventy-eight."

Pages rustled around the room.

Henry persisted, his heart speeding up. "It won't take long."

Davis ran his fingers through his thin brown hair.

"I'm tired of all this after-school tutoring all the time so you can 'move on.' I'm sure others don't get the problem, either."

"Speak for yourself, Wilty."

The class became deadly quiet.

"So," Henry began, "in this problem, I don't understand how…"

"Wilton. What you don't understand is we're not going over this again and that's final."

Henry sighed loudly and turned the pages of his textbook. "Fine. I asked a teacher a question and he's refusing to answer it. Cool."

Henry's face reddened at his rash comment. Davis glanced at the class and then walked down the aisle. Knowing Davis came for him, Henry stared into the textbook.

"Wilton, if you don't like this, you can go to the Office. If you say one more thing like that," Davis said sternly, "you will go to the Office."

Henry glanced up. "Whatever you say, Mr. Davis."

At the end of the class, Henry expected Davis to call him over, but he didn't.

In history, one kid asked if there would be another fight.

Henry smiled. "We'll see."

Now this is getting fun.

History class went better, but he hounded Mrs. Fields in English about verb tenses that always confused him. He pushed her to keep clarifying, until finally her face stiffened with impatience. Fields called him over after class.

"Henry, I'm glad to see you more involved in class discussion, but I felt you were a little pushy. In the future, please be more polite."

Henry shrugged. "I don't think I was being pushy. I just didn't understand the problems, and I wanted to."

"I think doing it with a better tone will be more helpful."

"I don't think anything was wrong with my tone. I wanted you to explain things better, especially for C students like me."

Her brow crinkled. "What do you mean? I instruct so everyone can understand, especially C students."

"Then how come we're still C students?"

Fields stopped at the question, which surprised Henry, as well. Her mouth opened slightly.

"Well," she said uncertainly. "You just have to work harder."

"Work harder. I've heard that before. What does that actually mean?"

"Well, study harder."

"Right. But what does that mean?"

"Henry, what are you asking?"

"I'm just trying to understand. You adults say work harder and study harder. What do I do to study harder? Give me the steps."

Henry raised his eyebrows, looking for an answer. One of the waiting students let out an impatient sigh. Fields' narrow, aged face tightened as though she was caged into answering.

"If you want to know how to study better, Henry," she replied. "I'll be happy to help you."

"Can you give me a few tips right now?"

"I'll be happy to set up a time for that. I have these students to talk to."

68

"Yeah, Wilton, I got another class."

"Alright. In the meantime, I'll go away and 'study harder'."

He chuckled and went to his locker to change books, then off to the cafeteria. Kam sat with Chloe and Becka at a small round table, eating away.

"What's going on?" Henry asked.

"The usual," Kam said.

"So what's with you in class?" Becka said. "You're annoying everyone."

Henry shrugged as he opened his drink.

"I'm just asking questions. Isn't that what we're supposed to do?"

"I guess," she replied.

"I've never seen Davis so ticked," Becka said. "I'm surprised he didn't toss you."

"Me, too." He chuckled gleefully.

Kam shook his head.

"Well, look," Henry said, "teachers are so used to us just sitting there like…like lumps on a log. They're not used to somebody all of a sudden pushing them to explain things better. Typical. When they challenge you, it's called good teaching. When you challenge them, you're rude. Well, they better get used to it." His face hardened. "'Cause I'm not gonna stop. Plus, it makes going to class more fun. I'm so freakin' bored in this place, I feel like putting a gun in my mouth."

He quickly raised his hands. "Figuratively speaking, of course."

The next week, exams came back. Henry worriedly waited in his seat for his math test, self-esteem on the line, thinking positively for a good grade. When he received it, he saw a big red C plus. He rubbed his forehead hard. *Shit.*

"Hey, Wilton got a C plus," someone said, looking over his shoulder. "After all those questions. Wow."

"Real smart, Wilty."

"Heck," Laurie said, "I got an A minus and I didn't ask any questions at all."

Other kids mocked Henry as he sat hunkered over in embarrassment, angry that he hadn't hidden his grade and irritated that a bully like Laurie had done better. His other exam results weren't much different. He spent the rest of day and evening moping about it.

The next morning during announcements, Peterson mentioned there would be a school assembly for the next afternoon. Everyone speculated what it could be about, being such a rare event. As Henry discussed it with his friends, the thought struck that possibly the attacks on him and his own complaints could be the reason.

This will be interesting.

He didn't let his poor exams stop his persistent hand-raising. He had come to enjoy it and how much it irritated others. He pushed past his sensitivity to their criticisms.

Screw them. Keep going. You'll never learn anything if you stop.

Henry became confident he might get somewhere, and that rare feeling of hope felt good to him, acting almost like some kind of outlet for him.

"Hey, Wilty," Trevor called out, standing around with Donny and Charles in the hallway. "I need ten bucks. I'll pay you back next week."

Charles burst out laughing.

"Are you guys still extortionists?" Henry called back over his shoulder. "You were doing that in the seventh grade. Time to grow up."

He retrieved his things. As he closed the locker door, the three boys surrounded him.

"Look out," Henry said. "Have to catch my bus."

Henry pushed himself between Trevor and Charles, who tripped him. Henry stumbled forward, his hand slapping against the floor to stop his fall. He straightened up.

"What did you do that for?"

"We don't like the way you're talking lately," Charles said, stepping toward Henry.

"Is that right."

"Going to the Office all the time," Trevor said. "Keep your mouth shut and leave us alone."

"Wilty, when we hit you, it's because you deserve it," Donny added. Trevor chuckled and shook his head.

"So you keep your mouth shut. We run the show around here, not you."

Say something.

"Stay away from me from now on and it won't happen," he replied as he walked away. "Jerks."

"Let's get him."

Henry heard them trot up. He pulled his pack off and blindly swung it around, hitting Charles in the shoulder and grazing his face. Henry skipped backwards.

"Ha, ha," he yelled, as he shouldered his pack and skipped away. "Come and get me, turkeys."

"Wilton."

Mrs. Roach, science teacher and wife of the gym teacher, came up to them quickly. Henry bounced down the stairs.

"What are you doing?"

"Yeah, we were just talking with him and then he hits us," Donny said.

"Charles was gonna attack me."

"I was not," Charles protested.

"Wilton, come back here," Roach demanded.

"Have to get my bus."

"Come back here," Roach exclaimed.

Henry got outside and trotted onto his bus just before it left. He plopped down with a heavy, nervous exhale and nodded at a few kids sitting nearby. He stared out the window.

It never ends. They're having fun and the teachers are letting them. He gazed out the window at the passing scenes. A corner of his mouth turned up into a vengeful smile, pinching into his cheek. *Your fun's coming. You can feel it now.*

Henry avoided Mrs. Roach throughout the next day so he wouldn't have to argue with her. That afternoon, everyone packed the auditorium, resounding with high-pitched chatter and laughter that bounced off the high, wood-paneled walls which rose up to a row of grimy, forgotten windows. Seniors sat up front and freshmen in the rear. The teachers took seats or stood along the walls. Henry had found Kam, George and Chloe and followed to sit with them. He saw Caleb a few rows back and nodded to him.

On the stage, the president of each class, including Robin, sat down on the chairs already placed there. When Ruzzo and Peterson finally arrived, making everybody wait, they lumbered up the steps onto the stage and everyone quieted down. Ruzzo stopped at the microphone and adjusted it to his lofty height. He cleared his throat and straightened his red-print tie. Peterson sat down behind him and primly crossed her legs.

Henry grunted.

"Problem?" Chloe asked.

Henry saw Robin say something to the freshman president and they switched seats, presumably, he thought, so she could sit next to Peterson. He then noticed for the first time how much they looked alike.

"Good afternoon," Ruzzo began in his sonorous tone. "I have called you all together today because of the recent rash of conflict here in school."

"Recent. It's been going on forever," Henry whispered to Chloe.

"I'm sure you've already heard about it or even witnessed it. I just want everyone to know that we do not condone physical attacks in this school in any way. We have zero tolerance for any of that, and this includes verbal attacks as well. It has come to my attention that some of you are saying bad things to each other. We will no longer tolerate that. What we will tolerate is respect for one

72

another. It is important that we speak to each other in a civil, respectful manner at all times. We respect the differences we see in each other. We don't criticize to the point where it is insensitive or hurtful to that person. You must keep in mind how the other person feels about what you are saying. If it is hurtful, then you stop." He paused a moment. "We will no longer condone any of this behavior. Going forward, any student who is caught behaving that way, hitting someone, or saying something that is demeaning, racial or otherwise, will be reprimanded, up to and including being expelled. It should not be difficult to do this, nor should this be difficult to understand."

Henry smirked.

"Now, even though it's November, I'm going to give you an early Christmas present. I'm going to wipe all your slates clean. Everyone starts over. Alright? So let's behave and get along. No physical or verbal attacks on each other. That's something we don't need or want. Are there any questions?"

Henry lifted his eyebrows. *Wipe the slates clean?* He thrust his hand into the air, a little too fast. He wanted to pull it back down but too late. All eyes turned to him.

Ruzzo frowned. "Yes?"

Henry pushed himself out of his seat, petrified into numbness.

"I'm...I'm wondering about the clean slates?" Henry called out weakly.

"I can't hear you."

"Um, what...what about the kids who a...already have clean slates? What do they get?"

He stopped a moment. "I mean, the kids who cause the problems get their slates cleaned but the others, the good kids, get what—cleaner slates than they already have? We don't get anything else?"

Even far away, Henry saw Ruzzo's eyes darken. "What you get is a pat on the back. Thanks for being good, Wilton."

Everyone burst out laughing.

Henry forced a little smile and nodded in respect to Ruzzo's mirthful remark. Robin whispered to Peterson, who shrugged. The audience quieted.

"So, so," Henry continued more boldly, "the bad kids get something for being bad and the good kids get…get nothing for being good." He stood silent for effect as his heart thumped. "Okay. Just wanted to get that clear. Thank you."

Peterson slowly shook her head. Robin did the same.

"We appreciate everyone being good," Ruzzo answered. "Follow the rules and respect one another and there won't be any issues. And we'll get through this year in good stead. Alright?" He examined the paper in his hand. "Now, I have a few more things…"

As Ruzzo moved on to those things, Henry looked at him peevishly and crossed his arms with clenched jaw.

"As usual," Henry fumed, "we get nothing."

"Wilton, you a-hole."

Henry turned around and crunched his forehead at Derrick, two rows back.

"Did you just hear what Ruzzo said? Or are you frickin' deaf?" Henry shook his head at him.

"What a stupid waste this is," Henry whispered to Chloe.

"Well, it might do something," she said.

The assembly ended and everyone filed out into the main corridor adjacent to the open courtyard. Henry's friends sped on ahead, and he let them go. A couple of girls passed him.

"Wilton, you're an idiot," one of them remarked.

"Right back atcha."

The girls laughed.

"Wilton."

Mrs. Roach walked up to him. "Why did you leave yesterday when I told you not to?"

"Did you just hear that girl call me a name?"

"Yes, I did," she answered.

Henry raised his eyebrows. "Well?"

"I will speak to them in a moment. More importantly, why did you leave yesterday when I told you I wanted to talk to you?" she continued.

Henry sighed loudly.

Roach's face twitched at the insolence and raised her finger at him. "Don't do that," she ordered. "When I tell you to do something, you do it."

"I had to catch my bus."

"I don't care about your bus."

"I do. And I wasn't going to miss it because of some stupid kids bullying me for the hundredth time."

"You hit Charles with your backpack. You hurt him."

"He's fine. But you didn't see it, so how do you know for sure?"

"He told me."

"He was coming up from behind to attack me."

"Well, he said he didn't do anything to you."

"He tripped me and I fell to the floor."

"Nevertheless, when I call you back, you come back," she insisted.

"Is that it?"

"No. You were rude in there. The principal made a very good speech about respect and then you disrespected him. Not too many of us think you are one of the good kids. You owe Mr. Ruzzo an apology."

"What did I do wrong?"

Mr. Roach walked up to them. "Your question was inappropriate."

"Well, how do I know until I ask it?"

"You shouldn't have asked it."

Henry smiled quizzically.

"But how do I know that until I do?"

"That's enough," she said, her dark eyes flaring. "Go to the principal and apologize." She walked away and her husband gave Henry a severe glance.

Henry couldn't figure whether that was an order or if she said it hoping he would. He went to his locker and then went home.

Over the next week, Henry noticed life at school became relatively peaceful. The bullies passed him by with hardly a glance. Even the Vultures kept their snide remarks to themselves. Henry sensed a friendlier air and kids kept to their own groups.

In this oddly new environment, the mouse rested. Henry walked straight down the hall without looking out for anyone, although still inherently anxious. Kids appeared to him cheerier and more relaxed.

"Now this is the way it should be," he murmured at his locker.

"What?" George said, arriving next to him.

"Huh? Oh. Just seems more chill around here. Easier."

"Hm. I don't notice anything," George replied, and they walked.

"Right." Henry smirked at his middling friend, never harasses anyone, never harassed.

"Did you win last night?"

"Beat them good. Scored a goal, too."

"Cool. You're gonna be captain in a few years."

"Watson and Banner are ahead of me on that," George lamented.

"Ya gotta show that leadership, dude."

"I need more goals."

"Okay, I'll watch your next game and tell you what you're doing wrong."

George snorted. "That'll really help. Thanks."

The boys went into the cafeteria. Henry peered around at all his chattering peers; their energy no longer annoyed him.

This is really good. I could get used to this. Maybe there is hope after all.

He refused to think about how long it would last. He went home a little happier and came back with less trepidation. He had wanted everything to change so badly, to rid himself of the burden of fear and helplessness.

Well, maybe this is it. You're finally free. You might not have to deal with these adult bullies after all.

But, by the beginning of the next week, his trust in this respite weakened. From the start, he couldn't believe the old way of life would simply disappear—the bullies liked it too much, he thought. They needed it too much. He wished he could somehow keep the good times rolling.

No way. Not with these kids, or these adults, in charge.

After classes, Henry went to the gym for a basketball game between his school and the one nearby. He climbed up to sit with Kam, who had his computer on his lap.

"How they doing?" he asked, above the chants, cheers, whistles and squeaking shoes.

"Not too good," Kam answered. "As you can see by the score."

"I left a few texts for ya. Did you get them?"

Kam shrugged. "Yeah, I've been busy."

Henry didn't believe him. Caleb and teammates sped up and down the court. While Caleb was the shortest of the players, he moved and passed sharply.

The crowd exploded over a swished three-pointer.

"Caleb's playing well."

"He is."

"Why don't you just tell me what's wrong?"

"Nothing."

"Well, you want to hang out this weekend?"

"I'll let you know."

"Oh, baloney. It's what I did at the assembly, isn't it? Now I'm the kid you don't want to hang with. Don't worry, dude, I'm used to it."

"Sometimes you just go too far," Kam said.

"No, Kam. They're the ones who've gone too far. Clean slates. That's laughable. I have to admit, though, it has been quieter lately. Like, you don't have everyone carping at each other, making fun of each other."

Kam shrugged. "I guess."

"Ruzzo may have said the right things, but, just by the sound of his voice, you could tell his heart wasn't in it."

"Sounded okay to me."

Middling.

"Peterson sitting behind him—what a pair."

After the game, Henry walked down the hallway with Kam. He laughed out loud at something Kam said, louder than he needed to.

The next morning, Henry boldly strode through the hallway, not avoiding or hiding from enemies.

I never should have had to do that. Never again. Then he declared the mouse dead.

Halfway down the corridor, meandering through the kids, he heard his name.

"Hey, Wilton."

Henry answered without turning. "Hey what?"

"Want to hang out after school?"

Laughter.

Henry did find that amusing.

"I'd rather put a knife in my eye," he replied as he opened his locker.

Henry put some books in and took some out.

"Hey," Charles said, "we asked you nicely."

"A bit rude, dude," Joe said.

"Get away from me, dude."

"Apologize for hitting me with your pack," Charles said.

"You tripped me. You apologize to me."

"That was an accident. Now apologize," Charles said threateningly.

Henry slammed the locker shut.

"Make me."

Those words fell out of Henry too quickly, and for the first time. Charles' forehead twitched minutely. Henry found Charles to be a lucky sort—short black hair, handsome, good with the girls. He got good grades, too. Better than Henry's. He could have a bright, funny demeanor, and that,

78

Henry knew, was what helped hide the bully inside and allow him to get away with it.

"Excuse me."

Henry started to leave. Joe stepped in his way.

"Whoa, whoa, whoa," Henry said, putting his hands up. "Don't get in my way. I thought you bullies got the message not to do that at the assembly."

"Don't call us that," Joe demanded.

"Then stop acting like it. Now get out of the way." No one moved. "Now!"

Joe and Charles stiffened at Henry's shout, which had a sharp and angry edge to it that Henry well knew and enjoyed. Other kids turned as if startled.

"What's going on here?" Mrs. Hernandez said, approaching them.

"They're in my way again," Henry said.

"No, we're not," protested Joe.

"Then get out of my way."

Charles smirked and motioned to Joe. They sauntered off.

"Hey, there you go," Henry said angrily but with a forced pleasant tone. "Now you're learnin'. Walk away nice and quiet. That's what I like to see bullies do. Nice and quiet."

"That's enough, Henry," Hernandez ordered.

Joe and Charles curiously peered back.

"Well, that didn't go very well," she said.

"They were harassing me again. Remember what Mr. Ruzzo said?"

"I do. And he also said we treat each other with respect."

"Were they treating me with respect?"

"Maybe not, but we don't call kids bullies."

"That's what they are."

"We need you to get along better."

"Yeah. Well, I've been trying to get along with them for years. I think it's time for them to get along with me."

Hernandez dropped her head and pressed her lips into a slight smile, as though, Henry thought, she found what he said ridiculous.

He stepped closer to her. "If they come to me and get in my way, they cause the problems. There they are. Simply tell them not to get in my way again."

"I'll talk to them," Hernandez replied with a grimace. "We just need to keep things calm and safe around here."

"For who?"

"For all of us.

"That sounds like I'm included. Wow, what a change." He threw his hand out. "Well, you teachers have talked to me enough. Let me see you talk to them."

"I will do so, Henry," she said impatiently.

"It only takes a few seconds. Let's walk down there together. C'mon."

"I said later, when I have more time."

Henry gave her an angry stare. "Well, I talked to them like that because you teachers don't. It's their job to pick on me and my job to accept it and like it. Right?" he asked sharply.

"No, Henry, that's not true at all."

"It's not?" He leaned in to her. "If they harass me again, Mrs. Hernandez, it will be your fault. So tell them to stay away from me."

He walked off and breathed steadily to ease his rage as he approached English class.

Good. Good. You're feeling stronger.

Henry heard someone in the classroom call out.

"Where's Wilty?" Laughter. Mrs. Fields, at the door, showed a slight smile.

"It's Wilton," he told the class as he sat down.

Henry's tension eased by lunchtime as he sat quietly with friends in the cafeteria.

"What's wrong?" Caleb asked. "You mad again?"

"Why not? Plenty to be mad about."

"Why? I expend my energy in other ways."

"How's that working for you?"

"Good."

"Yeah? You a hundred percent unbullied this week?"

"So far."

They laughed as though it were a private joke.

"Will you two knock it off?" Becka said. "Just let it go."

"What do you care? You're never bullied," Henry said. To Henry, Becka was another middling, untouched by harassment, and a bit haughty at times.

"I was picked on in the seventh grade because of my weight."

"I don't see any weight," Henry said.

"That's because I stay thin. Plus, you've always taken everything way too seriously. That's why they pick on you."

"Thanks, Becka. Apparently, you took it seriously."

"But I never let it run my life like you have. And I forget about it. "

Henry narrowed his eyes at her, a bit miffed that maybe she was right.

He turned to Caleb. "It's breaking down, though."

"What is?" Caleb asked.

"The truce."

"What truce?"

"Between the strong and the weak," Henry contemplated. "Between them and us."

"So how far are you going to push everybody?" Chloe asked. "Something's going to happen pretty soon."

"That's right," Henry muttered. "It is."

"You might really get kicked out," Caleb said.

"I'm sure they'll try, but it won't happen."

"Why's that?"

"Just a feeling. But watch yourself. Charles and Joe came at me. The vampires are rising again."

"Things will change just because they came after you?" Becka asked.

"Only a matter of time." Henry peered around for other victims. "I'll tell those kids over there. And if you two ladies can watch the Vultures to see if they bother Carla, let me know."

The girls laughed. "Okay, captain."

If the school returned to hell, Henry feared what would happen. Sitting in class, images of more arguments, fights or worse worried him. Taking them all on frightened him, but he would not back down.

They're all sick of you? Well, too bad. Kam doesn't want to hang out. Fine. He's not gonna help anyway. No one will. Back to the war.

"Can you answer that, Wilton?" Bronner said. "Wilton?"

"What?" he said hoarsely and cleared his throat.

"Wake up, Wilty," someone said.

"You want to answer the question?"

"Sorry. If you ask the question again, I'll try to answer it. And it's Wilton, by the way."

Bronner sternly repeated the question, and Henry gave him a correct answer. Being awakened from a gloomy reverie and giving the right answer so quickly made Henry sit up, energized. He got himself into the remaining lecture, happily annoying everyone. Although some kids in each of his classes still cared less about the whole asking questions thing and slumped in their chairs, a few more raised their hands. Henry wondered if he had influenced them.

Yes, he thought, maybe there is hope.

But reality always bit back. While on the bus ride home, reading over his paper, he pressed teeth against lip. He couldn't tell in any way if the paper would get him an A or just another C, much like his exams. He moved his hand over his worried brow and down his cheek.

There's got to be some way to get these grades up. You're not stupid.

The next day, Friday, Henry caught George at his locker.

"Hey," George answered quietly.

"Wanna get together and study tomorrow?"

George closed his locker silently.

"C'mon," Henry goaded. "Let's get Caleb and the girls and meet at the library." He raised his eyebrows sheepishly.

"Alright. I'll see if Kam wants to."

"No, don't. He's not interested."

"Wilton."

"How about noon?" Henry asked.

"Okay."

"Wilton, let's get to class," Johnson said.

Henry did not acknowledge Johnson and walked away.

"Wilton."

Henry kept walking.

"Wilton, stop when I'm talking to you."

Henry did.

"What is it?"

"Get to class."

"That's where I was going until you stopped me."

"Well, get going then."

"You know, Mr. Johnson, there are a lot of kids in this hallway and I'm the only one you're, um, saying that to. Any reason why?"

"Because I want to," Johnson said. "Now go."

"Are you picking on me, Mr. Johnson?" Henry said loud enough for others to hear.

Johnson stared silently.

"I hope not."

Henry liked how he held Johnson's stare to let him know he would not accept such treatment. *Frickin' adult bully. The teachers might be starting on you. You knew they would eventually.*

While walking down the corridor near the Office that afternoon, Henry passed Miss Stagg. He gave her a quick, uncaring glance. He only spoke with her once the year before about what classes he should take and a possible career path. Henry never heard many complaints about her as a guidance counselor, but then, she wasn't in the hallways very often, either.

"Hello, Henry," she said, brushing back her long, reddish-brown hair that Henry had found sensual. Her smile brightened her round, impish face. Mostly, he found her formal and all business, while young and new to the job.

"I'd like to have a talk with you, if that's okay. Do you have time later?"

"I have to catch my bus."

"It shouldn't take long."

He shrugged. "Okay."

"Good. I'll see you then."

Henry had an idea what she wanted. Ruzzo likely told her to talk to him. After classes, Henry stepped into Stagg's office and sat down in front of her desk. She moved aside some papers and a book and placed a file in front.

"Well," she said, settling back in her chair. "So tell me. How is everything with you?"

"About the same."

"No real issues going on?"

Henry pushed the corners of his mouth down. "Just the usual." He blinked back at her innocently.

"Well, they asked me to have a talk with you," she said, her elbows on the arms of the chair and her hands fiddling with a pen.

"How come?"

"Well, you seem to be having some altercations with kids lately, bickering with some of the teachers, the principal and vice-principal."

"Uh-huh."

"Do you agree?"

Henry thought a moment.

"Sometimes."

"Any reason why?"

"Well, some of the kids kinda pick on me and I'm tired of it."

Stagg pushed herself forward and placed her elbows on the desk

"Do you know why?"

"Why what?"

"Why they're picking on you."

"Because they like to, I guess."

"Do you think you're dealing with it okay?"

Henry nodded. "I think so."

"Well, other people don't."

Henry nodded. "Apparently."

Stagg placed her pen down.

"Who are those people picking on you?"

"The bullies."

"Yes. I hear you like to use that word. We don't like labeling people."

"It is what it is." He rested an ankle on the other knee and relaxed even as his stomach tightened.

"And who do you think these bullies are?"

"Well," Henry began. "There's Derrick and Jeremy, Frank, Billy, Charles, Donny. Um, Todd and Joe. And then there is Robin and Meaghan and Laurie."

"You think they're all bullies."

"They are."

"I have asked some other students about you and they're kind of frustrated, even concerned, about your behavior. Like they don't know what you're going to do next."

"You've asked around about me?"

Stagg nodded. "Yes."

"Well, of course they're going to say I'm the problem."

"Aren't you? These names you've given me. I know some of them are strong-minded kids, but calling them bullies is a bit of a stretch."

"Did you know Jeremy pushed my face into my locker and I was attacked in the locker room?"

"Uh, no, I didn't."

"Did you know Billy attacked me twice? And Laurie and Meaghan are cyber attacking other girls. And Derrick slammed me in the head with a book? And Robin is just flat-out mean?"

"I don't have any information about that here, so I can't address that."

"Any reason why they wouldn't give that to you?"

"I will have to ask them," Stagg replied. "But you reported all this, correct?"

85

"Yes. That's why Billy and Jeremy were talked to. Derrick, too. But, they've spoken to them before, and it didn't work. It never does."

"I can try to help you by speaking to these kids as well."

"And these kids you talked to never mentioned I've been attacked?"

"Yes, some did. But they also believe that you bring it on yourself. The Office has received calls about you, too."

"What calls?"

"Anonymous."

"Really," Henry said, both surprised and perplexed. "Must be Safe2Tell. Well, I've done nothing that bad."

Stagg folded her hands on her desk. "Apparently, others don't agree."

"Miss Stagg, I grew up minding my own business, keeping to myself. I never caused problems and I don't want any. So why would I bring it on myself?"

"Sometimes it can happen without you noticing it."

"Is that right? Wow."

"Exactly. So, over the next few days, check your behavior to see if it invites these kids to heckle you. Try to avoid the places they go."

Henry pressed lips together to avoid smiling, even laughing.

"It's difficult to avoid the boys' room, the locker room, the gym and the cafeteria."

Stagg nodded as a slight smile came to her thin, red lips.

"I'm talking about non-essential places."

"What are those?

"Places you don't have to be if you think they might be there."

Henry nodded slowly. "So, the bullies can go wherever they want, but I can't."

Stagg sighed. "Sometimes discretion is better."

Stagg sat in thoughtful silence.

"What do you do to avoid them?" she asked.

"I hide around corners and behind other kids. Should I continue doing that?"

"If you feel that's necessary and if it will avoid conflict."

"Apparently it does."

"Keep doing it, then. In the meantime, what can we do to improve your relationships with other kids?"

"Tell the bullies to knock it off and leave me alone."

"You have to connect with them somehow, Henry."

"No, I don't. Now, I have some friends. Would you like to speak to them?"

"I can do that."

"That may give you a more rounded view of the situation. Can you also bring those other kids in and talk to them? That might change their behavior and things will get better."

"Okay. But, overall, Henry, opening up and being more conversational may help," Stagg said. "School can be difficult, no doubt. Just try not to let things bother you."

"But they do," Henry returned softly. "And I don't think I have to take their BS anymore. I have every right to defend myself."

Stagg frowned. "Against boys like Derrick and Billy, it will be difficult for you to do that if they get angry and attack you. Things can get out of control very quickly. And we don't want you to get hurt."

"So it's the strong versus the weak?"

"You just want to protect yourself. If they say something you don't like, ignore it." She waved her hand. "Just let it roll off you like water off a duck's back."

"Then go get a duck."

Stagg's face froze.

Good. Good line.

"I'm doing nothing wrong," he continued. "I've already ignored them and avoided them long enough. Not anymore."

Stagg quickly rubbed the side of her nose.

"I don't know, Henry. But we have to do something. I want to help you, but we can't keep going on like this."

"That's right."

"As you may know, we have counseling sessions here that can help you deal with these issues. And I think you should see another counselor to help deal with your anger issues."

"I've heard of those classes."

"We have kids like yourself come together on a Saturday morning to talk things out."

"What things exactly?"

"Dealing with bullying and what strategies you can use to de-escalate a particular situation."

"Well, you definitely need a class like that in this school."

Henry held back a smile. Stagg pursed her lips and stared.

"Tell me," Henry said, adjusting himself in the chair, "while I'm in that class learning how to deal with the bullies, what are the bullies doing?"

"What do you mean?"

"Well, while I'm in this class on a Saturday, where are Derrick and Donny and Billy and Frank?"

Stagg gave a slight shrug. "I, uh, don't know."

"They're probably hanging out at home or together, enjoying life and having fun while I'm taking up my precious little time in a class learning how to deal with them."

Stagg blinked as if confused.

"We just need to avoid unnecessary conflict," Stagg said.

"So you want me to keep running and hiding from these kids?"

"I'm not saying that."

"What are you saying then? I don't understand."

"I'm saying that getting along better will solve a lot of issues."

"Obviously."

She raised her hands.

"That's all I can tell you."

"Yes, I know," Henry said. "There are a lot of problems in this school. You're never out there to see it, anyway."

Stagg pulled her head back. "Well, I disagree. Before you started acting up, everything seemed to be just fine. You're going to have to change your behavior or…"

"Or what?"

Her face tightened. "That's for Mr. Ruzzo to decide." She pulled the file in front of her and opened it. "Looking at your grades, they're mediocre at best. You have no extracurricular activities. You don't seem to be contributing to the school in any way." She looked at him challengingly. "Not much to hang your hat on, is there?"

Henry agreed with her, except for the last thing.

"Oh, I'm contributing," he said. "Trust me, I am. Okay, look. Call those kids in here and simply tell them to knock it off. That will help a lot. You might be surprised at what you'll learn, instead of just coming after me. At least that will be fair to me. Can you do that? Because if they stop, I stop. No more anger issues. Problem solved."

Stagg pursed her lips, as if, Henry thought, she didn't need the work.

"I'll see what I can do."

Henry gave her a smile and stood up. "Well, I have to catch my bus. Thank you for your time, Miss Stagg, I think this talk was really, uh, enlightening. If we both do our parts, I think the abuse will stop."

"Abuse."

Again, Henry tried to hide his amusement.

"Can I give you a few more names, please?" He reached out as if wanting pen and paper. Stagg obliged and Henry wrote down the names of all the kids, victims, he had known.

"There you go. Call those kids in as well. They've also been very bullied around here. Can you do that for me?" he asked.

"I will speak to them."

"Let me know how it goes. Well, have a good night, Miss Stagg."

He stood with a smile waiting for her to answer. She frowned.

"Good night, Henry," she said, with a dissatisfied expression, as if, Henry believed, the talk didn't go as she had planned.

He trotted out to his bus, chuckling to himself.

Yup, she's a bully, too.

Thanksgiving arrived, along with the big football game. Everyone filed into the gym to cheer the team on to victory on the last school day. Henry sauntered along with the herd and, as he got closer to the gym, he took a quick left and went to the boys' room. He hung his pack on the stall door and sat down with his tablet to play a few games. He could hear faint cheering and the school band playing.

"I'm supposed to clap for the same assholes who bully us all the time? Not really."

The holiday passed uneventfully, the football team got crushed and, back in school, Henry sat in the stands relaxing with Caleb in gym class. Some of the boys, including Derrick and Donny, shot basketballs, and a group of girls on the other side of the court worked out. The gym lit up from the late autumn sun streaming in through the upper windows. Roach appeared with a basketball under his arm and got everyone running up and down the court and then on to sit-ups and push-ups.

"C'mon," he yelled out, as several boys struggled to finish. "Get that heart pumping. You're not in shape. Let's go. Let's go."

The boys were still panting when Roach told them to form two teams for a game, with two kids from the school basketball team, Jonathan and Hakim, as captains. Caleb got picked first and Henry, as usual, near last. He used to care about that—it embarrassed him. Now, he just waited patiently to be picked so they could get on with it. He exhaled sharply.

"What's wrong, Wilton?" Roach asked.

"Nothing. Just waiting as usual."

Roach smiled.

"Well, play better and you'll get picked first."

"Thanks, Mr. Roach."

Henry's name was finally called and the game began. Once out on the court, however, Henry got the urge to actually do something. Derrick and Donny, on the other team, cut into Henry simply for being out on the court.

"I'll take wimpy," Derrick said to his team.

Derrick stood tall and tough as Henry, dribbling, backed up his enemy all the way to center court. Derrick tapped his crotch against Henry's butt with each backward move.

"Knock it off," Henry yelled.

"Thought you'd like that."

Jonathan ran up and took Henry's pass.

Angry, Henry threw out caution. He dribbled well and made a quick darting move one way, spun around and put the ball through the hoop, completely fooling Derrick and delighting himself. He then backpedaled away, giving Derrick a smile and pointing at him. The other guys got on Derrick for allowing Henry to beat him.

But Henry had to defend Derrick, who dribbled to the other end, backed Henry up toward the basket, and suddenly whipped out his elbow. Anticipating it, Henry jerked his head back just in time.

"Hey, watch it."

Derrick pushed one arm into Henry's face and threw the ball up one-handed but missed the basket. Henry bumped him, and an already off-balance Derrick fell to the floor. Jonathan grabbed the ball as it came off the rim and they all sped back up court. Henry gave Derrick another smile. Jonathan, at the other end, weaved through defenders for an easy lay-up. Henry watched, and, as he turned, he was hit in the face. He cried out and dropped to his knees, holding his face, more as an act than from actual pain. The play stopped.

"What did you do that for, Derrick?" Jonathan said.

"Shut up," ordered Derrick. "It's part of the game."

Henry looked up holding one side of his face, his eye half-closed.

"You moron," he shouted.

"Yeah?" Derrick said. "Get up and say that."

"You frickin' moron."

Derrick threw down his fist. Henry let it strike him on the forehead as Roach called out.

"Alright. Knock it off. I can't leave you guys alone for two minutes."

Henry rested himself on one elbow, holding his face.

"Oh, we were just playing," Derrick said with disgust. "He takes it too seriously. Then he calls me names."

"We don't call anyone names."

Henry sat up, holding his mouth.

"And we don't hit each other, either," Henry replied, glaring at Roach. "Look at this. He sucker-punched me." Henry held out fingers covered in a thin film of blood from his mouth.

"No, I didn't. He's making it up as usual."

Roach helped Henry to his feet.

"Let me see," Roach said, pulling Henry's hand away. He took Henry's jaw to inspect it.

"It was an accident," Derrick said. "C'mon, let's play."

"Yeah, we starting up the game or what?" Donny said.

"Wilton, I'm trying to help you. You better go down to the nurse."

Henry, his face crimson, pushed Roach's hand off.

"I'll be fine. Get him down to the Office and get him suspended," Henry demanded.

Roach's eyes widened at Henry's outburst. "It's over, Wilton. If you don't want to play, you can sit down."

"Well, what happens to him?"

Roach sighed.

"Alright, look. No more hitting each other," Roach said to everyone. "And no more calling names."

"We're not supposed to hit each other," Henry persisted with raised voice. "And that's what one of your bullies did."

"Don't call me that," Derrick said.

"I'll call you what you are." He glared at Roach. "Now get him down to the Office and get him expelled," he blurted, and darted for the locker room.

Everyone in the gym had stopped to watch.

"Wilton," Roach called out. "Come back here."

"I'm out of this stupid class."

In the locker room, Henry checked himself in the mirror, the pounding in his chest slowing down.

"Whew. Good job." He raised cool water to his mouth. The bleeding wasn't bad, and he pressed at a red mark under his left eye.

"I might need a little make-up."

He touched a throbbing lower lip.

"He should be here any second."

Henry felt proud of himself. Speaking so boldly to Roach was fun. It really made him feel better.

Roach came in. "Wilton, come with me."

"Why?" Henry said in a low but pleasant tone. "Where we going?"

"To the Office. Let's go."

"Why?"

"Your behavior out there was unacceptable."

"So was Derrick's."

"I think we should discuss this with the principal. Let's go."

Henry continued to look in the mirror, touching the sore spot. He spoke just above a whisper.

"Your bully coming with us?"

"Never mind. Let's go."

"Only if he's there, too."

"I said move."

93

Henry glanced at him a moment, then said, "Okay, let's go."

In the hallway, Henry sped up, leaving Roach several steps behind. He looked back. "C'mon. Let's go, let's go."

In the Office, Roach told Henry to have a seat.

"No, I'll go in with you," Henry said.

"No. I said sit down."

"I want to make sure you tell him the truth."

Roach's mouth curled into a scowl. Henry shuddered at the sight of a teacher showing such an expression to a student.

"Again, Wilton?" Ruzzo said, as Henry stood in front of him.

Henry touched his cheekbone.

"Wilton shouted at me in front of the class."

Ruzzo sat back.

"Explain it to me, Wilton."

"Derrick attacked me while we played basketball."

"Why did he do that?"

"Why don't we call him in and ask him?" he replied, pushing boldness.

Roach sighed. "Derrick says it was an accident. And you called him a name."

"It was no accident and everyone knows it. He hit me 'cause I made him look bad in front of everybody and he couldn't take it. I want him expelled now."

Ruzzo slammed his hand on the desk.

"This is the problem, Wilton," he shouted. "Your demanding tone. You don't demand anything from us. We demand it of you!"

Ruzzo's sudden outburst startled Henry. Silence ensued for a moment as Ruzzo sat back and then rocked himself. Roach stood still.

C'mon, keep going. Say something.

"Just…just call Derrick in here and we'll get this over with," Henry said with an appeasing tone.

"We'll talk to him," Ruzzo replied.

"What's wrong with right now? You don't have a problem talking to me."

Ruzzo's eyes dropped impatiently. Roach crossed his arms.

"Well?" Henry's lips quivered, anticipating a Ruzzo explosion.

"I'll call him in after you leave and speak with him."

"Remember the assembly? You said kids will get expelled if they attack someone. Zero tolerance."

Ruzzo nodded. "May get expelled."

Henry chuckled. "Oh, I see."

Ruzzo gave Henry an implacable stare. His hedging on punishment did not surprise Henry.

"I know...I know what will happen if you call him in. And that's a big 'if'. Here's what will happen. You'll say, 'Now Derrick, don't hit anyone anymore, okay?' Wink, wink. And Derrick goes, 'Okay, Mr. Ruzzo. I won't. Wink, wink.'"

Henry glared into Ruzzo's eyes.

"I have to get back to class," Roach said, sounding exasperated.

"Mr. Roach, please tell Caleb, Donny and Jonathan to come in here. They can be witnesses to this crime. Thank you."

"This isn't about the attack on you," Ruzzo said

"So you admit there was an attack."

"You have five nights detention for your flagrant disrespect of a teacher during class," Ruzzo called out.

"What, disrespect to a teacher who saw me assaulted by two of your football players and lied about it?" Henry said. "I don't think so. Derrick attacked me again. He's attacked enough kids. He will be expelled."

Ruzzo shrugged. "This conversation is over."

"I think it's far from over." Henry stood and stared. "I'll be back in tomorrow."

"Go back to class now."

Henry immediately turned and walked out. In the hallway, he put hands on his hips, his heart thumping. Where before he felt small and scared in front of the principal, now he perceived himself taller and bolder, capable of challenging the big bully more. He let his anger do his talking and forget the consequences. He rubbed his stomach.

Alright, calm it down. You did well. And you're not going to detention.

Back in the locker room, Henry dressed and returned to the gym to watch the basketball game still going on as if nothing had happened. He leaned his elbows back and stretched out his legs, two spots on his weary face throbbing. He didn't think there was much conviction in Ruzzo's voice about detention. Derrick was running up and down the court, concentrating, playing hard. Henry caught Roach's eye, waved, and gave him a little smile. Roach turned away.

He liked being out on the court for once, playing well. But ugly fate once again put an end to his fun.

Of course. What else?

Derrick saw Henry and flipped his victim a middle finger.

That night, Henry wondered what would happen in the morning after not going to detention, and why no one called the house about it. Would Derrick get his rightful punishment?

"If they don't do it, you'll have to go back. You can't let this one go."

After three hours of homework, he went down into the basement to return a screwdriver to his father's workbench. Heading back to the stairs, he glanced at the bottom drawer of his father's desk. He opened it to check out a war pistol locked in a clear plastic case. The gun, which his father had received from a great uncle, was a black, unimposing, semi-automatic pistol with four bullets lying near it. A few years ago, his father had let him hold it unloaded and he pulled the trigger a few times. He hadn't touched it since, but he knew where the key was. He stared at it a moment and then closed the drawer and went back upstairs.

He joined his parents watching the ten o'clock news. The big news story reported the discovery of a plan by two students at a high school in another town to harm some other students.

"Why am I not surprised?" he said out loud.

As the reporter spoke into the camera, the scene cut to a school representative who gave some limited information about the incident and then on to a few concerned students who spoke about the frightening possibility of danger. Henry watched a few minutes, and then his eyes froze on the TV screen. Cameras, lights, microphones, interviews, police cars.

"Whoa," he murmured, transfixed by a sudden idea. "Of course."

He dropped his head back and laughed mutedly at the thrill of it. He pictured himself in front of the cameras telling the world his own story.

"Of course what?" his mother asked.

He stood up and bowed slightly. "Nothing. Good night."

Henry let the idea sparkle in his mind. The corner of his mouth turned up vengefully as he dropped onto his bed. "Perfect. Tell the world what's going on. On the nightly news." His eyes narrowed. "They didn't care about you. So why should you give a screw about them?"

He jumped up and leg-kicked the air.

"Oh, this is great. Yeah, you'll get away with it," he whispered. "Ha. What are they gonna to do to you? You're fifteen."

He realized he may have some power after all. Hope.

In bed, with his small journal pressed against his arched leg, Henry excitedly wrote it all down.

"So, this is the plan. Expose them all. But how you gonna pull it off?"

After a solid night's sleep, Henry stuffed books, computer and food into his backpack and his diary into his back pocket. He mused about how long it would be before he was summoned to the Office, or if Derrick would even be suspended.

He met up with fellow meeks Freedman and Bradley in the hall.

"Hey, guys, wait up."

"What's up?" Freedman said.

"Okay, look. I have a plan."

"What plan?" Bradley asked.

"To get the bullies. By the time I'm done, they won't bother us again."

"Henry, don't drag us into this," Freedman said. "You're already making it hard on yourself."

"Tell me you're not tired of getting shit on."

Freedman, tall, slender, curly brown hair, had been a favorite target of the bully squad since middle school. He stood silent.

"So, what do you expect us to do?" Bradley asked impatiently.

"If they come up and do something, simply yell at them. Tell them to get away from you. Bring attention to it so a teacher comes over. Then, tell the teacher. Get angry."

"Didn't do you much good in gym class," Freedman said. "Derrick is still here."

"Not for long," Henry said ominously. "Start writing down all the times you've been attacked. Keep a diary of them. See ya."

In class, Henry watched Derrick walk in, relaxed and assured, as though no punishment would ever touch him. He clamped his mouth tight and would only wait a few more hours for his enemy to get kicked out.

"Hey," he said to Jose.

Jose nodded reluctantly.

"How did you do on the test?" Henry asked, pushing Jose to talk.

Jose sighed. "Fine."

98

Henry smiled. "You still have that book Derrick hit me with?"

"Yeah, I do. Wanna see it?"

"You mean do I want to see the weapon? What happened to you, Jose? You were never a bully before."

"I'm not one now."

"Yeah, you are. As soon as you took the book from Derrick. He almost split my head open."

"You're alright." Jose got up to talk with a few other kids.

Henry shook his head. *The birth of a bully.*

"Henry Wilton," Bronner announced as he placed papers and briefcase on his desk, "you are wanted in the Office."

"Uh, oh," one kid said.

"Buh, bye, Wilty."

Henry froze. The expectation had become reality. His nerves twitched as he stood up amidst staring classmates and headed for the door.

"And bring your books," Bronner added.

Henry gave the teacher a side-glance and went back to his desk. He smiled to himself, believing Bronner had waited until he was in front of the class before telling him to take his books. As Henry left the room, Bronner started lecturing and closed the door on Henry's heels, never looking at him. Henry's mouth clenched.

Oh, yeah? I'll be back. I'll be back for you, asshole.

Henry stopped in the empty corridor and let out a long, heavy sigh. He had thought of this for a long time but now realized he didn't plan on what to say.

"Only one way to find out."

Images of his life in school came to him as he headed to the Office: Years at the hands of unbridled kids who humiliated, disgraced and ignored him, and his own failure to do anything about it. With every slow step, he passed by the lockers he was slammed against; notices on walls promoting hard work, respect for others and events and activities he knew little about; and classrooms full of students getting educated—robots in his mind, who sat there accepting the school as it was. A few classroom doors were open. Some of the kids looked out at him. He glanced at Mrs. Roach, who stepped out of the room as she lectured. Henry turned back to look at her. He nodded to her and smiled.

In the Office, he thought Mary's eyes showed pity as she pointed him to Peterson's office.

Don't worry, Mary. I'm not going anywhere.

Yet, he felt himself physically weakening, and could not stop it.

C'mon. Ya gotta step up here.

He wanted to show at least a façade of strength. Peterson sat officiously at her desk, her folded hands in front of her.

"Sit down, Henry," Peterson said with little emotion.

"Why is Derrick still here?" he said, hiding nervousness by taking the offensive.

Peterson pursed her lips at Henry's impudence.

"Why isn't he expelled?"

"Never mind that. This is about you."

"Excuse me?" Henry raised his eyebrows.

"This is about your behavior."

"What about it?"

"You have been unruly, disrespectful and, frankly, scaring everyone."

Henry pulled his head back with surprise. "How am I scaring anybody? I'm the one who's been scared."

"People don't know what you're going to do next with the way you're behaving. It's creating too much tension, and we've had enough."

He chuckled. "You've had enough. I've been living with that for years. I don't see you doing anything to help me."

"We have tried to, Henry. But you've become too confrontational, and you exhibit anger toward teachers and students. We believe your behavior will worsen and possibly cause harm to others, yourself, or both."

Henry chuckled. He crossed one leg over the other and settled back in the chair with forced relaxation. Peterson leaned forward.

"And we have to make a decision that is in the best interests of the school. You're suspended for ten days, during which time we will pursue expulsion. If you have all your personal items with you right now, please leave any books and school materials on the desk here. We will call your parents and have one of them pick you up. Do you have anything to say before we do so?"

"Would it make any difference?"

His gut tightened.

"You only have yourself to blame."

He nodded.

"Has anyone even talked to Derrick?"

"Mr. Ruzzo has spoken to him," Peterson said.

"I don't believe he has. I'd like to ask him."

"I don't think that's necessary."

"Consider it a last request from a wrongly condemned man. It will only take a second." He lowered his eyes at her.

Peterson sighed impatiently and called Ruzzo.

After a few minutes, Ruzzo slowly stepped in.

"What is it, Wilton?"

"Derrick hasn't been suspended?"

"This is about you. And I'm afraid we've come to the end."

Henry's cheek twitched. Fury rose steadily.

Alright. What are ya gonna do?

Ruzzo showed a slight smile. "You're too unstable, Henry."

"I'm unstable. What about those kids who've abused me?"

Ruzzo nodded. "No one has abused you," he said calmly. "We will recommend to your parents that you get therapy, especially for your anger issues." He rested himself on the corner of the desk. "You have a lot of problems, Henry. And I don't think we can help you with them here."

Henry felt pulled in by Ruzzo's soothing baritone. Was he right?

"You just can't cope with life, Henry," Peterson added caringly. "Or with people. There's a lot wrong with you. Therapy may help you understand yourself and all the problems you're causing for yourself, us, your parents. Maybe time away from school will help."

"This may be too strong a school environment for you," Ruzzo added. "We demand the best from everyone and we don't think you're able to handle it. You can always find another school that better fits your abilities."

"What, a school without bullying? Does that even exist?"

"Well, of course. You're in one right now."

Henry stared at Ruzzo a moment and then at Peterson.

Wow. Keep going. Don't let them.

"The only end I see is...is these bullies getting suspended. And you can start with your number one bully right now."

"Listen to me."

"No! You listen to me." Henry jumped to his feet before he knew it, silencing the two adults. He breathed out exasperatedly, and slowly sat back down. He eased himself for a moment. Then he leveled a gaze at them.

"Are you ready?" he said, fatefully. "Are you ready for the change of life?"

His heart pumped fast as he tried to speak as slowly as possible.

"These kids of yours, these bullies, go free while I suffer." He shook his head. "I've given you all the chances and all the time in the world. Not anymore. Suspend Derrick or I'll call the superintendent."

You will?

Ruzzo raised his bushy, black eyebrows.

"We have already spoken to the superintendent."

Peterson smiled faintly.

"Does he know what's going on around here?"

"What is going on around here, Henry?"

"Bullying."

Ruzzo sighed. "You have stretched that idea to the limit."

"So...so the attacks on me by Derrick and Billy and Frank are just my imagination. Calling me names, blocking me in the hallway, and pushing me and other kids into lockers. For years."

"And a lot of that's your own doing," Peterson remarked.

"So you're blaming me for the attacks on me. I pushed myself into the lockers. I punched myself in the face in gym."

Peterson sat back and glanced up at Ruzzo, who remained seated and staring at Henry.

"Why don't we call the superintendent anyway? You don't mind, do you? After all, it's not really happening"

"Henry," Peterson said in a soft tone, "we are sorry. We can't help you anymore."

Keep going. Don't let them.

"Then I'll call the police."

What?

"Let's let them decide if there's abuse going on around here."

Ruzzo puckered his brow.

"Wilton..."

"All I have to do is give them a call, and in just a few minutes there will be police cars right outside your window." Henry raised his voice. "And I'll accuse you of aiding, abetting and condoning assaults and bullying in this school."

Wow. Good.

"I'll expose this school for what it really is. A rathole. With a bunch of rats running around biting each other all the time."

Peterson furrowed her brow.

"You don't care about kids like me," Henry said. "You...you just want to protect yourselves and your own."

"Wilton," Ruzzo began.

103

"And who do you think comes after the cops? TV. Newspapers. I'll tell 'em everything. Ha. They will lick this up. And you two bullies will be right in the middle of it." He grinned maliciously. "Your faces on camera for everyone to see."

Peterson found that amusing.

"I doubt they will come because of a phone call from one student."

Henry sharpened his tone. "Oh, I think they will. They'll be a bit curious. I'll make sure they know who you are and what you are and what you've done. Principal Bully and Vice Principal Bully. Ha."

"Alright, that's enough," Ruzzo demanded. "You will not continue to speak to us like this. I will have Officer Lentine remove you from the school."

"And then I'll call the police. A lot of the attacks on me and others are crimes. Actual crimes."

Ruzzo and Peterson stared.

Henry relaxed a bit, enjoying their silence, hoping they didn't hear the thumping in his chest. He believed he gained more power and theirs diminished with each liberating word, even though he was making it all up as he went along.

"Ha. Who would have thunk it? Adult bullies." He shook his head slowly. "Fooled me. Fooled a lot of us. A pair of adult bullies."

"Alright, Henry, that's enough," Ruzzo cautioned.

"Oh, that's right, you don't like to be called bully." He shrugged. "Hey, it's just a word, right? Just a name. You shouldn't let it bother you. Because, as you know, sticks and stones, well they can break your bones, but names," Henry shook his head, "names can never, ever, hurt you." He tilted his head to one side. "And you practice what you preach, don'tcha?"

Henry stood up.

"You adults," he continued, derisively. "You're so useless and worthless to good kids like me. All my life, I obeyed the rules. I did everything I was told. I kept silent. I turned the other cheek. I walked away like a man, with my tail between my legs while you bullies laughed at me. And got no respect for it. Nothing. Just a bunch of *crap*." He pointed at them. "And you knew it."

"That's enough."

"You were never going to talk to them. And why would you? They're your kids. To you they're doing nothin' wrong. *I'm* the problem. You make *me* the problem."

Henry laughed.

"And then you try get rid of me? It's gonna be the other way around!"

Good. Good.

Peterson drooped a little. Ruzzo remained set in place with arms folded. Henry gave him a sly grin. A knock came at the door and Mary stuck her head in.

"Is everything okay in here?" she asked with concern.

Mary looked to Ruzzo and Peterson for confirmation.

"It's alright, Mary," Ruzzo said.

She slowly closed the door.

"What you're accusing us of is horrible," Peterson said, tiredly. "We're not doing anything of the kind. We're not your enemies, Henry. We've tried to help you. And you need help."

"I thought you were helping me, with all that baloney to keep me in line. And all you did was help yourselves. And yet," Henry said, raising his shoulders and showing his palms, "I...I understand. You see me as a nice kid, never complaining, so you take advantage of it, like all you bullies do. Give you an inch and you take a mile."

Ruzzo slowly shook his head at Henry, who suddenly sprung around to the back of the chair. "We've been such suckers," Henry bellowed. "My people are such suckers, such weaklings!"

"Who are 'your people'?" Ruzzo asked.

"The meeks. The kids picked on, humiliated, all your victims. Everywhere. Those who don't want to admit who they are, not even to each other. Suffering in silence. And our silence is what you want." He chuckled. "You know, I can't blame you for doing what you've done. Ha. We just do what you tell us, because we believe you. And…and the way you have us in the palm of your hands, the way it's all set up, is so good, so, so—oh, what's the word—um, elegant. Yeah. You have us in such a way that whatever we do to fight back, we're in the wrong. It's…it's crazy. You've created this…this world so that your people and my people are in their perfect places. Where you learn who the kids are to get and we learn to keep our mouths shut after we get it." He rubbed his eyes. "I have to commend you bullies. A perfect system. It's so strong that it takes something strong enough to change it. And that something is me."

Henry surprised himself by saying that. But, in doing so, he affirmed to himself that he had achieved a position of power, and he would not turn back. But that didn't stop his nausea. His body quivered, though not noticeably, and he gripped the back of the chair again so his hands wouldn't shake.

"But, then, I'm just a kid. What can I do? Right?"

The two adults remained silent.

"Okay, so here's what's gonna happen. As soon as I leave here, you will get Derrick in here and suspend him. That ought to shut the bully down a little. Then you'll expel Frank and Billy."

Henry breathed in deeply

"No discussion. No more stalling. That's what you'll do." He pointed to Peterson's desk phone. "Now." He gave Ruzzo a slight, victorious smile.

"I will not."

"If you don't, my father will sue."

"When I spoke to him, it didn't sound like he would do something like that."

"But he will if I'm expelled. That causes a lot of problems for parents, doesn't it? Plus, if I'm expelled, don't I have a right to a hearing to talk about it? I can bring in

106

witnesses, right? And so can you. And I can still go to class. That will be a lot more fun for me than it will for you."

He glared at Ruzzo. "You don't know what I can do."

Henry let a slight, brazen smile form in the silence.

"It's your choice." He raised his phone. "And you got ten seconds to make it. I'm missing class."

Henry was just as angry with his gurgling gut as he was with Ruzzo and Peterson, unable to control the tension inside.

"We don't give in to threats, Wilton."

"They're not threats. Just what I'm going to do. Alright, I tell you what. I'll serve three days in school for yelling at Roach, but Derrick gets five at home for attacking me. It's better than going through a long, drawn-out expelling that I have a good chance of winning. Imagine the abused kids in this school who will join me. There are a lot of them."

C'mon, bully, do it. I gotta get outta here.

"Or I go public and drag you with me. And I don't think the superintendent will like that. Do you?"

Henry watched both adults think about his proposition.

"One phone call from me will cause a lot of issues for everyone."

Henry gave Ruzzo a bold, angry glare.

"I don't know about you but I think this is a pretty good compromise. You know what Derrick has done. And the next time, he might really hurt somebody. And that will be on you."

Henry held Ruzzo's stare to match the principal's strength.

After a few more moments of thinking, Ruzzo glanced down at Peterson.

"Call Derrick in."

Peterson hesitated a moment, apparently to show her dislike of the decision. She got on the phone and had Derrick summoned.

"There ya go. That wasn't so difficult, was it? Now get Billy and Frank in here and expel them."

"No. We already made the decision not to do that, so we can't expel them now."

"They didn't even get detention for attacking me." Henry snickered. "We'll see about that."

Henry pulled out his diary from his coat pocket. He took Peterson's pen off her desk with a smile, and sat down to write, his hand slightly shaking.

"What are you doing?" Ruzzo asked after a moment.

"Oh, this? It's my, uh, diary." He rubbed his nose. "I bring it to school and I write down all the wonderful things that happen to me."

As he wrote, Henry felt them staring at him.

"Can I see that?" Ruzzo asked.

"Sure. Almost done." After a quiet minute, he offered Ruzzo the notebook. "Please initial on this page here what we just discussed and everything I've written is true."

Ruzzo took the notepad and started to read. He flipped through the pages.

"This goes back a long time."

"Yeah. A few years. Sign, please."

Ruzzo turned while reading.

"Hmm," he said. He gave the notepad to Peterson, who also perused it. "You mind if we look through this?"

Henry shrugged. "Sure. I'll be back for it later." He went to the door.

"Henry," Peterson said, "I'm calling your parents to discuss this."

"No. We can handle this ourselves."

"Any reason you don't want them know?" Russo asked, as though challenging Henry.

Henry let out tense breath. "Well, you know, my mother keeps a good home for me and my father. And I don't want to track in the stink and the muck and the crap from this school into her nice, clean house."

The two adults stared.

"So, I'd rather take care of things myself and I'll go home with nice clean soles on my shoes."

He gave them a barely perceptible smile

"Nevertheless," Peterson finally said. "We will call them."

"Fine. Then you'll have to explain all the attacks on me. Just look through the notepad and see for yourself. It's pretty detailed—the kid who was jumped, the kid who attacked, date and time." He opened the door. "Oh, and from now on, whenever someone blocks my way in the hall, I will do whatever it takes to get him out of the way. Whatever it takes. So, if you don't want any problems, tell your bullies to knock it off. It's up to you. Have a nice day."

Henry let the door close with a loud thud, startling Mary and two students standing there.

He rushed to the bathroom, all wound up and his gut knifing him. A few boys were there talking and he went into a stall. He laid his forehead on his arms, breathing steadily and airing out damp armpits. He could only feel the immensity of what he had just done. All the things he said— had he exorcised his fears? he wondered. He couldn't believe all the things that came out of his mouth. He believed he was beginning to think.

"I guess it did make a difference."

He finally left the stall and leaned forward against the sink, breathing in deeply, exhausted. He smiled at himself in the mirror. The change in his life happened so quickly, he could hardly believe it. But he still didn't like it. He wished he didn't have to do it. Now he didn't know what to do next, or what Peterson and Ruzzo would do, as he entered a new world. He wondered what they were talking about right now. He washed his hands and threw cold water on his pale face. Now, the thrill of seeing Bronner again.

This will be good.

He stepped in through the door dramatically and gave everyone a big smile.

"Hi. I'm back," stopping Bronner in mid-sentence. "And I'm sure you're happy about that." Henry crossed the room slowly with a big yawn. Bronner frowned. "So, where are we?" he asked sitting down, pulling things out of his pack. "I have some questions for you."

"You don't need to interrupt the class like that, Wilton."

"Oh, sorry."

Peterson called and spoke with Henry's mother about his detention, but didn't tell her about their long discussion. Henry defended himself as usual, and his father scolded him as usual. Henry took it in stride, including being grounded the rest of the year. He knew he wouldn't win, and didn't fight with them. He was too tired for that. He got a victory that day and now needed to channel his energy toward schoolwork.

He couldn't wait to get to back to school. Everyone chatted about Derrick's suspension. Henry showed as much surprise as everyone else, avoiding suspicion that he had something to do with it.

"Wow, hard to believe," he said.

"See, miracles can happen," George said.

Henry chuckled. "A Christmas miracle. But, I have detention."

"Why, what did you do now?" Sharonda asked.

"I yelled at Roach. Which was fun."

"You're getting crazier all the time," she added.

Henry looked at Sharonda. "That right? Well, I'd rather be crazy than go back to normal."

But Henry couldn't stop anxious thoughts about what Ruzzo and Peterson might do, Derrick returning the next week, finals looming, and papers due. He noticed Peterson and Ruzzo were not in the hallways as much. No one bothered him, either. He believed Derrick's suspension may have helped him there, too.

He strode easily into the library and right over to Carla.

"Hi."

"Hello."

"How ya doin'?"

"Good."

He pulled books and computer from his pack.

"I am so far behind."

"Uh-huh."

Not much was said as they sat there for almost an hour. He wanted to ask if she had any more cyber attacks but didn't know how to bring it up.

"Hey, did Miss Stagg talk to you?"

"Miss Stagg? No. Why?"

"Well, I told her I thought you were being cyberbullied. So I asked her to talk to you."

Carla stared as if she were processing what Henry had said. "Excuse me?" She jumped up and slammed her pen on the table. "You had no right to talk to her about me. Who do you think you are? You're the only one getting bullied around here." She shook with rage and threw her things into her pack. "You mind your own business from now on and stay away from me."

"Carla, you admitted you were being cybered. You have to let someone know."

Henry looked around the library after she stormed out. All the other kids there wondered what happened.

"I guess she didn't like what I said," he said to them, embarrassed. "Well, probably shouldn't have said anything."

Back in the hallway later, Jeremy confronted him.

"Fuck you, Wilton."

"What?" Henry said.

"You think getting Derrick kicked out will do anything?"

"Me. He got himself kicked out. I mean, c'mon, Jeremy, look what he does? He's insane. It's only a matter of time."

"You've stepped way out of line."

"What?" Henry said incredulously.

"Just watch your back," Jeremy warned.

"Yeah, I know that's the direction you'll be coming from."

Henry liked that answer. It made him feel free and easy, for now. He headed to Stagg's office.

"Hey," Henry said to Kam as he passed by.

"What's up?" Kam said.

Kam kept going as if he couldn't talk, or, Henry thought, didn't want to.

Henry got to Stagg's office and knocked. Stagg called him in.

"Hi."

"Hello, Henry."

"Uh, did you ever talk to those kids? Those names I gave you?"

"I can't tell you if I did or didn't, Henry."

"Why can't you?"

"It's private."

"Then how do I know if you did or not?"

"You don't."

"But these kids are causing a lot of problems for me and others, too. I have the right to know if they've been talked to. They have to be stopped."

"Apparently, there is some disagreement about that."

Henry quickly exhaled. "Well, I know you didn't talk to Carla. When I asked her, she jumped down my throat."

"You shouldn't have done that."

Henry narrowed his eyes. "If I don't see a big change in their behavior starting now, I'll have to assume you didn't. And that's not good."

"Alright, Henry. You'll have to speak with Principal Ruzzo."

"Again, talk to Carla. She's hurting."

Stagg looked down at papers on her desk and resumed her writing.

"Wow," Henry said after closing the door. He shook his head. "Unbelievable."

In classes, he felt eyes on him.

He talked to Caleb.

"Does everyone think I got Derrick suspended?"

"Yes."

"Great. Thanks."

"How'd you do it?"

"I just told them it was the right thing to do, and, shock, they did it. You're as happy as I am about it."

"He hasn't bothered me too much lately."

"Remember when he told you to put your finger through his belt loop?"

"Hey, Wilty," Laurie called out. "How's your girlfriend?"

"What?"

"Amazon," Meaghan said.

"Who's that?"

"Who do you think, Wilty?" Robin said. "Carla. She was screaming at you in the library."

"Lover's quarrel?"

"Wilty has a lover?" Charles asked.

They laughed.

"None of your business."

"Everything's our business around here, Wilty," Robin added, grinning.

"Yeah, you keep thinking that, Madam President," Henry said sarcastically.

Robin pierced Henry with her black eyes.

"Charles, did Hernandez ever talk to you?"

"About what?"

"About bullying me that day with Joe."

"No. And we weren't bullying you. Just talking to you. Trying to be your friends."

"If I hadn't said anything," Henry said, returning to Caleb, "Derrick would still be here, doing what he does best."

"What happens when he comes back? Might be worse."

Henry ruminated about just that over the next several days and about the big talk with Peterson and Ruzzo. He had pushed himself through the fear and the emotional limits that had always hemmed him in. He had gained some confidence, but he remained very unsure of the consequences, and he ran on instinct. He felt like he was wandering aimlessly in a fogged-in landscape with no real direction, just hoping he would end up at the right place. In his room, he wrapped his arms around his knees and rocked himself.

You're doing good. You're fine. You've done nothing wrong. They have. Remember that.

To Henry's relief, Jeremy's threats turned out to be hollow. Henry did his time after school. When Derrick returned the next week, Henry couldn't help a little dig.

"Hey, buddy. How was your little vacation?"

He smiled. Derrick and his friends didn't.

Over the weekend, Henry relaxed and hit the books. He helped his mother bring plants to the church for the holiday season and brought several in from the back of the car. Reverend Isabel Garcia helped.

"Haven't seen you in a while, Henry," the minister said. As tall as Henry, with short, black hair streaked with a little gray, she exuded congeniality and sincerity that made her popular. "How've you been?"

"Oh, doing the best I can, I guess."

Henry placed a few plants at the top of the stairs leading to the apse.

"Any problems you want to talk about?" he asked, while Henry's mother was outside.

"No, I'm good. Why?"

"Your mother mentioned you're having some challenges at school."

"She did, huh? Well, always challenges. But I think I have a good idea now how to handle them. It's a terrible school. A lot of bad kids."

"Must be difficult."

"It has been. It won't be a terrible school after I'm done."

"What do you mean?"

"There are some dangerous kids there that need to be taken out."

"What do you mean?"

"Expelled."

"Oh. Have you spoken to the principal about this?"

Henry chuckled. "Oh, yeah. We've had our talk."

"That's Principal Ruzzo, isn't it?"

Henry nodded. "Correct. You know him?"

"Yes, I've met him. He seems to be a strong character. I'm sure he'll help you."

Henry chuckled. "Oh, yeah, he will help me." He went back to the car for more plants. "Whether he likes it or not," he mumbled.

"Well, if you ever need to talk, let me know."

Henry smiled. "I will."

His mother engaged the reverend, relieving him of further discussion.

The week of final exams arrived. Henry had practiced breathing and visualized being relaxed and letting it all just flow out. So easy. But none of it worked. At the end of the week, he sat on his bed in his usual posture—arms folded, staring, feeling wasted. He cringed at the sight of himself hunkering there in front of each exam, trying to be in control but descending into a tornado of inner rage as he stared at the awful pages, feeling fear and failure and the fear of failure.

He slowly shook his head. "Shit, what are you going to do?" he said out loud. "Wow, all that work. God damn it. All those hours, questions." He pressed fingertips to his brow. "Nothing comes of it. You're so weak. You're so fucking weak."

He shook his head at how fruitless his quest for academic achievement might be, or anything else, for that matter.

"Nothing comes of anything in my life," he muttered to himself. "Damn adults. You did this to me. You're the reason I'm a total failure. I'm gonna get you all for what you've done to me." His eyes hardened. "It's coming. Yes, I can feel it. It's coming."

His mother called him down for dinner. A steaming bowl of beef stew, one of his favorites, waited for him. His mother placed the coffee pot in the middle of the table. He blew the food on his spoon and ate quietly.

"Tastes good, Mom," Henry said softly.

His mother gave him a bemused smile.

"Thank you," she said, as she flipped her napkin onto her lap. "So how was your day? Exams done?"

"Yes."

"How did it go?" she asked.

"Lousy."

"Why is that?" his father asked.

Henry shrugged. "I don't know."

"You studying hard enough?" his father said.

Henry chuckled. "Yeah. I study real hard."

But that's not the problem.

"We all feel your behavior over the last semester was not very good," his father continued. "We're concerned and we want to see something better from you."

"That depends on everyone else."

"You just do your part," he said. "And everything should work out."

"I always have done my part."

"We haven't seen that."

"How many times have I been in trouble in my whole school life?"

"Well. I'm talking about now."

"Stop the bullies, you stop the problems. And I will need more help from you to do it. You have to do a lot more than just blame me or have a pleasant conversation with Admin. I've learned that."

"We will help you as much as we can," his mother said. "Come to us if things get tough for you."

"Oh, I will. Just get ready. They're not gonna go down easily."

"Who?" his father asked.

"The bullies."

His father sighed and shook his head.

"Now, changing the subject," his mother said. "We have to go shopping tomorrow. I'll need your help with the presents."

116

"Sure, anything so we don't have to talk about school."

Upstairs, he at least felt happier with Christmas vacation coming up next, since he desperately needed the break. He picked up his phone and played a few games that relaxed him.

The last day before Christmas vacation arrived and Henry came to school weary of life. He decided to be glum and indifferent in his morning classes and spoke little. He wished that he could leave feeling successful and at ease for the future. Now, he just wanted to get home to the comfort of his room.

He made sure, though, to tell his friends a have a good holiday. But he also wanted to do the same with enemies. He passed Derrick, wishing him a merry Christmas. His number one enemy ignored him. Derrick was noticeably subdued since returning. He must have been talked to by someone, Henry thought. Maybe his parents.

Wow, parental involvement. What a concept.

But Derrick's quietness gave Henry some worry. Too quiet, he believed.

He smiled broadly at Charles and Trevor.

"Merry Christmas, bullies."

He laughed out loud and walked away cheerier now.

Donny weaved his way through the crowd toward him.

"Merry Christmas, Donny," Henry said nicely.

"Choke on a bone, Wilton."

"Back atcha."

He cleaned out his locker and headed for the bus. Down the hall, Mrs. Roach stood outside her room and he went straight for her.

"Merry Christmas," he said to her with a smile.

She frowned.

"Well, you have a nice Christmas, Henry," she replied. "But you should know that I'm Jewish."

"Oh," he said. "Well, my apologies. I didn't know. Happy Hanukkah."

"Thank you," she said patiently. "Hopefully, you will think about what has occurred over the past few months and come back behaving better."

Henry's eyebrows rose.

"Oh, I will," he said softly. "And I hope everyone else does, too."

He held her stare a moment. "See you then."

He bounced down the stairs to find Bronner in the hall. Henry smiled wide and wished him a good holiday. Bronner slightly nodded.

"Aren't you going to wish me a merry Christmas back?" Henry asked, a bit surprised.

"Merry Christmas," Bronner replied not unkindly, without turning around.

Henry sighed deeply and happily. He walked out into the cold, late afternoon and boarded the bus for home.

The big, yellow machine rumbled through the streets, making its periodic stops to let excited kids escape into the holiday air. Christmas lights brightened stores and homes. Henry breathed out in relief, enjoying the luminescence of the season. It lifted him as a nice break from the pressure and darkness of the usual world. The tightness in his chest eased. His laid his head against the smudged, foggy window as the busy town rolled by, for now, free of the decadent place he loathed.

He got off the bus with a group of other kids from the neighborhood. The kids were all upbeat as they talked about different things in the frosty air. Henry smiled tiredly, and, when he reached his house, he said goodbye to them, wishing them a good holiday. He opened the mailbox and pulled out letters and magazines. His two-story house reflected the season—single, white candles in each window and a spotlight his father had placed on the grass to illuminate the front of the house, centered by the wreath hanging on the front door.

The brightly lit kitchen, warm and inviting, smelled of something good. He placed the mail on the counter to the right and dropped his pack. Opening an upper cabinet, he took down a box of crackers.

"Well, hello," his mother said.

"Hi."

"How was last day?"

"Good. Any last day is good."

"Don't eat too much. Dinner will be ready soon."

Henry smiled at her. "Okay."

He popped in a few more crackers, then put the box back.

After a quiet dinner with parents, he went up to his bed, laid back and stared at the ceiling. The cat pushed the door in and sprung up next to him. Henry yawned wide and deep. Turning to the cat, he pushed her down on the bed and rubbed her stomach. She swatted back playfully. Henry breathed in deeply and exhaled latent tension as he stroked her fur. The cat stretched herself out and yawned as well. Henry blinked and cringed.

"You know," he said, "we have to do something about your bad breath."

She swiveled her head over and stared at Henry. His mind slowly drifted and all tension melted away. He felt what he believed was total relaxation and let tiredness close his eyes.

Growing up, Henry had welcomed the difference the holiday season brought: the public camaraderie and the ideals of love and peace. This Christmas joy flipped on like a light in a black room, changing anger to tranquility, a pounding heart to a restful one, a vengeful smile to an honest one. He did wonder why he couldn't have it and hold on to it—have it all year long. He always had to manufacture the sensation of it.

"Things never last, cat. Enjoy it while you can."

As he lay there thinking about this, he admitted, coldly, reluctantly, that the flush of holiday joy was not only temporary but unreal. Fear simply stood aside and waited with a smirky smile until the annual exuberance weakened enough to easily vanquish it. The world forgets too easily, and life would return to the conflict and killing that made the hope of Christmas a complete fraud. Love, peace, hope, joy—they were like butterflies in his mind.

Henry confronted for the first time those happy lies he grew up with; those he told himself for sheer emotional survival. "No more," he sighed. "Time to let them go. Childhood is over." But as he got closer to returning to school, the dread always crept back in.

"That's what life is really about. Fear and misery. But, at least now, you know what to do. You might be able to save yourself."

Christmas wasn't just about the gifts or the lights or ephemeral merriment. Henry believed in the words of Christ and felt akin to Him. While he didn't go to church too often anymore—his parents let him decide that—he always attended Christmas midnight mass. Sitting in a pew in the middle of a packed church, Henry sang the carols and listened to the choir. He found something ethereal about a group of candle-lit faces in unified voice lifting his broken spirit for just a moment and raising innocent images of a better world he had yet to see. He banished that. Peering around at the faces in the pews and balconies, a corner of his mouth turned up bitterly. He slowly shook his head as if he knew better.

Why are we even here? What are we doing? Is this ever going to make any difference...?

Henry inhaled deeply.

Alright, stop. Relax. This is Christmas, not stupid school. Take a break, for God's sake.

Henry exhaled silently to calm himself. He listened to the choir's soaring, albeit imperfect, voices echo through the century-old church. He closed his eyes to seek something good and kind and meaningful. He wondered if anyone else searched as well. Then he grimaced at his frailty for easily falling into that childish, hopeful crap. He could not believe in that anymore.

Let it go. It's all fake.

Henry cleared his head. Reverend Garcia, in burgundy robes, came to the lectern and spoke to the congregation with humor and sympathy, but no originality. She gave the same message of the season with the typical Biblical passages and verses, which was fine with Henry. Christ was the only reality for him this time of year—all year long, actually. He noticed very little of that in anyone else, except maybe his mother.

Then, Henry caught someone familiar through the heads of the congregation. His eyes narrowed. Charles sat there with two adults, a little girl to his left and a boy to his right.

What the hell?

Henry stared knife-like at him.

Where did he come from?

A bully defiling his church. There he sat, Henry fumed, like a good Christian boy, strong and sadistic, uncaring of the pain he caused himself, Caleb and others. Like the good bully that he is, Henry thought, Charles wasn't even thinking about that. Henry's breathing quickened and his father turned to him. Henry pulled air into his nostrils to settle himself.

"Problem?" his father whispered.

Henry dropped his head back to level, ignoring his father. His face hardened in furious thought. Charles, the evil presence in his church, reminded him of the interminable conflict waiting for him. He concluded that if he wanted his happiness, his sanity—indeed, his life—he would have to fight for it in a war everyone but him saw was wrong. If that's what those kids, those adults in that school want, Henry nodded, that's what they'll get.

You've held back long enough. It's your time now. He glanced at Charles again. *Get ready, asshole. I'm coming for you. All of you.*

The pastor concluded and Henry reluctantly stood up with everyone else to sing *Joy to the World*. For the first time, Henry did not sing.

Why should I? This whole thing's a joke. These people don't have a clue.

Would Jesus think his battle wrong? Henry wondered. Forgive your enemies, He said. Hmm, Henry mused, forgive. How? How can forgiveness apply to people who have hurt so many, and with no mercy? He had believed. All his life, he had behaved. He had practiced do unto others.

And what did it get you? Absolutely nothing.

He breathed in audibly. His father turned to him again.

At the front of the church to the left of the apse, the figure of Christ hung on the cross, beaten body drooping and half dead. Henry could relate. But then, after gazing at the figure a moment, he brightened. He knew the way out now, the way out of his dark, oppressive life. Now the time had come to use his newly-gained power against those kids and adults who never helped him. He didn't want to do it—it will cause a lot of pain. But he had no other choice, and he finally accepted his destiny. He felt an unusual confidence for what must come.

As voices of a hundred sang in unison around him, he stared at the sorrowful figure on the wall with a heart now as hard as the books that had assaulted him. In two thousand years, nothing had changed.

You couldn't beat your bullies. But I will. I'll get them for the both of us. I'm gonna get them all.

Vengeance is mine, sayeth the Lord.

Henry shook his head.

Sorry. Not this time. Vengeance is mine.

PART TWO

PART TWO

CROWDS OF STUDENTS FUNNELED INTO THE FRONT ENTRANCE of their school under a cold, grey sky on the first day back. Henry stepped off the bus onto the sidewalk as other bus kids passed around him. The school still appeared to him like a foreboding old prison daring him to enter. After ruminating for over a week, Henry understood what he had to do. His shaky confidence pushed him forward, but his doubt remained as big as the building itself.

Henry gazed up at the tall, glass façade that projected itself from the building. He noticed through the white reflection painted on the windows the ghost-like figures of Vice Principal Peterson, Mr. Davis and Mr. Johnson looking down on him and frowning, as if, Henry thought, with some concern. He gave them a faint smile. He enjoyed that as he passed underneath them.

Now, in the middle of the large foyer as kids passed by in all directions, his eyes hardened.

It's time, people. Your time has come.

He surveyed the hallway at his locker, greeting a few kids nearby, seeking out his enemies. Throughout the day, Henry tried to relax in his classes as teachers discussed the curriculum. But by the afternoon his anxiety had returned like the bully that never goes away. He knew why—just being in that damn school. The same horrible space, the same failure, but also the trouble that lay ahead. Fear flowed through him relentlessly.

C'mon. We talked about this. Get angry. Stay angry. It's the only way.

Anxiousness still had its way with him. But he understood quite well now that controlling emotion would take time and that anger could defeat the fear bred deeply in him.

Patience, dude, patience. C'mon. Breathe. Do the breathing.

In Mrs. Fields' class, he barely listened to her lecture, depressed that he had a lot to prove in and out of the classroom and only five months in which to do it. Henry had planned his war on two fronts: against the bullies and against his own deficient mind. To get energized, he pushed his hand into the air and did so incessantly, desperately, throughout the class, questioning every little bit he did not understand and even a few things he did. Hearing the annoyed mutterings and sighs of classmates amused him.

"Wilty, you're the pain that keeps on hurting," Charles said.

Okay. Small steps. Give as good as you get.

"And you're the bully that keeps on bullying, Chuck."

"Don't call me that."

"Don't call me Wilty."

"We have to put a muzzle on the meek," Trevor added.

"That right, Trevy?"

"Alright, enough," Mrs. Fields said.

"Wilty's a bit of a smart-ass today," Laurie said.

"Shut up, Laurie."

She darted a surprised glance at him.

"You want to meet your old friend again?" Trevor said, holding up a book. Some of the kids chuckled.

Henry kept his smile. "Try it and see what happens."

"I said enough," Mrs. Fields demanded. "Any more threats like that and we go to the Office, understand?"

Henry's pulse quickened at the repartee. He had never before degraded someone's name as they had always had done to his. And that was the first time he had heard a teacher speak like that in class. Something changing? he wondered.

Derrick lounged his tall frame in the corner chair. He remained as subdued as he was after returning from suspension.

Henry pulled a piece of paper from his pack. "Hey, Derrick." He held up the paper for Derrick—and the class—to see. Derrick looked at it and saw the words, 'you suck' written across it in his handwriting. Henry burst out laughing. "Right back atcha, buddy." He dropped his forehead onto his arm in laughter, still holding up the paper. Derrick looked back passively.

"Let me see that," Fields said.

She gave Henry a stern look.

"This is inappropriate."

"In this school? You're kidding, right?"

"Why did you write this?"

"I didn't. Derrick did. In September."

"No, I didn't," Derrick replied casually, as though expecting to be believed.

Fields let out an exasperated breath. She dropped her hands

"C'mon, Derrick, tell the truth. There are witnesses here who saw you do it. Right?" Henry glanced around. "Anyone? And then he slammed me in the back of the head with a book. Of course, he did it with my back turned like the coward that he really is."

The classroom quieted.

"Alright, Henry," Fields said. "Let's stop this nonsense."

"Yeah, Derry," Henry added. "Stop the nonsense."

Henry heard more impatient sighs and mumbled words around the room. He suspected that the kids blamed him for all the bickering and wouldn't dare blame Derrick, Trevor, Jeremy, Robin, or Laurie. He gave Derrick a little smile. Derrick nodded back.

He's gonna explode.

After class, Mrs. Fields called Henry over.

"Henry," she began, sitting on the corner of her desk. "You're still having these arguments. Is there anything I can do to help? We were hoping for better behavior this semester."

Henry chuckled. "Yeah, tell them to stop."

"Well, you said the same things to them."

"Only to defend myself. You see, they shouldn't be talking like that to begin with. But they do because you let them get away with it."

"I did warn them to stop."

"A little weak, but you did. How come you're just talking to me about this and not them?"

"You could have just ignored their comments and let it go."

"Again, listen, they shouldn't be talking like that to begin with. That's the problem." Henry stepped toward her. "You stop that, the arguments will stop. They mess with me, I mess with them. You're an enabler of bullying, Mrs. Fields, because you're afraid of them. All you teachers and parents are. They completely control you."

"They do not, Henry," she stated. "Obviously you still refuse our help." She began gathering up her papers. Nervously, Henry thought.

"This is my school now. Things go my way. You'll have to decide which side you're on."

"There are no sides here, Henry. And you're very angry."

"And why do you think? They were bullying me, and Trevor threatened to hit me. I'll expect you to report this."

Fields stopped. "I'm not going to report every verbal scuffle you kids have, nor do I believe Trevor was serious. But I will speak to him."

"I hope so," Henry said, releasing some anger. "Because it was a threat. Heck, if I said something like that, you'd have me in the Office in a second."

Fields stared stiffly as Henry walked out, and she didn't call him back.

Around the corner, Henry leaned against the wall and blew out some tension, trying to calm himself. He closed his eyes. He wondered if it was too much, too soon.

No. That's what you gotta do. The sooner, the better. Be careful, though.

In the library, he eased into a chair. "Step one done," he said to the other kids there. "I talked back to them. How dare I do that to the kings of the school?"

They looked at him strangely.

Good enabler remark, too.

But, by challenging them like that, Henry realized he had crossed into enemy territory for his treacherous journey to freedom, with every word and gesture critical to success. His body trembled, so he breathed softly and calmly.

C'mon. Keep going. This is the way it has to be.

Near class time, he bounced down the stairs.

He caught up to Sharonda.

"Hey."

"Ah, hi there," she said as they made their way through the corridor.

"How was Christmas?" he asked.

"Good. Yours?"

"Not bad. Get everything you wanted?"

Sharonda stopped.

"Pretty much."

"What's the matter?"

She sighed. "Nothin'. So things gonna go better this term?"

Henry thought about her question a moment, but had to tell the truth.

"Depends on everybody else, Sharonda."

"Some of us are worried."

"No need. You haven't done anything wrong. Only those who have should worry. But I need your help. If you and Chloe and the girls see any abuse going on, you have to report it. Help me out."

"Alright. I gotta get goin'. Later."

Sharonda's tone concerned him. Neither Kam, Caleb nor George called him much anymore. He always had to call them.

Shit. If they go, what are you going to do?

He wondered how he could straddle the fine line between clashing with enemies and not alienating the friends he needed.

Well, they're middlings. You've already given them a chance to help. You knew you had to do this yourself.

Henry put up a bold front and hummed to himself loud enough for everyone to hear, until he was bumped hard by Derrick.

"Watch where ya goin', Wilton."

Henry glowered at him.

Later on, though, Henry found Derrick talking with Mr. Davis down the hall, both turned slightly away from him. Henry's eyes widened.

Perfect. You have to do it. C'mon. He tensed up and couldn't get himself to move. *C'mon, idiot, do it. You gotta do it now.*

He took in a deep breath and weaved through a maze of kids, aiming at Derrick and Davis, hoping they wouldn't notice his approach. Them talking so amicably, and another teacher treating a bully with such respect, burned Henry. As he got closer, his heart skipped and his lips parted with anticipation. He bumped Derrick so hard the books he held dived to the floor.

"Oh, sorry."

Derrick and Davis stared in surprise

"Wilton," Derrick shouted. "Pick 'em up."

"Wilton," Davis said. "Come back here."

Henry bounced down the stairs, kids pulling out of his way. He grinned wildly as he pranced into class, dropped into a chair and opened a book. Robin, Laurie and Meaghan sat nearby whispering. Carla seated herself stoically in a far corner. Kam, George and Caleb chatted next to him and he joined them. Mr. Bronner walked in.

"Wilty," Meaghan whispered after a few minutes into the lecture. "Let's go with the questions."

Henry shook his head a little. "Nah, not yet."

"Good," Robin added. "Give us all a break."

"Well, there you go," Henry replied.

"Well, there you go," Robin mocked.

"Vultures."

Robin frowned. "Why are you calling us that? What does that even mean?"

"Yeah, it doesn't even make any sense," Laurie added.

Henry chuckled. "I'm sure it doesn't to you."

He felt something hit his head. A crumpled piece of paper rolled onto the floor. He smirked at the girls and slowly shook his head.

That night in his room, Henry replayed the exhilaration of being the aggressor when he bumped Derrick. And he got away with his sneak attack, which felt empowering. But there would be consequences in his bully world. He got up from the bed and paced the floor, rubbing the back of his neck nervously.

He imagined enemy territory as a wide, grassy plain, spreading endlessly to the horizon. No meek had ever dared venture there. He thought he had the advantage because they didn't know he dared it. The only strategy he could think of at the moment had him braving the day-to-day skirmishes he expected and whatever they would lead to. Henry felt a strange, righteous confidence about his survival—that he had already won the war. He just had to make it through the battles.

But other work had to be done. He moved books aside on his desk and centered his computer. "Alright," he said out loud, placing his palms on the desk. "Let's get this stuff right. You got to get some good grades out of this."

A while later, he got an idea. He brought up a blank page on his computer and typed in "Support no bullying. Tell Admin to stop the abuse!" and created three columns for kids to write their names in and printed it out. He chuckled as he signed his name at the top, then slid it into his notebook.

"Ha. Let's see who signs this."

The next morning, Mrs. Tompkins told Henry to go to the Office. Mary directed him in to Principal Ruzzo's office, where Davis stood by with arms folded.

Henry smiled as he closed the door.

This will be good.

He widened his eyes innocently.

"Yes?"

"Apparently you caused a problem yesterday," Ruzzo began.

Henry screwed up his face. "What problem?"

"You bumped into Derrick and knocked his books to the floor. Mr. Davis told you to come back to pick them up but didn't. Why?"

"Oh, that." Henry shrugged. "That was an accident. I'm sure Derrick could pick up his own books. He's a tough kid."

"When a teacher tells you to come back, you do so," Davis remarked.

"Oh, you mean like when Richard Gillo dumped my books and computer on the floor last year and you told him to pick them up and he just walked away and you told him to come back and he didn't and then, uh, you told me to pick them up instead and when I said no you had me down in this office. Remember that?"

Henry raised his eyebrows at Davis, expecting an answer.

"That's enough," Ruzzo said. "It doesn't matter what happened last year."

"And a few days later," he said to Ruzzo, "I asked you if you spoke to your big football player and you looked at me mad and said you would. You were trying to scare me off, like a weakling should in your school. You never spoke to him. You lied. Why?"

"This about you, Henry," Ruzzo replied, unfazed by Henry's accusation.

"Well, I guess since nothing happened to him, nothing happens to me. Ha. And I'm not even a stupid athlete. That's about it. Have a nice day."

At the door, he waited for the two gentlemen to say something, but they didn't.

"And if you have a problem with this, we can always go to the superintendent and discuss it with him. I'm sure he'd be very interested in hearing about this. And other things as well." He frowned and closed the door.

Henry skipped back to class, heart racing.

Wow. Just walking out. Now let's see what happens. He shook out his twitching muscles.

He passed Derrick, talking with Todd and Kevin.

Henry grinned.

"Well, if it isn't my favorite bullies."

"Beat it, Wilton," Kevin said in a low tone.

"So, Derrick, did you pick up your little books yesterday?"

Henry chuckled. Derrick glared.

"I was called into Ruzzo about it. But he didn't do anything. Now I know how it feels to get away with it. You know, like when you hit people in the back of the head with a book and nothing happens to you?" Henry nodded. "Feels pretty good."

"I'm going to hit you right now if you don't get outta here," Derrick said.

"No, you're not. You're not gonna do anything. None of you are."

Todd slowly stepped behind Henry.

"What were you doing with those books, anyway? Don't you know they're used for reading?"

Henry laughed out loud and left them silent.

But he was nervous about approaching Carla. Would she yell at him again? He decided to brave it, as she walked toward him.

"Hi."

"Hello," she replied, not unkindly.

"You still mad at me?" he said with a sheepish smile.

"No, Henry, I'm not."

"I know I went too far. Sorry."

Carla kept walking with Henry right next to her.

"Forget about it, Henry. Just don't worry about me so much."

"But, just out of curiosity, did Stagg really ever talk to you?"

Carla stopped and sighed. "Yes."

Henry raised his hands. "Okay. I'll stay out of it. But, you know, if you want to talk anytime, let me know. We're in history together again. Maybe we can study together."

"Right. I'll let you know."

Carla disappeared into a classroom.

Well, I don't think she hates you. Leave her alone a while.

At day's end, Henry sat with Chloe at a long table near the auditorium, struggling with math and hoping to get her to help.

He sighed. "Frickin' algebra. What did you get on problem ten?"

"Nothing yet."

He threw down his pencil and sighed.

"Doesn't matter anyway." He closed the textbook. "Even if I get it right here, I'll get it wrong on the test. Just can't think. Drives me nuts."

"You're too nervous," Chloe said, rapidly typing on her phone.

"Yeah, slightly. Tests always trigger it."

"You need a shrink."

Henry chuckled. "I'm not the only one around here."

"Hey, you're my math tutor. You gotta help me."

"Not really. You'll have to find somebody else for that."

The outside door opened.

"Hey, Wilton," Charles called out, in a friendly tone, Henry thought. "C'mon out and join us."

"Why?"

"C'mon."

"Okay, hold on. I'll be right out."

Henry looked at the door suspiciously.

"Yeah, right."

He got his things together.

"Well, alright, I gotta catch the bus."

He pulled his pack onto his shoulder.

"See ya tomorrow."

"Okay," Chloe said. "Are you going out there?"

"No. If he comes back in, tell him I had to go do something."

On his way, Henry tacked his sign-up sheet amidst an unkempt mass of other notices on one of the billboards. He stood back and wondered who would dare write their name under his. He laughed out loud and went home.

The next morning, in his first class, his friends didn't appear happy.

"What's going on?"

"You haven't heard?" George asked.

"No. What?"

"Caleb got jumped," Kam said.

Henry sat down slowly. "When?"

"Yesterday."

"Who did it?"

"We think it's probably Jeremy, Joe, Trevor. That crowd," George said.

"Yesterday," Henry muttered. "They must have got him right outside in back of the auditorium."

Kam nodded. "How did you know?"

"I was there. Chloe and I were doing math in the hall. Charles tried to get me to come outside, but I went home."

Chloe nodded.

"Lucky you did," George said.

Henry looked around. "Is Caleb here?"

"No."

"Damn it. I should have gone out there. Then it would have been me. Caleb didn't have a chance against them."

"Nobody would have," Kam said. "I heard they pushed him around in a circle until he dropped to the ground and cried. Then they almost stripped him down. Somebody stopped it."

"They were smoking and drinking out there, too," George added.

"God. This frickin' place. It gets more perverted every day. Did anyone record it?"

George shrugged. "Probably."

"They wanted me, not Caleb. They know they can do whatever they want with all the teachers and the Office hating me. They know they can get away with it. Guys, c'mon, we got to get together on this."

Kam considered Henry for a moment. "We can all call Safe2Tell," he said. "Make sure they know about it."

"This is Caleb. We have to stand up to this. There's no way we can ignore it. I'm going to the Office to really make sure they know about it."

"You're actually doing that?" Kam asked.

"That's where the problem is."

"Good luck with that," Chloe added.

Henry ignored her comment. But what a golden opportunity for his cause, he thought, as he hurried through the hall.

You let yourselves go too far this time, assholes. Thank you.

Billy and Frank stood around looking relaxed. They hadn't bothered him or even looked at him so far, likely, he thought, because they knew one more altercation would get them kicked out for good. So they ignored him. But he wasn't going to ignore them.

"Hey, Frilly," Henry said. "How's it going?"

Billy sneered. "What did you say?"

"Frilly. Frank and Billy." Henry laughed and kept going.

At the Office, Ruzzo was out and Peterson was busy. He decided to go back later and went to class shaking his head, holding down fury and frustration and wondering how Caleb was doing, or feeling.

Henry sought out Charles.

"Hey, what's up?" he asked him.

"What do you want, Wilty?" Joe said.

"It's Wilton. So, what did you want yesterday when you asked me to come outside?" Henry asked Charles. "Too bad I had to go do something."

"Yeah," Charles said, grinning, "you missed out."

"On what?"

Charles turned away and moved some things in his locker.

"That wasn't good, what you did to Caleb."

Joe and Charles exchanged glances.

"What do you mean?" Charles asked.

"You know what I mean."

"We don't know anything about that," Joe said.

"Everybody else does except you. Weird, huh?"

Charles shrugged. "We didn't do anything."

"Why did you want me to come out, then? That's where Caleb was assaulted. But I left, and you grabbed him instead."

Joe's arms hung tough from a beefy torso. "Prove it."

"Oh, I will." Henry nodded firmly. "I'm going to the Office about this. I'll make sure they know. Because I doubt they do." He backpedaled. "Get ready. Whoever did this is gone."

In second block, Henry sat quietly exasperated, and asked no questions. *They're showing everyone who's boss. No one's gonna stop them. You're the only one.*

After lunch, he saw Frank talking with two other boys and aimed for him. He came up from behind and bumped into his old enemy. He peered back with a smile. "Oh, sorry, buddy."

Back in the Office, Peterson agreed to meet with him. She placed her glasses on the desk and folded her hands, waiting stiffly for what Henry had to say. He sat down.

"Just wanted to know if you heard about Caleb."

Peterson shook her head.

"No."

"I didn't think so. He was assaulted. Outside behind the auditorium yesterday afternoon."

Peterson moved in her chair uncomfortably, deeply frowning as though concerned.

"Does anyone know who did it?"

"Yeah. Caleb. And the kids who did it. And those who watched it and did nothing about it. There are usually plenty of those."

Peterson pinched her lips.

"Caleb's not here today. When he comes back, though I don't know why he would to this school, talk to him and find out who assaulted him. Okay?"

Henry gave Peterson a steady stare.

"Alright," she said, seemingly tolerating Henry's tone. "We'll look into it."

"Good. I'll come back tomorrow to see how you're doing."

Henry abruptly turned for the door.

"No. You don't have to come back. We'll handle it. Thank you for letting us know."

She looked back down at some papers.

Henry shivered at her arrogant and flippant tone.

"Excuse me?"

"We'll handle this."

"And I'll help you."

"No, Henry."

"Well, you've shown me that you and the principal are not too good at handling these issues." He stepped up to the desk and glared into Peterson's eyes. "Caleb's a good friend of mine. This isn't the first time he's been assaulted, like me, but it's going to be the last. The bullies who did this will be expelled."

"Henry, that decision will be made when the time comes. Thank you for bringing this to our attention."

"Do you remember the conversation we had just last month? I pretty much told you what I would do if you didn't straighten things out around here."

"Yes. I remember. They were the ravings of a frustrated young man who's having a very difficult time handling life. You spoke to us very disrespectfully. However, we are doing everything we can to address any legitimate concerns."

"Ravings. Look what's happened now. We're into the first week of school again and someone gets assaulted. What are you addressing? Same old, same old as far as I can see. You work harder polishing the floors around here than stopping the abuse."

Peterson stared challengingly at Henry. He could sense she was trying very hard to maintain some semblance of authority.

Stay with it. Fight her.

Henry pulled at the edges of his jacket and wanted Peterson to notice. He held a steady, hard gaze at her.

"I don't think you understand how seriously bad this is."

"Something like this can occur, and we do take it seriously."

"Well, with the way you've handled everything else, I trust you as far as I can throw you."

Peterson grimaced.

"I am sorry you feel that way. Now, we will handle this as quickly as possible."

"I'll be closely watching you." At the door, he turned back to her. "You know what I've always found interesting?" he asked, leaning on the doorknob. "Whenever something happens to one of your bullies, you seem to know about it right away. But when something happens to kids like me, you don't hear about it at all. Why is that?"

Henry raised his eyebrows.

"So, it always seems like when something happens to me, you don't hear anything about it, but when I do something to one of your bullies," he said, sneering, "you people are all over me like a bad stink." He liked that word, sharpening the t and the k. "Hope you do the right thing."

Henry let the door shut hard on its own.

You're going to get these bastards. You're gonna get them. You're gonna get them. You're gonna get them. He closed his eyes and took a sip from the water fountain. *Alright, calm down.*

Caleb did not show up the next day, and Henry empathized with his humiliation. He called Caleb's phone several times but no answer. He figured Caleb didn't want to talk. Instead of going to his house, he waited to see if his friend would return the next day.

In the afternoon, Henry decided to spend a few minutes in the gym. The volleyball team came close to winning the first game. Joe, Charles and Trevor spiked and dived, moving fast, high-fiving. Cheerleaders chanted. Fans shouted. Henry double-stepped up the stands to sit with Adam and Stanley, two middlings who were also Caleb's friends. Henry eventually asked if they knew who had assaulted Caleb. Stanley said he didn't know. Adam said nothing.

"Were you there, Adam?"

"I don't want to talk about it."

"What did you do? Did you try to stop it?"

"How?"

Henry sighed impatiently. "Has anyone talked to Caleb? I tried calling him but he's not answering."

"I talked to him yesterday," Stanley replied.

"How's he doing?"

"Okay, I guess."

"Is he coming back?"

"He'll probably be back tomorrow."

"Okay, look. We have to do something about this. Let's go to the Office and just tell them who it was."

"Let it alone," Adam said. "Caleb will be fine."

"Are you sure? Something like that does something to ya."

Both boys looked at Henry, who brooded a moment.

"Okay, you don't want to get involved. Fine. At least call Safe2Tell. You can do that right now."

"He's right," Stanley said to Adam.

"I'll call it after the game," Adam said.

"Peterson said she didn't know about it. That means no one else who was there called it in. Frickin' kids. They don't give a shit."

Two adults a few rows down looked back at Henry.

Henry sighed as he watched the game. "Alright. So let me put it this way so you won't exactly be squealing. If I said they were three of the kids who did it, say nothing if you agree and say anything if you disagree."

"Wilton, forget it. I'm not doing that," Adam said.

"C'mon. You won't get into trouble. I'll give you names."

Adam sighed. "No, Henry."

Henry looked at the players.

"Okay. If I said that Charles and Joe did it, would you disagree with me? Say anything if you do, silence if you don't."

Adam watched the game.

"Yes if you do. Silence if you don't."

Adam said nothing.

"Oh. Then who are the others?"

He looked again at Adam.

"Okay. Trevor."

"Nope."

"Really. Umm, ah, Sharonda."

"Hardly," Adam said.

"Donny."

"No."

"Kevin."

Silence.

"Roach."

Adam chuckled.

"Todd."

Silence.

"Derrick."

"No."

Henry added a few more names, but Adam disagreed with them.

"Oh, Jeremy."

Silence.

"Should I keep going?"

"No. Please."

"Okay, thanks for sharing. Don't forget to make that call."

Henry got up.

"How can you sit there and watch those kids play volleyball after what they did to Caleb? Look at them. They don't give a shit." His voice rose. "They're not even thinking about it. To them it was just some fun to forget about. They have no conscience, no guilt. They're monsters. Created by their do-nothing parents and these teachers and Ruzzo and Peterson."

Some spectators peered up at Henry again.

"We get it, Henry," Stanley said.

"No, I think I'm the only one who really gets it."

Adam grimaced.

Henry went into the hallway and dialed Safe2Tell for the first time, not trusting that Adam would do so.

"So, kids used this to complain about me?" Henry mumbled. "Well, two can play at that game."

He related Caleb's assault into the phone and the kids responsible and hung up, satisfied at having done it.

"We'll see what that does," he whispered. "Probably nothing."

"You talking to yourself?"

Christy smiled at him.

"Guess I am," Henry replied. "That's what this place does to ya."

Christy surprised Henry by talking to him at all. They had spoken only a few times. He had been in some of her classes the year before, but not this year. To Henry, she had both looks and brains, elevating her to a level far above his. Her long, light brown hair (silky, in his mind) framed a bright, oval face, and she always wore chic clothing, from jeans to skirts. He saw her as a princess who carried herself as if she knew it. But it was confidence, not conceit, he thought. She had dated a senior not too long ago.

He sat down. "Whatcha reading?"

She lifted the English book. "Oh, AP?"

"Uh-huh."

"Heck, I can hardly get a B."

Henry returned to his gloominess.

"What's wrong?" she asked.

"Ah, there's always something wrong around here?"

"Like what?"

Henry laughed quietly. "I didn't think you'd know."

"Know what?"

"The madness."

"Huh?"

"Nothin'."

"You know, you always look angry," Christy remarked. "That's what kids say about you. You have angry eyes."

"Really. Do you think there might be a reason why?"

"Why?"

"Well, when you're always getting jerked around. But, you wouldn't understand."

"Oh."

After a moment of silence, he asked her if she'd heard about Caleb.

"Yes, I did," she said quietly.

"What are we all going to do about it?"

"About what?"

"What happened to Caleb."

Christy thought a moment.

"What can we do?"

Henry pressed his lips together sadly. He knew that would be her response.

Queen middling.

"Actually, we can do a lot. They just don't want us to know it."

"Who are they?"

"The Office. I'll just have to do it alone," he said. "As usual. How about Carla? Have you ever seen her being bothered by some of the girls?"

"Ah," she sighed, "well, occasionally."

"Alright." He decided not pursue the discussion with her. "Good talk. Hey, have any advice how I can get my grades up?"

Christy's face puzzled. "Study harder?"

Henry smiled. "Good advice. Okay. Bye."

Study harder. What does that even mean? Never works for me.

Upstairs, Henry pressed fingertips to forehead. "Damn it," he whispered. "You got to end this. C'mon, Caleb, get back to school."

"Wilton," someone called out.

Henry came out of his thoughts to look at Mr. Davis. "Yes?"

"What are you doing standing there? Get to class."

Henry looked around. "Really? You mean just like all the other kids you see here? Or just me?" Henry smiled sharp and thin.

"Everyone."

"There they are. Tell them," he said loudly.

Several kids turned. None smiled.

Davis came up to him. "Get to class now."

Henry jumped back and held up his hands. "Hey. Whoa. Whoa. Are you gonna hit me?"

The teacher stopped.

"Yeah. Okay. You...you just stay right there." He backed away. "You're scaring me. Stay right there."

"That's enough, Wilton."

Downstairs, Henry snickered at Davis' surprised reaction.

Be ready. The teachers will come after you.

Henry spotted Billy ambling through the hall, his untouchable bully status deeply irritating him.

Okay. Let's do this.

He stopped in Billy's path.

"Hey, buddy, what's happening?"

Billy looked Henry up and down as if he were an insect. "Get the fuck out of the way, asshole."

Henry shrugged, maintaining a calm demeanor.

"Hey, language, language. Just saying hi."

"I said get out of the way."

"Hey, I'm just standing here. You can go."

Henry showed Billy an insolent smirk. Billy stepped around. Henry blocked his way again.

"Where ya going, anyway? Can I come?"

Billy stared at Henry. "Wilton, you better move your ass now."

"Bill, what's wrong? Hey, if ya don't want to talk." Henry nodded to the side. "Go ahead."

Billy broke his knife-like stare and moved past. Henry leaned to the side and brushed Billy's arm. He stopped as if to attack.

"Oops, sorry."

Henry gave him a challenging smile, but Billy kept walking.

"Let's hang sometime."

Billy shook his head.

Ooo-hooo. Now that's a really big change. Just don't get cocky.

Henry hummed his way to class, and went home for the weekend anxiously triumphant.

Caleb returned to school on Monday. Henry saw him at the other end of the hallway. He appeared deeply sad and tired to Henry. As Henry headed to class, he glanced with vengeance at Jeremy and Charles, who talked pleasantly as if the world was theirs.

Not for long.

"Hey, guys. What's up?"

"Keep walking, Wilty," Jeremy replied.

"Caleb's back. We'll find out today who assaulted him."

"What?" Jeremy said.

"You heard me. Get ready, bullies, you're gone."

"Don't think so," Jeremy called out.

Henry got into the classroom before Caleb to see how his friend would be greeted. He looked around at the kids near him. Caleb came in, followed by Mr. Bronner.

Murmuring rose up. Henry heard "naked boy is here" and a few stifled laughs. Caleb sat down with a reddened face. Henry changed his seat.

He tapped Caleb on the arm.

"Hey," he said softly. "What's up? I called you last night."

"I know."

"Good to see you back."

"Wilton," someone said disparagingly behind him, probably, Henry thought, for sitting next to Caleb.

Henry darted an angry glance behind him.

"Problem?" he said to Donny, sitting at the desk behind him.

Henry dropped his elbow onto the desk.

"Turn around," Donny ordered.

"Make me."

"We can do that after school, meek."

"Let me know where, a-hole," Henry replied, then turned around.

Good. Let's get it over with.

Donny slapped Henry across the back of the head.

"Hey. He just assaulted me."

"Dope slap," someone said.

Donny raised his hands. "I didn't do anything."

Bronner looked over the scene. "Will you guys stop sniping at each other?"

"What, that's it? There are witnesses here." He looked at Donny. "Just like when you assaulted Caleb last week."

"I wasn't part of that. Just ask Caleb. Right, Caleb?"

Caleb hunkered in embarrassment.

"Right, Caleb?" Donny demanded sharply. "Tell the truth."

"Just forget it, Henry," Caleb said quietly.

"See?" Donny smiled.

"I know someone who was there. He said you were one of them. You too, Todd."

Todd shrugged. "I wasn't there, either."

"The bullies get away with it again."

"That's it," Bronner said. "Conversation over. This is not meant for class. Take it to the Office."

"Already have."

"Alright," Bronner said, stepping around to the front of the desk. "Look. We've had too much conflict in this school over the past year and it has to stop."

"You can blame Wilty for that," Todd said.

"We can all do better than this," Bronner emphasized, ignoring the remark. "Be better. It's a new term so let's all relax and get along. Stop the constant arguing. I know you can all do it."

Henry snorted. "It's not conflict. It's abuse."

"Conversation over," Bronner said. "Now we have work to do."

He began writing on the blackboard.

They're winning again. Just glossing it all over.

With Bronner's back turned, Henry whipped his hand around wide enough to strike Donny, and barely missed his face.

Donny looked back in shock.

"Hey, he tried to hit me" he said incredulously.

Henry shrugged. "No I didn't."

"Wilton did," Jose said.

"No, I didn't," Henry sneered.

"You all want to be suspended?" Bronner shouted. "Now knock it off."

Donny leaned forward. "You just signed your death warrant."

"Screw you," Henry whispered.

"We'll talk about this after class," Donny warned, punching a fist into his other hand.

Henry yawned gapingly at him.

Outside in the hallway after class, Henry pulled Caleb aside.

"How you doing?"

"I'm fine, Henry."

"Hey, Wilton," Donny said. "There's a dirt road behind the stands at the park. Be there after school."

"What for?"

"I'm gonna teach you some manners."

Henry gave Donny a condescending smile and rubbed the bottom of his nose. "You?"

"Yeah, me," Donny replied angrily. "Be there at four o'clock."

"You make sure you're there."

Donny grunted and shook his head.

"Look, I know this is tough for you," he said, returning to Caleb, "but let's go down to the Office and you can just tell Peterson who assaulted you. We can get those kids kicked out today. We can't let them get away with this."

"Who's we?" Caleb asked.

"They know they can do anything they want. Right now, they're laughing it up as if nothing happened. They're not even thinking about what they did to you. But you are. Right?"

Caleb clamped his mouth tight, seemingly impatient with Henry. Henry could see Caleb's eyes focused on something, as though thinking about what Henry had said. Henry flushed with a little bit of hope.

"Look, it's scary. I know. I'm scared all the time. But we can do this. We can stand up together."

Caleb's small, smooth-skinned face crinkled up in dismay, almost like he was about to cry.

"You didn't tell your parents, did you? Tell them tonight and they can sue this rathole. I'm getting Ruzzo and Peterson in line, so tell your parents."

"I don't want to talk about it, Henry. Forget it."

"You can't forget about it. You never will. That's my point."

Two kids glanced at them.

"Keep walking," Henry said to them.

"Look, ten years from now, you'll regret that you didn't stick up for yourself and do something, fight them or get them expelled."

"Stop it!" Caleb barked, so loud that everyone in the hallway stopped. "Leave me alone." He stomped away.

Henry froze, not only at Caleb's outburst but by how he looked—a face contorted in pain, revealing what Henry thought was inner torment. He gave an embarrassed shrug to everyone and went to the Office to see Peterson.

"I have some something for you," he said.

"What is it?"

Henry handed her a page he'd ripped from his notebook.

"Those are the kids who assaulted Caleb. I got them from someone who was there."

"We have been getting calls about what happened to Caleb. We will call Caleb in so he can verify this."

"He's here today."

"Okay. Thank you."

"Uh, how about right now?"

"We'll get to it, Henry," Peterson replied curtly. "We're very busy today."

"Oh. Are there other student assaults you're working on?"

Henry cocked his eyebrows at her.

"I think I said last week that this is the most important thing," he said, placing his hands on his hips. "Because that's the way I want it and you should, too. But, hey, if you're that busy, I can call the police and have them come up and do it, and you can do all that important work on your desk. You don't mind, do you?"

"Henry, we'll take care of this."

"Like with everything else?"

The green glint in Peterson's eyes sharpened to a point where, Henry thought, it could cut glass.

"Have you noticed you haven't heard from his parents?"

She sat silently, guiltily in Henry's mind.

"You may want to call them. But, then, why would you? You really don't want parents yelling at you, do you?"

"Why wouldn't he tell them himself?" Peterson asked.

"Because we're too embarrassed to, that's why. Ashamed. And you know that and you take full advantage of it." *Ooo, that was good.* He leaned forward. "And you remember the conversation we had about the strong kids and the weak kids, right? So, in your way of thinking, Caleb should just walk away from this and laugh it off. Right?"

"That's not what we were talking about. This is much more serious."

"Are you going to call him in?"

In a burst of temper, she pulled her computer in front of her, located Caleb and had him summoned.

"Now, that wasn't so hard. And what happened to Caleb almost happened to me. Charles tried to get me outside. But I didn't go, and they grabbed Caleb instead. I want those bullies gone by the end of day tomorrow. Make sure it happens, alright?" He grinned. "Bye."

"Henry," Peterson called out. "Here is your sign-up sheet." She placed it softly down on the front of the desk.

"Oh, yeah. I forgot about this."

"You put it up without permission."

"That's true."

Someone had scribbled the words *"Wilton's an idiot"* on it and scratched off the word *"no"*.

"Ha, look at that. Well, why don't I put this back up?"

"No," Peterson snapped.

"Why not?"

"We have anti-bullying policies in place. We don't need that."

"Yeah. But how come they're not working? Look what's happened to me and Caleb. Ha. No one signed the sheet."

"What does that tell you?" she asked.

"They're too scared, that's why. Afraid of retaliation. Which is why I put it up, to prove it. Do you really think that everyone believes you're doing a great job stopping abuse in this school?" He chuckled.

Peterson's eyes widened. "That's enough. We're doing the best we can. We will deal with Caleb's situation."

"No. Caleb's assault. He was assaulted. On school grounds. On your watch."

"I can't talk to you anymore about this. Go to class."

"I'll be back. See ya."

Peterson exhaled sharply.

Using the word assault, Henry thought, put Peterson in a position she was unaccustomed to and her mask of red anger showed it.

Good. Keep pushing.

But the defaced sign-up sheet amused him.

The word spread quickly that Henry would fight Donny. A lot of kids said they would be there to watch the massacre.

Henry made his way to the library where Carla sat with forehead on her arms, very still, as if asleep. She appeared to Henry like she didn't care that her books, computer and phone were open to silent theft, common in his school, as though she were saying, "take them, I don't care anymore."

Sharonda and Chloe passed behind him.

"She doesn't look too good," he said.

The girls dropped their packs and pocketbooks on a table.

"Well, she's had a tough time," Sharonda said. "Some of the girls got on her in the locker room yesterday."

"The Vultures?"

"They put up pictures of girls going at it on her locker door."

"Why?"

"Look," Chloe said, "there is more going on than you know."

"Probably."

Chloe sighed. "She's lesbian," she whispered.

"Really. Does everybody know?"

"Most of the girls have suspected for a while," she said.

"So, you don't put up pictures."

"They do."

Henry grunted. "I know Laurie and Meaghan are cybering her. I don't know why she doesn't do anything."

"Henry, get with it, please," Chloe said.

"Well, I don't know. What are we going to do?"

She slowly shook her head. "I don't know."

"Yeah, but being gay, that's old nowadays. I mean, there are lots of kids in schools who are gay and they're accepted."

"And a lot of kids that aren't," Chloe said.

"The other thing," Sharonda added, "is there are a few teachers here who don't like that, either."

"Hmm, Mrs. Roach," Henry murmured. "So she knows all about this."

Sharonda nodded.

"Well, what did you do when you saw it happen?"

"I walked away," Sharonda said. "I couldn't watch."

"We don't walk away anymore, remember?"

"Well, Henry, sometimes it's best," Chloe said.

"No. It's easy. Someone must have recorded it."

"Probably."

"Okay, ladies. What are you gonna do? You're going to report it, right? Call Safe2Tell, find out who recorded it and persuade them to take it to the Office."

Chloe smiled. "Okay, boss."

"Gee, she's lost weight, too. We gotta help her. Let's go over to say hi."

"I think she needs the rest," Sharonda said.

"It's the wrong kind of rest. C'mon."

Henry sat down at Carla's table.

"Hey, Carla?"

Carla opened her eyes and blinked a few times. She sat up and wiped some drool off the corner of her mouth.

"You okay?"

She cleared her throat. "Yes, I'm fine."

"You don't look fine."

Carla pushed her hair back, pulled her pack closer and put her things into it.

"I said I'm fine, Henry."

"You're lucky your things are still here."

Carla filled her pack.

"I heard they were harassing you in the locker room today. Let's go to the Office and report it. You don't have to take that from the Vultures anymore."

"You think it's so easy, don't you, Henry?"

"No, it's not. But I'm getting a handle on the Office. I've gotten them to do things."

Sharonda and Chloe arrived. "Hi, Carla," Chloe said.

"They'll go with you to give you support. We can all do this together."

"No. I only have four more months left in this place and I won't be back."

She abruptly got up and walked into the hallway. Henry followed.

"Carla," Henry said, exasperated again. "Listen. Going to another school defeats the purpose. They end up winning. And they want you to go to another school to get rid of you. That's what they want me to do. If you and a few other girls who get harassed go to the Office and complain, that will help a lot. If boys like me complain, they shrug it off. But if girls start complaining, that changes everything. Do it, Carla, do it for all of us."

Carla's thoughtful expression got Henry believing he may have broken through.

"It's scary. But I've fought my fears the last year and...and it's getting better. You can, too." He took a step closer to her. "Carla, you can be who you really are. It's just taking that one big step."

"I don't know if I can. Other girls will just take their place, anyway."

"No, they won't. Not if we take charge. I've already started. The next school you go to will have their own group of vultures. Stay here and let's fight them."

"I…have to go."

Carla left Henry staring. *Wow, she's got it bad. She's given up.*

He sat down with Chloe and Sharonda.

"How'd it go?" Chloe asked.

Henry glanced at her angrily. "If you were there, you'd know."

"You went after her so fast, you didn't give us a chance," Sharonda said.

"Good excuse."

Sharonda narrowed her eyes. "Alright, that's it. We're tired of you talking to us like that."

"If you'd help more. Call Safe2Tell and then go to the Office about it."

"Not here, Henry. We'll do it privately."

"Oh, yeah? Watch this."

Henry dialed Safe2Tell and reported Carla's condition and that she was being cyberbullied and sexually harassed in the locker room. He named Laurie, Meaghan and Robin, although he couldn't cite any proof. Henry ended the call, held his phone out, opened his fingers and dropped the phone clacking on the table.

"See? Easy. Your turn."

"We don't have to do it that way."

"I want to stay friends with you. But I can't if you're not going to help."

"Friendship is based on that?" Sharonda asked.

"Yes," Henry replied with finality.

"Henry, this is her problem," Chloe said. "She has to solve it herself."

"God, Chloe. We have to solve it together. Alright, you've made your choice." He got up, slung his pack onto his shoulder and walked off.

When he passed Stagg's office, he knocked.

"Yes, Wilton, what is it?" she asked.

"Did you ever talk to the bullies?"

"Again, I can't tell you that."

He sighed and looked at her.

"The best thing to do is speak with the principal."

"You heard what happened to Caleb?"

Stagg sat back. "Yes," she replied sadly.

"And there's no bullying going on around here? They wanted me, not him."

"Well, I'm sorry. Matters are worse than I knew."

"Well, since no one's behavior has changed, I assume you didn't talk to them. I will tell my parents and file a lawsuit against the school for negligence."

Stagg nodded slightly. "That is your right."

"If you want to help, I strongly urge you to talk to Carla now. She's hurting."

Henry closed the door. *She doesn't care. Nothing will happen to her anyway. She's above it all.*

Henry dropped into a chair in his next class.

"What a school, huh?" he said.

"What's wrong with it?" Andrew asked, as though insulted.

"What's wrong with it?" Henry shook his head. "Forget it."

"Good idea," Andrew returned.

Henry bristled at Andrew, the middling. Henry envied him, hated him.

In the same school but a different world.

Mrs. Tompkins dropped bags on her desk.

"Ignorance is bliss," Henry said. "Alright for you."

"I don't think ignorance is bliss, Wilton," Tompkins remarked. "It's dangerous."

"Yeah, it is."

"You have something to say?"

Henry glanced at her, then around the room. His classmates stared back at him. They appeared to him concerned, as if wanting to understand him. But he couldn't trust them.

"No. What's the point?"

At home, Henry could only think about Carla and how to keep her from leaving. *You have to stop her. Shit. You have to get her to the Office somehow. If you don't, they'll win.*

Emotionally exhausted, he laid back on his pillow just to snooze a moment and ended up sleeping for two hours. He pushed himself over to his desk to do what homework he could.

The classrooms burst open as everyone rushed into the hallways at the end of first class the next day, and Henry hunted down Caleb and finally found him in a side hall, talking to Trevor. Trevor had about four inches on Caleb, a wider, lineman frame, which made Caleb slight and small in comparison. His arms were crossed over his chest, feet apart, his brown-haired head moving slightly as he spoke, appearing like Caleb's superior. Suspicious, Henry sidled slowly along the wall.

"…and things will be okay. Alright?"

"What will be okay?" Henry said.

Trevor turned sharply, appearing startled. "Oh. Wilton."

"Talk to ya later," he said to Caleb.

"What did he want?"

"Nothing," Caleb replied, glaring at Henry. "You got them to call me in, didn't you?"

"Who?"

"Peterson. They pulled me into the Office to talk about what happened."

"What did you tell them?"

"Nothing. And I told them why. I want this to end. Now leave it alone."

"No, I won't. And if you had any self-respect, you wouldn't either. It's time you stood up for yourself. Walking away doesn't work anymore. Not in my school."

"Oh, who do you think you are, Henry?"

Caleb disappeared around the corner.

Then someone whistled, as a man would to a woman, producing a burst of laughter.

Henry rushed up to see who whistled. Donny, Wyatt, Pam, Robin, Gray and other anonymous kids who hung out with them were gathered around looking at a phone.

"Hey," Henry called out to them. "Is that a video of Caleb being assaulted?"

"Beat it, Wilty," Wyatt said.

One girl, with a little smile on her face, passed him shaking her head.

"Let me see."

Gray looked up. "It's none of your business, meek. Get outta here."

"We'll see about that, bully," Henry warned.

"Don't call me that," Gray warned.

Wondering whose phone they watched, Henry peered back. Pam put the phone into her pocketbook.

Henry couldn't pay enough attention in his next class, after that. He rubbed his forehead. *You have to push Caleb. You know what's best and he doesn't. Wait a minute.*

Henry rushed to the Office after class and got in to see Ruzzo.

"I know someone who has a video of Caleb being assaulted," he said, breathless.

"Who?"

"Pam."

"If you surprise her, you can get it."

Ruzzo eyed him thoughtfully. "Alright."

"You have to do it now. Any second, she could delete it."

"Are you absolutely sure she has it?"

"Yes. I think it's likely. Are you not going to check?"

"We will find out."

"Okay." Henry could only walk out and hope.

Then rumors spread that Carla was in the hospital and no one knew why.

"Hey, Wilton," Donny called out above the hallway noise.

"What?"

"You didn't show up."

"Show up?"

"Yeah, we were gonna have a little boxing match."

"Oh, yeah. Sorry. Got busy and forgot. I tell you what. Let's try it again after school. Four o'clock."

"One more chance, asshole. Everyone's gonna be there."

"Okay. I promise. Can't disappoint the crowd." He smiled.

But Carla in the hospital? Henry ruminated all day about it, and could only hope it wasn't true. If it was, he knew why.

After third block, he saw Peterson talking with Robin and Meaghan, and leaned against the lockers waiting for them to finish. They spoke pleasantly, and seeing them smile and laugh so easily sickened him. What the heck could they be talking about like that amidst all this horror, he thought, some of which they caused? And with Carla in hospital? But he wasn't surprised.

Girl bullies.

They exchanged niceties, and he stopped Peterson in the middle of the corridor.

"Well, what did Caleb tell you?" Henry asked.

"He didn't want to talk about it," she replied reluctantly.

"Really. Did you try to do anything to get him to talk?"

"There's nothing we can do, Henry. If Caleb is uncomfortable telling us anything, we have to respect that."

"And you're taking full advantage of that, aren't you?"

Peterson's face flinched.

"So the kids who assaulted Caleb are walking around here scot free, you know it, and you're doing nothing about it. What's wrong with this picture?"

"Excuse me," Peterson said.

Henry side-stepped to stop her.

"Where you going? I'm not done."

Peterson gaped. Henry pushed his face close to hers.

"What's the matter? Don't like being blocked in the hallway? Happens to me all the time."

Peterson flushed with anger.

"Move out of the way, Henry."

"I gave you those names and Adam in my class gave them to me. Call him in. There are different ways to get kids to talk and you know what they are." Then he smiled. "I'll be in to see you later."

His smile mutated into a glare as he bolted away from her.

Amazing. Even after our big talk. They're out of their minds.

He marched down the hall, believing no one should get in his way.

The evening didn't go much better for Henry, who increasingly believed that Carla did something to herself. The dread and anxiety layered on his mind like blankets, and he rocked himself and breathed rhythmically. He wondered how much longer he could hold on. And homework awaited.

"How can I get better in class if I'm always thinking about this? I'm so tired." He tapped his head with his fists. "Damn, Carla, you shouldn't have done it. Well, you don't know yet. Maybe she's alright."

He yawned deeply and had to lie down and sleep. He woke an hour later and went to his desk.

Henry slumped in his classes the next day. He stayed away from the Office and wanted nothing to do with anything, but couldn't escape Donny.

"Hey, where were you, asshole?" Donny asked, stopping him in the hallway.

"What?"

"You know what."

"Oh, shit, Donny," Henry chuckled. "I just have a lot of things going on. I can definitely do it today. I'll meet you there."

"Oh, bullshit."

"Seriously. Be there."

"Forget it, you fucking coward."

"Just be there," Henry said, and chuckled at Donny as he walked away.

Down the hallway, Jeremy had his arm around Freedman's shoulders, saying something to him, rubbing the meek's ear. Henry knew Freedman was too scared to stop him.

C'mon, Freedman, do something.

Then the sight of Billy and Frank strolling along together up the hall, still in his school, laughing, arrogantly free and unpunished, he could no longer tolerate.

He sighed. *It's time.*

"Frilly," he called out, "what's happening?"

He stopped in Billy's way.

"Where you off to, buddy?"

"Wilton, I'm going to fuckin' pop you if you don't move."

"Gee, just talking to ya. The thing is, we don't talk enough. Why don't the three of us hang out this weekend? Get to know each other better. Be buddies. Stop all this violence. What do you think, Frank?"

"Yeah, sure."

"Get outta the way," Billy whispered.

"You know, you should see someone about these violent impulses," Henry continued. "I've been told that kids who are bullies are bullied at home. Is that true? Are you both abused at home? Were you abused growing up? Did your mothers not hug you enough? I'm trying to help you understand yourself so you can stop being the biggest fuckin' jerks in the school. I think you can be better people. Let me help you."

Henry smiled. Frank slowly stepped behind and disappeared. Billy dropped his head as he let out a quick laugh, then he glanced around as though looking for someone—teachers, Henry knew—and Henry got himself ready. Billy stepped forward and, in a flash, pushed Henry back. His arms flew into the air, and he landed on the floor hard on his backpack, his head ricocheting back, striking the polished floor. He shouted, as much in pain as for attention. Frank, who had got down on all fours behind Henry, casually got up on one knee, and Henry, knowing what he had to do, booted Frank in the back. He landed on his stomach. Henry jumped up and aimed his shoulder into Frank's head and gave him three quick punches to the corner of his eye. His stomach churned as his fist finally met skin and bone and, in that instant, he had joined violence.

Billy watched as though surprised for a moment, then threw a wide-arcing roundhouse. Henry withstood it and whipped his leg around into the bully's knee. Billy buckled over in pain. Henry gasped as Frank's beefy arm wrapped around his neck. The grip ratcheted up so fiercely that Henry feared a neck snap. He threw fists behind him, landing somewhere on Frank's face with no effect. Billy, red rage on his face, came back at Henry, who kept flailing his legs to keep the bully at bay. Frank whipped Henry down and pressed him into the floor.

Henry shouted again.

"Alright, stop," Mr. Berry shouted.

Berry and Henry pulled at Frank's arm and finally loosened it.

"Frank, stop."

Berry struggled to pull Frank off Henry as Billy watched. Frank butted his shoulder against Berry. Tompkins, Johnson and Lentine rushed in and finally forced Frank to release his victim, who lay on the floor breathing hard.

"Stop it," Johnson shouted at Frank, nearly on top of him.

A crowd had gathered once again. Henry, now on his back, coughed and swiveled his head slowly as the sharp pain eased. He sat up.

"These two are crazy," he tried to shout in a raspy voice, his face flushed. "I want them gone."

"He started it," Billy said.

Lentine took Frank by the arm. "We'll sort this out downstairs. C'mon."

"Yea, Frilly," Henry said, getting to his feet. "Let's go."

Henry forced a smile.

"C'mon, Franky, move it," Henry added.

"Shut the fuck up."

"Hey, hey, did you hear that?" he asked Berry.

"Just move it," Berry said.

Henry grinned at the onlookers, but noticed fewer of them smiled. They appeared to him nervous, even scared.

Don't blame me. Not my fault.

"Alright, back to class, everyone," Tompkins said. "Let's go."

"Just some bullies being bullies," Henry told them.

"Quiet, Wilton," Johnson said.

Back in the Office like old times, the three boys waited to be called in. Henry folded his arms across his chest.

"Well, I guess this is it. You two clowns are finally done. And it was so easy to do."

"If that happens, dumbass, we'll come after you," Frank said.

He looked straight into Frank's vacant, black eyes.

"Frank, tell me once and for all. Did you throw away my science project in the seventh grade?"

"What?"

"Did you throw my science project in the dumpster in the seventh grade? You remember. I accused you of doing it."

Frank thought a moment.

"Yeah. I remember that. Yeah, I did."

"Why? I worked hard on that thing."

"Seemed like a good thing to do at the time."

Billy snorted.

"There must be a reason. C'mon."

"I don't know. It was a long time ago."

"But, but there were other projects closer to you in the room. Why didn't you just grab theirs? Instead, you came across the room and took mine. Why me? Why have you always been after me? Huh?"

"I don't know. Just something about you."

"I've never done anything to you. But you've always come after me. What about that time in the auditorium in the eighth grade when that kid grabbed me from behind and got me in that headlock? I honestly thought he was gonna break my neck. I didn't even know the kid. But you were sitting right next to him."

"Oh, yeah," he chuckled. "Yeah, that was pretty bad."

"You said something to him to get him to assault me. What did you say to him?"

Frank thought a moment. "I think I just said you called him a name or something."

"But why me, pal?" Henry said, raising his voice. "Why have you always targeted me?"

"Relax, Wilton," Frank said with an uncertain expression. Regret? Henry wondered.

"Excuse me," Mary said. "Please keep it down."

"Why, Frank?"

The door opened.

"Why is there yelling out here?" Peterson asked.

"Why, Frank? Why?"

"Wilton, that's enough."

Henry threw his hand out to stop Peterson.

"Why, tough guy? Tell us all why. Why me?"

"Because you're easy," Frank replied with his bully smile. "It's fun watching you get mad and frustrated."

"But don't you ever feel bad about all the pain you caused me and other kids around here? It never bothers you?"

"No, not really."

"Why?"

"Because you're weak, Wilton. I hate weak kids. Everyone does."

"No shit," Billy added. "You can't stick up for yourself. We've given you plenty of chances to do that and be a man."

"So what? Who cares about that? No, there was never anything wrong with me. It was all you. And the stupid teachers and the vice principal here and your moron parents who let you get away with it!"

He gagged from anguish and cleared his raspy throat. "Well, you're outta here now. You're done! You mental deficient."

"That's enough, Henry," Peterson said. "Now sit down over there. You two come in."

Henry walked into the hallway to get some water. He sat on a bench in the foyer and glowered, his mouth shut tight and his eyes bulging with rage. He noticed some kids peek at him warily.

Several minutes passed until he heard, "He's out here."

Peterson called for him. He didn't move.

"Henry," she said coming up to him. "Come into my office."

"Get away from me," he mumbled, staring into the floor.

"Come in with me now."

Henry sat like a glum statue.

Peterson dropped her head patiently, and then sat down next to him.

"Okay, Henry, tell me your side of the story."

Henry turned to her slowly.

"You have to say something, Henry."

"You want me to say something?" he said in a very low voice. He stood up. Peterson separated her hands, as if expecting something to happen.

"Those two psychos are gone. They've assaulted someone for the last time." He leaned toward her. "If they are not gone by the end of the day, you're gonna see how weak I really am."

"That's another threat, Henry."

"You know what you have to do."

"Do not leave. We're not done here."

"Oh, we are very done," Henry exclaimed. "God gave you two ears and one mouth. Close one and open the other two."

Peterson closed her mouth, seemingly at Henry's impudence.

"This is *over*. You're at fault for all this. You and their stupid parents."

Peterson said nothing. Henry walked upstairs and stood in the main hallway as kids passed around him, staring with unblinking eyes as sadness engulfed him.

"Strong and weak," he whispered. "If that's the way you want it, that's what you'll get. You fucking fools. You still think I'm weak? You don't know what I can do."

Henry got bumped from behind.

"Get outta the way, Wilty," Charles said as he passed by with Joe, who looked back at Henry and chuckled.

Henry stared knife-like at them. They both turned to look at him again. Kids glanced at him as he stood there, but eventually he got himself to class.

He passed Berry standing at his door. "Say good-bye to two of your bullies," he said.

At his locker, Henry slowly pulled off his pack, neck muscles sore, a throbbing in the back of his head, cheekbone and lower lip.

Okay. Now let's see what happens.

He caught Caleb walking by without stopping to talk.

"Change your mind yet?"

"About what?" Caleb said, slowing down.

"Going to the Office," Henry replied impatiently. "Billy and Frank are gone. This is a good time to get the others kicked out, too. We can end this now."

"Henry, we get hurt for narcing like that. Even if those kids do get booted, they have friends in here that can make it rougher than it is now. And what about out there? They can get us out there, too."

"I understand that, dude. But if we have to be in here eight hours a day, why should we have to take this bullshit?"

Caleb let out a heavy sigh.

"At least we'll go down with some self-respect. You don't have much of that, do you?"

Caleb glowered at Henry. "Fuck you." He bolted and disappeared among the other kids.

Henry pursed his lips, unhappy he let his mouth run off again.

At home, he learned that Peterson had called his parents again, and Henry had to go through another drawn-out discussion. He now sported a red spot on his cheekbone. His lower lip had swelled quickly and now restricted his speech. To him, they were badges of courage. But after he explained to them exactly what happened, they, for the first time, expressed more frustration with the school than him. Henry jumped on that.

"You can help me here," he said. "You have to go down to the rathole and tell them if I get assaulted one more time, you'll bring in the police."

"I'll speak to them again tomorrow," his father said. "But how many more times do we have to do that?"

"Dad, you have to be tougher with them. They're bullies. You can't be nice to them. Tell them to expel the two kids who assaulted me. Then they'll be two less kids I'll have to worry about. And I want you to complain about Miss Stagg."

"Who's she?"

"She's one of the school counselors. We talked last month. She was supposed to talk to the bullies and she hasn't, and she's not going to."

His father shook his head as he sat in his chair with the newspaper on his lap. His mother, on the couch, fiddled with the rings on her fingers.

"But we need you to do your part, too, Henry," his mother added.

"Stop saying that," he said, exasperated. "I've been doing my weak kid, don't let it bother me part for too long."

That silenced the room.

"You were always a nice, quiet little fella growing up," his mother said. "You were never a problem until all of a sudden you're angry and acting out."

Henry sat down next to her. "And why do you think that is, Mom? Why?"

She slowly shook her head. "I don't know. I wish I understood."

"Time to do your part. Stop the bullies and you'll stop the problems. Simple. This isn't rocket science, people."

"There will always be bullies in your life, Henry."

"Well, so far so good." He got up and started up the stairs. "Call them tomorrow. I have every right to walk down the hall without being assaulted. What's happening is all their fault, and useless adults who let them get away with it. Ow, this damn lip," he added, raising his voice in anger. "Maybe you gave in to the bullies, but I'm not. Now call them tomorrow and end this once and for all. I want this over with. 'Cause if you don't, I'll do it for you. And you're not gonna like how I'll do it."

His parents sat silent against the rage as he climbed the stairs and slammed the door shut. He knew the futility of any more words. He grabbed his math book and started to work.

Later, his father knocked on his door.

"Henry," his father said, in a moderate tone.

Henry said nothing. Once again, his father came up to smooth things over after an argument and show some reason, a routine Henry was tired of. What was said was said, and nothing was going to change that. His father tried the locked doorknob.

"Henry, open up. I want to talk to you."

Henry shook his head at his father's useless plea.

"I can't talk. I'm studying."

His father knocked harder.

"I said open up."

"I can't. I'm busy."

"I don't care. Open up."

Henry jumped off the bed and slammed his fist against the door.

"I'm studying," he shouted, punching the door. He fisted the door again and thought he would put a hole in it. "You like to bang? How—about—this?" He belted the door with each word. "Now get the hell away from me. How am I supposed to get better grades if I can't study?" he blared. "How? You take me away from it. They do. I can't think. I can't do anything." He banged on the door again. "Now get away from me. You're useless."

He went back to the desk. His father stood quietly, maybe stunned.

"John? Can I talk to you?" came his mother's voice.

His father hesitated but went downstairs. Henry could hear muffled words from his parents. He eased the thumping in the chest so he could get back to schoolwork. He stared fixedly, unable to ease the madness boiling inside. He wanted to cry.

"Lousy father," he mumbled. "The person who's supposed to help me the most helps me the least. Typical stupid parents."

Then he closed his eyes and breathed slowly. He had to keep it together, which was becoming more difficult. His own rage disturbed him.

Henry's throbbing lip intruded on his sleep. He fell into thoughts of his fight, beating Billy and Frank on the hallway floor in his vengeful dream. His body thrust around and his mind sparked with violence as he played out the battle under the covers. His rage mounted with each moment, pounding his fist down at enemy flesh and bone with a force he could not muster for real. He bolted up, panting.

"Stop it. Stop. What the fuck. You can't do this anymore." He exhaled sharply and rubbed his face. His heart drummed and he let out long breaths to slow it down. "Sleep. You need sleep."

His head dropped back on the pillow and he wiped away tears. He squeezed his hand into the fist that struck Frank.

He became slightly nauseous at the thought that he had finally crossed the line—hitting another human being.

"You're one of them now. You can never go back." He also knew the next time he hit someone would be easier and stronger. His victory added power to his offensive as he pushed forward through enemy territory. "It's the way it has to be. The old you is gone. "

In the morning, Henry filled his pack, including his notebooks. He could do nothing about his swollen lip, which later became the butt of a few jokes. He looked around for Frank and Billy.

"Hey, guys," he said to Charles and Kevin downstairs, proud to show off his new face, but careful with the pain.

"Chicken out?" Kevin asked.

"Huh?"

"You were supposed to fight Donny, remember?"

"Yeah, well, taking on Billy and Frank was enough of you bullies. Donny's not worth the time. Have you seen Frank or Billy?"

"They're around here somewhere," Kevin said.

"Not for long. They're getting expelled. Just like you guys should."

"Don't think so, idiot," Charles said. "You're the only one getting expelled. That's the rumor. Everyone hates you. No one's gonna do anything for you."

"No, they're definitely gone," Henry said. He walked away, and then stopped. "Hey, I'm curious. Do you think Frank and Billy are good kids?"

Charles shrugged. "What?"

"Do you think Frank and Billy are good kids?"

"Yeah."

"Really. Do you think I'm a good kid?"

"No, you're an asshole."

Henry nodded. "Right. 'Kay, thanks."

He shook his head. No surprise there.

In Bronner's class, he smiled at everyone and asked if anyone had heard anything about Carla.

"I haven't," Sharonda replied.

"What is your obsession with her?" Becka asked.

"Nothing. Just wondering. You see, I care about her and what she's going through. How about you two?"

Sharonda sighed. "I'm not talking about this with you anymore, Henry."

"Then go to the Office and tell them you saw Carla bullied in the locker room. Or at least call Safe2Tell."

He stared at them for an answer.

"I called," Sharonda said. "Chloe, too."

"Alright, thank you. Now, look," he whispered, "why don't we all go to the hospital to see Carla? I think she tried suicide." The girls looked at each other. "And I think you believe that, too. So let's go over to see her on Saturday, if she's still there."

"I'll let you know if I can," Sharonda added.

"Good," Henry sighed. "That will be good."

After his next class, Henry heard his name called. Mrs. Hernandez nodded for him to come with her into an empty classroom. She glanced over his shoulder as if to ensure they were alone.

"Henry, I just wanted you to know that there are some teachers here, including me, who are on your side. We know what's been going on and we believe in what you're doing. We've discussed among ourselves how we can help you. So, as soon as we come up with the best course of action, I'll let you know. And, I'm sorry we haven't done more before this. But this is a sensitive issue, even with us teachers."

"Uh, okay," Henry said. "I didn't think any of you cared."

"Some of us do, and I'm sorry we haven't helped you sooner, especially me. We don't like being a part of this, either. So I'll get back to you and let you know what we come up with. In the meantime, hang in there. But don't do anything rash, okay? That will hurt your cause. Can you do that for me?"

"Sure. You realize how many kids have been hurt because of all of this?"

"I understand that. That is our big mistake."

"You never spoke to Joe and Charles that day, did you?" Hernandez sighed.

"No, I didn't. And I'm sorry.

"Did you report it or anything?"

"No. I didn't feel at the time it rose to that level."

"Well, how can I trust you?" he asked boldly. "How can I trust any of you adults? I don't. I don't trust anybody."

"Then we'll have to earn that trust. Give us a chance. It's...more complicated with us, Henry. Even with adults, we can be timid. We have let things go too far for too long"

"Well, then let's all get together and go to Ruzzo. You know he's a bully."

"It's possible we can do that. I'll let you know. Okay? It should be soon. But keep this between us. Alright?"

"Fine. But I need your help, and we can stop all this pretty quickly."

"I know. And we're going to. Just give me a little more time. Alright?"

"Sure."

"Okay, we'll talk soon."

Hernandez went to the doorway, glanced up and down the hall as if not wanting to be seen, and scooted away. Henry reeled with thoughts and questions. He pulled his hand soothingly across his taut forehead.

"Wow. This just gets crazier. What's wrong with these people?"

But he gained some confidence from it as he strode down the hall. He felt better knowing he had allies with some power to help him, while not believing in them.

He was told go to the Office after history. Peterson wanted to see him. He stopped at his locker along the way.

Okay. Be tough.

He walked into her office. "You know, you should name this chair after me," he joked as he sat.

"I wanted to see you, Henry, about this altercation with Billy and Frank. Billy insists that you goaded him into the fight. Is this true?"

"Well, they're obviously just saying that so they won't get expelled, which I assume you haven't done yet."

"They both said you called them a certain name and you harassed them and bumped into them and wouldn't let them pass in the hallway."

"So. That's acceptable behavior around here."

"No, it's not, Henry."

"That's happened to me for years. You read my diary. And no one did anything about it. But it doesn't matter what I said to them. We can use words all we want. But, in my school, we don't assault each other. Now call them in here and expel them."

"We haven't decided that yet," Peterson said.

Henry narrowed his eyes angrily. He pressed his hand against his jacket pocket.

"What, you thought last month was a joke? You think because I'm a kid you can just ignore me? After all this abuse, you still protect your own?"

"Calm down, Henry. If anything, we are trying to protect you. You're acting out way too much. We have received more calls about your behavior."

She's starting again. Move it.

"And you've received calls I've made about other kids' behavior. I'm sure you're talking to those kids, right?"

"We have been speaking to several kids about their behavior."

"Call the principal in, please."

Peterson hesitated.

"He will want to hear what I have to say. Trust me." He lowered his eyes.

Peterson relented and they waited for Ruzzo. Henry pushed his hand inside his jacket. Peterson watched him. Her face tightened. Ruzzo sauntered in.

"Did my father call you today?"

"Yes, he did."

"And what did he say?"

Ruzzo glanced at Peterson.

"He wants whoever attacked you expelled," Ruzzo said. "I told him you were part of the reason for the fight."

"Look, Henry, we understand the problems," Peterson said, "and we are putting a stop to it. We don't have to be confrontational anymore."

Her voice sounded lame to Henry.

"Pardon me if I don't trust that, and I'm not the only one around here who feels that way."

"It's just you, Henry," Ruzzo stated.

"My father can cause a lot of headaches for you."

Russo smiled slightly. "I don't think he will. He agreed that if you did partly cause it, then you should be punished as well."

Henry stood up, raising his voice. "Oh, enough of this crap. You didn't take me seriously then. Now you will. Everyone will." He reached into his jacket. "I'm going to do something I should have done before." His eyes flared. "Are you ready?"

Peterson jumped up. "David, he has a gun."

Ruzzo's eyes popped. "Wilton!" He jumped forward.

Henry pulled out his hand—and held his phone. Ruzzo froze, only a step away from Henry, his ruddy, red face a picture of fear.

Henry looked at them wide-eyed.

"What is wrong with you two?"

Ruzzo blinked. Someone knocked quickly at the door.

"Is everything alright?" Mary asked, her thin face taut with concern.

Henry pinched his face as though confused. Ruzzo dropped his arms to his side.

"I don't know, Mary," Henry said. "I don't know what happened."

"It's alright, Mary," Ruzzo said hoarsely, staring at Henry. "Call in Officer Lentine, please."

Mary looked over the scene and closed the door softly. Peterson threw her pen on the desk and sat down and lay her forehead in her hands. Henry didn't think Ruzzo could move that fast.

"What? You thought I had a gun? Are you kidding?"

"Wilton," Ruzzo said softly, "I'm removing you from the school as of now."

"All I have is my phone and I'm going to use it right now if you don't call in Frilly as I stand here. And what's going on with the kids who assaulted Caleb? I want them in here now. You know who they are."

"Wilton," Ruzzo said. "We cannot tolerate you in this school any longer."

"You two are amazing. After our conversation last month, when I took over this school."

"Stop it," Ruzzo barked, but showed a shakiness from his near-death experience. "You've done nothing of the kind."

Henry raised his face to the ceiling. "Ha. Hangin' on. In denial. But, I understand. You've been in control for so long I can see how difficult it is to let go. I come along all of a sudden and take it away from you. Actually, I shouldn't have expected you to just roll over without a fight."

He snickered at them while working to keep his voice steady and his own body from shaking. Ruzzo's reaction had startled him.

"You bullies have run the world long enough, and look what you did with it. It's my world now and you'll do exactly what I tell you, when I tell you. Or, I make my phone call. When I call the cops and cry assault into this phone, you know what will happen. In three minutes, all hell will break loose."

Ruzzo let out a loud sigh and shook his head.

"Let's do it right now. If you're calling Lentine in here, let's go all the way."

Henry dialed 911 and held it out to Ruzzo.

"Go ahead, press the little green button."

Ruzzo looked at the phone. Henry gave him a daring glare.

"Go ahead. I've done nothing wrong in here. All I had was my phone."

There was a knock at the door. Lentine came in.

"How can I help?" he asked.

Ruzzo thought a moment.

"I guess we have things under control here, Matt. Thanks."

"Sorry to bother you. Mr. Lentine," Henry said, and smiled at Ruzzo.

Lentine looked the scene over. "Okay." He closed the door softly.

"Time to call them in, Mr. Principal. They don't belong in this school anymore."

"Neither do you," Peterson said, looking boldly at Henry.

Henry stared out the windows behind them. "You know, I like the entrance area out there. Great place for a news conference. What do ya think? Let's finally do it. As soon as the TV crews show up, I'll be right out there waiting for them. Picture me telling the world what's been going on in here. Remember, it doesn't matter if…if what I say is true or not. Once I say it, cry assault and call you Principal Bully and Vice Principal Bully and the teachers, too, you'll never be rid of it. But the school system will get rid of you."

"Alright, Henry," Ruzzo said, stepping forward, "None of what you've said will work. You have no proof. Vice Principal Peterson and I are in no way a cause of this alleged abuse you scream about."

"You have my diary."

"I don't believe all those incidents occurred. They easily could be made up."

"Really. I can always get those kids to come in here and back them up. Write their own diaries, too."

He smiled at Ruzzo.

Henry reached inside his coat, pulled out three more notebooks and threw them on the desk. "There you go. More of those, uh, incidents. A lot of the kids assaulted in those notebooks are in this school. Yeah, let's call them in right now and ask them. You want to? We all can have a nice little chat."

Peterson took up one of the notebooks and flipped through it. Ruzzo stood silent.

"Tell you what, let's have the police come over and do it since you're, uh, always busy. The superintendent, too." He walked around the chair and spread his arms out. "Let's have a full-blown police investigation. What do you think? The media will love it. And they will hound the both of you, here and at home. I'll make sure of it."

Henry held his phone out. "Go on. Press it. I dare you. I double-dare you."

Ruzzo kept his glare on Henry.

"Well, what's the matter, Principal Bully? Problem?"

Henry waggled the phone in the space between them.

"Call Frank and Billy in here—now. And this will all be over."

"No."

Henry snorted at Ruzzo's defiance, admiring it. "Yeah, you were a bully, weren'tcha?"

"In school, big, tall, tough, played sports? You enjoyed the power. You liked it. Picking on weaklings like me, watching us standing in front of you scared, assaulting us in the bathroom, in the locker room, outside. Yeah," he whispered. "You liked the power, didn'tcha? You liked it. You enjoyed it." Ruzzo remained, to Henry, disturbingly unmoved. "You loved it so much that you took it right into adulthood and right into this school. They do say power is a turn-on."

Ruzzo stepped forward. "That will do."

Henry stepped forward. "You gonna hit me?" Henry shouted. "Go on, hit me. I know you want to. You want to end it all right now? *Hit* me."

"That's enough," Peterson exclaimed, rising from her chair.

"Is that right, girl bully?"

"Wilton," Ruzzo demanded. "You are in way over your head."

Henry's shakes and twitches diminished as each minute passed, faster than before, giving him strength. "Did you really think I bought that bullshit you gave me about the weak kids bowing to the strong in order to keep the peace? And…and you were looking at me as if that's how the world really is and I should obey like the obedient weakling I am. Told to me by the alpha male and female." He shook his head. "Not in my school. Not in my world. Those days are *over.*"

His shout echoed around the room and he laid the phone on Peterson's desk.

"You see, I'm no longer a meek. I'm actually the strongest kid in the school. And that becomes your biggest problem, or should I say your biggest nightmare."

Ruzzo pursed a little smile. "I don't see you as the strongest kid in the school."

Henry copied Ruzzo's smile. "I know, and that's your biggest mistake."

Henry leaned his elbows forward and stretched himself easily over the edge of the desk. He then hovered the tip of his index finger over the call button and rapidly tapped his finger on both sides of the button.

"You have ten seconds."

He looked from Ruzzo to Peterson, then down at the button, tapping. What would he do if he pressed it? he wondered. What would he say? Could he handle it?

"Time's up. What's it gonna be?"

Ruzzo, with arms folded, stared down at Henry.

"Well, Vice Principal Bully? What should I do?"

"Henry," she said in a soothing tone, "take your phone and go to class. We will take care of everything here, and it will be okay."

For the first time, Henry thought, she was actually being nice.

"Will they be expelled?" Henry asked.

"We'll let you know."

Don't do it. She's suckering you again.

"Too late."

Henry pressed the button. Ringing. Henry's eyes widened.

Good luck.

Peterson reached over, snatched the phone and jabbed at it to disconnect the call.

Henry straightened up as she dropped the phone in front of her. Ruzzo remained impassive, arms folded over his chest.

"Well?" Henry demanded, while greatly relieved. "We can keep this in-house, nice and quiet. You know Frank and Billy are bad and it's too late to help them."

Henry fixed his stare onto Ruzzo, whose sharp, hard eyes made him shudder. To Henry, it was like looking into a black soul that never saw light.

After another moment of stubbornness, Ruzzo told Peterson to call in Billy and Frank. Henry reached for his phone.

"And make sure they never come back."

Alright. Good. Keep going.

"Now what about Caleb's attackers?"

Both adults remained quiet.

"Well?" Henry commanded.

"We are coming close," Peterson said.

"Good."

Ruzzo glared intensely, hatefully, Henry thought.

Henry smiled the bully smile back at him. He thought Ruzzo would explode.

Henry made his usual turn at the door. "So you thought I had a gun. Nah, I couldn't do that. I'm not one of those crazies. I don't need a gun or a bomb to do what I want to do. I have this." He raised his phone. "This is my weapon. And my computer, too." He glanced at the phone. "Social media's great, isn't it? So easy. Yeah. You see, I don't want

178

you to die. I want you to live. I want you to suffer like I have. And you only suffer if you're alive. And I want you healthy and strong for what's to come."

"Alright, Wilton, you got what you wanted," Ruzzo said. "Now get out."

"You know, there are problems all the time in this school. And when something finally blows up between kids, you adults jump out of the woodwork to find out who's to blame and who's to punish—the easy part. But where are you when the problems are festering, when we need your help? You're nowhere to be found."

Henry opened the door.

"Okay. So you know what you have to do. The school will be a lot better for it."

"The school or you?" Ruzzo asked.

"Both," he snapped. "Because if I'm better, the school is, too."

He looked at Peterson. "You know, you're not as brave as he is, but you're smarter. My advice is to get out now while you can, or he'll drag you down with him."

He gave them both a look of warning. He stuck his head back in, smiling.

"Oh, you can keep the diaries. I have exact copies."

He let the door close on its own and asked Mary for a pass.

Henry smiled victoriously. "Still here, Mary."

As he ambled through the halls of his school, Henry didn't think about what just happened, nor did he get sick over it, although his nerves twitched and his insides trembled. He held on through the skirmish, survived and sped away. He couldn't help but be amazed that he had done it again—challenged them. He chuckled to himself, because he could give up Peterson and Ruzzo to the world any time he wanted. Just not yet.

I'll finish them off myself.

Up in his room after dinner that night, he went straight to his desk for school work. He no longer wanted to sit on his bed, back against the wall, arms folded, agonizing about the day's events, angry he didn't do better, lamenting, wishing and hoping.

"Fuck that shit. Didn't do you any good anyway. Hope. Hope is for suckers. Hope is for people who can't change anything, or too scared to. You know what you have to do, so do it. And no more night fights, either."

When he resolutely started homework, the vengeance that burned him up inside made his eyes hard below his dark brown eyebrows and the corner of his mouth turned up slightly. He summoned for himself a stern demeanor revealed by a hardened face, tight lips and a steady, disciplined gaze. He decided he would smile only for advantage. There was no reason to do otherwise. The world didn't deserve it.

The halls buzzed the next day that Billy and Frank had been suspended, and Henry sensed that everyone believed they wouldn't be back. He strode the corridors with a deliberate quick step and hummed so everyone could hear. He greeted kids with a "Hey, how's it goin'?"

Then he was pushed against the lockers and lost his balance.

"So you got them kicked out," Donny said, with Joe at his side.

Henry righted himself. "What are you babbling about?"

"You fuckin' chicken shit."

Henry shrugged. "I had nothin' to do with it."

"Bullshit."

"C'mon," Joe said to Donny. "Forget it."

Henry called out to them. "They're coming close to pulling in the kids who got Caleb, ya know. Getting worried?"

Donny and Joe ignored him.

The rest of the day, Henry allowed himself some relaxation, though the school fear in his chest, albeit reduced considerably, stuck to his insides like an old appendage. But he felt a depth of relief he had dreamed of for years, a liberation of sorts, with his two ancient enemies finally dispatched.

You did it, buddy. You did it. Stay tough. Just a few more to go.

At lunch, Henry passed two tables full of bullies, munching away and passing food among themselves. Henry hadn't seen them gathered together like this before and wondered if they were displaying unity for their two fallen comrades. Sitting with them were other anonymous kids, who Henry despised as being weaker hangers-on, following the bullies around like puppy dogs with no minds of their own. Roach was there, too, talking amicably with them, as if showing support, Henry thought.

"What do you want, Wilty?" Jeremy said.

"Well, look at this. The Bully Club." He looked at Roach. "And their advisor. Oh, ho, where's my camera when I need it? Good photo for the yearbook."

He laughed out loud, walked over to his friends and dropped his tray next to George.

"Hey, sad about losing two of your members? And they'll be fewer of you as time goes by."

Henry winked at Roach and sat down.

"Henry, what you doin'?" Sharonda asked.

"Yeah, then he sits with us," George added.

"Relax. They never bother you." *You're middlings.*

A few minutes later, Roach stood behind him.

"Wilton."

Henry ignored him.

"Wilton."

"What?"

"Come with me."

"I'm eating."

"Come with me now."

"I'll talk to you after I'm done."

"I said now."

"Hey, are you yelling at me?" Henry said. "Do not yell at me. We'll talk after I'm done."

Roach grabbed the back of Henry's chair and pulled it back.

"Get up."

"Hey, hey, okay," Henry said out loud so everyone could hear. "Don't get violent. You're scaring me."

Henry stood up toe to toe with Roach.

"What do you want?"

"Let's go."

"For what? I've done nothing wrong. As usual."

Henry stood and folded his arms, his pulse quickening more from anger than fear.

"Move it," Roach demanded.

"Where to?"

"Hallway."

"Well, let's hurry up. My food will get cold and that's a lot more important than you are."

"See ya, Wilty," Charles called out.

"Be back in a sec."

"Wilton," Roach said outside the cafeteria, "look, why are you antagonizing those kids. They were doing nothing wrong. What's the problem?"

"Oh, c'mon, I was just joking. They shouldn't let it bother them."

"Billy and Frank are gone and maybe they deserved it. But these other kids that you call bullies, they're trying to get through the day just like you, and they don't need your wise-ass remarks. And now I have to talk to you about it."

"Just like you talked to those kids who made fun of me in all your classes? Just like you talked to Gray and Wyatt when they were pushing me around that day? And you lied about it."

"I did not lie."

"Tell them stop calling me that name?"

"What name?"

"You didn't hear them calling me a name?"

182

"No."

"Wilty," Henry exclaimed.

Roach stared a moment.

"Well, the boys have always called you that. I didn't think it bothered you."

"What boy wants to be called Wilty? My name is Wilton."

"Stop yelling."

"But we weak kids have to take all the bullshit from you tough kids, don't we?" he said. "Take it and walk away, right? Isn't that how it's supposed to work in this hell hole?"

"I don't have time for this."

"This is what we're going to do. We're going back in there and you're going to tell those wonderful boys of yours to stop calling me that name. Then you're going to tell Donny to quit threatening to assault me after school."

He headed to the door.

"C'mon. You can do something good for me for once." He opened the door and waited.

"Fine, Wilton. Anything to end this nonsense."

They stopped at the bully table.

"Alright, guys," Roach began. "Stop calling Wilton, 'Wilty'."

They burst out laughing.

"The poor kid."

"That's enough," Roach demanded. "Donny, I hear you're threatening Wilton after school. Don't do it again."

The boys quieted. Henry smirked at them.

"Well, thanks, Mr. Roach. Thanks for helping me out for once."

"Go eat," Roach said, glowering at him.

Henry sat down and put a fork into his food. "A lot of good that's gonna do. Great. Now my food's cold."

"They're not gonna like you for that," George told him.

"Tough. What are they gonna do about it?"

"So, did you find anyone who recorded what happened to Carla?" he asked Sharonda.

"I asked, Henry, but everyone I spoke with said they deleted it. Probably because they didn't want to be caught with it. And they wouldn't have gone to the Office anyway."

"Nice. But now you can go to the Office and tell them what you saw, and give them those girls' names so they can be called in."

"Ah," Sharonda chuckled. "That might be a bit much."

"We don't have the right to do that to other girls," Chloe added.

"You do have that right if they refuse. I gave Adam up to Peterson. He saw what happened to Caleb. Hopefully she calls him in. I'm sorry, she will call him in."

"Yeah, and I'll bet Adam won't be too happy about that," George said.

Henry groaned. "Too bad. We got more important things to worry about than who likes who. This isn't grade school, you know."

"Henry," Kam said, "aren't you getting tired of all this?"

"Of course. But, I gotta keep going until it's done."

"Until what's done?" Sharonda asked.

"Until the bullies are gone."

"Don't think that'll ever happen," Chloe said.

"Have to give you a lot of credit for hanging in there," George added.

Henry sighed in frustration. "Two are gone now. And we found out who assaulted Caleb, with no help from him."

"No one should be forced to do something," Chloe said.

He chuckled. "You know, you guys will never understand. You'll never really get what Caleb and I go through."

"We do, Henry," George said. "But it seems like you're causing as many problems as you're solving."

"I can't cause problems that are already there," he snapped. "But I need support. And I just wish I got more." He stood up. "But I understand. We're just never going to meet on this. We're in two totally different worlds. You've never been in my situation. That's why you get mad at me.

You're in your own happy little bubble. Well, have fun in there. I'm out here dealing with the real world." He stood up. "I won't bother you with this again."

"Good," Kam said, glaring up at him. "Probably better that way."

Henry looked at each one of them. "Fine. Have a good day."

As he left the cafeteria, he heard, "Bye, Wilty."

The rest of the day, he just wanted to relax and listen to lectures and not be taken away by all the problems distracting him from better grades.

C'mon. Forget everything else and just listen. You're too far behind.

"Hey, Wilton," Tom said from behind him in science lab.

"What?" Henry said, writing in his lab book.

"Did you find out who got Caleb?"

Henry sighed patiently. "Yes."

The room quieted.

"Who?"

"I can't say. But you'll find out."

"He doesn't know anything," Trevor sneered.

"Yeah, I do. And so do you. You were there."

"No, I wasn't."

Trevor's insistent tone made Henry believe him.

Henry fell into a pall of sadness coupled with dull anxiety. He wondered what Carla actually did to herself. Maybe he could find out something from Ruzzo. With Peterson busy behind her closed door, Ruzzo agreed to see him.

"What is it, Wilton?" Ruzzo said, eyes down as he wrote at his desk, which enraged Henry.

"Look at me," Henry demanded. Ruzzo did. "From now on you look at me when I walk in the room." He rubbed his forehead. "Now, what did you find out from Adam? Did he give up the names?"

The principal sat back, accepting Henry's outburst tiredly. "Yes. We believe we have the students who attacked Caleb."

"Assaulted Caleb. He was assaulted."

"One of them is in with Mrs. Peterson now."

"Good. I'll expect them gone today."

"It will likely be tomorrow."

"Make sure. Or I'll make my little phone call. And this time, it will go through. Now," he continued, slowing himself down, "let's talk about Carla."

Ruzzo sucked in his cheeks.

"Have you heard anything about her?"

"We are not at liberty to say."

"Oh, really? I was the one trying to be her friend, more than anyone else around here. Now what happened to her? We're all going to find out eventually."

Ruzzo placed his pen down carefully. "I cannot tell you. You will have to find out for yourself."

Henry kneaded his forehead as both fell silent. "She tried to hurt herself, didn't she?"

Ruzzo cleared his throat. "You better go to class."

"Oh, my God." Henry wanted to cry out, but held it off. "Well, you better hope she's alright. 'Cause this is on your head. She was abused in your school, and you all knew what was happening to her and did nothing."

"I knew nothing about it," Ruzzo insisted.

"Baloney. And if you didn't, that's even worse. Sitting here in your ivory tower. Some teachers knew what was happening to her. I told Stagg to talk to her again, and I'll bet she didn't. And you're supposed to know. But you don't care."

"That's hardly true, Wilton," Ruzzo said, unconvincingly to Henry.

"That is true or this wouldn't have happened."

Ruzzo rapidly shook his head.

"One of my people down—again. You have a lot to answer for."

Ruzzo's eyes lowered menacingly at Henry

"What is wrong with you?"

The visage of Ruzzo's glare both repulsed and frightened Henry. He thought it was that of a man finally caught up in his own web of hate with no way out.

Stomping out, Henry had to take a breather as tension wound him up tight. He felt ill again. He went into the boys' room and sat in a stall, placed his forehead on his arms and couldn't stop a few sobs.

"I want this to end so bad. I can't take much more."

He dozed deeply on the toilet for a few minutes until other boys came in and woke him. His hand had fallen to the floor. When the room was finally empty, he washed his face. The cheering in the gym reminded Henry of the school basketball game. Caleb wasn't playing, and the team played badly, but he didn't care. He needed to relax. Carla's possible flirting with death scared him, and he felt some guilt for not helping her more.

Damn it, Carla, I hope you didn't.

Players and refs ran back and forth, and kids and parents in the stands shouted and clapped. He could relate to some extent, for he had thought about suicide, too.

That night, with Carla's situation occupying him, Henry gave up on schoolwork again and went downstairs for something to eat. He joined his parents watching the news. A story came on about a pair of sisters in their seventies who received a visit from a high school classmate. The man, along with other boys, had bullied the two girls mercilessly to the point where the sisters were ostracized all four years. The man had felt guilty and remorseful about it and always wished he could apologize to them. His wife finally tracked down the sisters, and the man met with them and gave them that apology. They had lunch together, the first time the two sisters had lunch with a classmate.

Henry waved his hand out.

"Unbelievable. He's felt guilty about that all his life. Look at them. It's almost a lifetime ago."

His mother nodded.

"That's crazy. How many other people are like that? Millions? See, I'm not going to leave school with any scars, and I'm going to make sure no one else does, too."

"Just make sure you do it the right way," his father said. "Bring it to the principal respectfully and he can do something about it."

Henry snorted. "Be respectful and nice to the people bullying me? Doesn't work that way, Dad. Not anymore. Good night."

Henry headed straight back to the Office after second block the next day and had to wait almost twenty minutes to see Peterson.

He walked in and sat down in the chair.

"What is it?" Peterson asked tiredly.

Henry held back a smile at her lament.

"What about those kids?"

"What kids?"

His eyes widened. "What do you mean, 'what kids'? The kids who assaulted Caleb. Don't mess with me, Mrs. Peterson."

Peterson moved her computer to the side impatiently.

"They have been suspended."

He nodded slowly. "Good. Well, who are they?"

Peterson hesitated.

"Who are they? We'll all find out eventually."

"Jeremy, Charles, Todd, Joe and Kevin."

He let go a sigh of relief. "Well, make sure they never come back."

"We gave Kevin two weeks' suspension."

"Why?"

"His behavior record was better than the others, so, if he gave us some details, we would give him a break."

Henry felt he could not disagree.

"Make sure the others don't come back."

"We will try."

"Excuse me?"

188

"As you have pointed out, it can be difficult to permanently remove anyone."

"Oh, I'm sure you'll find a way. Now we have three more to go."

"What do you mean?"

"The Vultures."

"Who are they, Henry?"

"Laurie, Meaghan and our class president. And their friends. Aren't they you're favorites?"

"Well, what did they do?"

Henry eyed her suspiciously. "I think you know. You've received some anonymous tips about Carla being assaulted or cyberbullied. I ought to know. I sent some of them."

"Alright, we have received those complaints."

"Anyway, they've abused Carla and other girls for a long time, humiliated them. I know Laurie and Meaghan are cybering her."

"How do you know that?"

He removed a piece of paper from his pocket and dropped it in front of Peterson.

"Here are names of some of the girls who witnessed assaults on Carla. Bring them in and ask them." He turned at the door. "I have to say you're doing well. I'll be in to check on your progress tomorrow."

Henry walked out. He liked doing that, leaving his orders to be carried out. He went to the library and sat at the same table Carla came to so often for, Henry believed, what little peace she could get. He folded his hands on his lap while staring ahead at nothing, breathing easy. He thought what little anyone else had done to help her.

All week, everyone talked of the five boys who were kicked out. Henry again noticed kids giving him glances. The noise level in the halls muted. Lockers closed normally, but conversation occurred in low tones, maybe from the shock of all the kids expelled. He enjoyed that.

He saw Caleb.

"Well, they're gone. What do you think?"

Caleb shrugged. "I don't know, Henry. Good, I guess."

"You guess?"

Caleb shook his head. "What am I supposed to say?"

"How about thanks?"

Caleb grimaced. "I'm not like you, Henry. I accept who I am, and you should, too. We're not strong and we never will be. That's life. If shit happens, let it go. Fighting back just makes it worse."

"Makes it worse at first," Henry replied. "Then things get better. I've proven it. Christ, Caleb, you've bought into Ruzzo's world view. The strong sit at the table while we sit on the floor collecting the scraps. No, I've changed that. That world is dead." Henry breathed out quickly. "You don't have to live like that. Look what I did."

"What did you do? Did you stop them yourself? No, you got other people to do it for you. Did you take them out and beat them up to stop them? No. You had other people fight your battles for you."

Henry turned away impatiently. "And that took a lot of guts for me to do. I wanted to make them do it 'cause they're supposed to."

"That's in here. What about out there? Who's gonna protect you?"'

"I don't know. But in here was the first step. Out there is next. But one thing's for sure, I'm no longer a meek."

"Good for you. Hope you're happy."

"Are you happy, not giving yourself a chance like I did?"

"Chance at what?"

"At being happy. Living with self-respect. Because I don't think you are. And how much longer can you live like that?"'

Caleb backed up. "I'm fine, Henry. You live your way and I'll live mine."

Henry stared at Caleb as he sped off, a friend he knew could be lost for good.

What is wrong with him?

Henry later sat himself in the library and took out his books and computer, again attempting to stick to homework and papers to pass in. He settled back, yawned deeply, and realized how always tired he seemed to be.

As he worked on math for a while, a hard bump from behind startled him. Wyatt strutted by, after which Trevor reached over and pushed a book off the table. They glanced back at him and smiled.

Henry stared at the book. *I don't believe it.*

"Get back here and pick it up," Henry said.

"What?" Trevor said.

"Pick it up."

"Pick up what?"

"Now!"

"Watch it, Wilty."

"Shut up and pick up the book." Henry slowly got up and walked over to them.

Two kids left the room.

Henry put his arm out, as if ready to escort him back to the table.

"Let's go. C'mon."

Trevor smacked the arm away. "Who's gonna make me? You think you run the show around here 'cause more kids got kicked out? That'll never happen, asshole."

The future quarterback sat down and watched like a king above the fray.

"Pick it up, asshole."

Mrs. Tompkins trotted in.

"What's going on?"

"What do you think?" Henry said. "The bully quarterback bumped my chair deliberately, and he pushed my book onto the floor. Tell him to pick it up, please."

"Trevor," Tompkins sighed. "Pick up the book."

"I didn't do it."

"Pick it up," Tompkins repeated firmly.

Trevor laughed. "It's just a fucking book."

"Don't talk like that."

"We're waiting," Henry said.

"Trevor?" Tompkins said.

Trevor snorted. He ambled to the book, picked it up slowly and threw it onto the table—a loud, sharp slap echoed through the library.

"Good. Now get the hell outta here and don't bother me again," Henry said sharply, glaring boldly at Trevor to emphasize his demand.

Wyatt chuckled. "C'mon, let's go."

"Look over your shoulder, meek," Trevor warned.

"Hey, he just threatened me."

"Enough, guys," Tompkins said. "It's over."

"Tell them not to come near me again," Henry warned.

"I will. And if they do, you let me know immediately. Okay?"

Henry looked at her suspiciously, but she seemed sincere.

"Alright," he said in a calmer tone. "I will."

He got on his phone and called Safe2Tell to report Trevor and Wyatt, and also mentioned the help that Tompkins gave him.

Wow. Good to see for once. Maybe things are changing.

By the end of another long week, Henry just wanted to go home to his room. He peered around his last class as kids murmured among themselves. Derrick talked quietly in class, and Henry gave his old foe a hard glance with a slight smile. The continuous presence of Derrick in his classes—in the world, for that matter—offended Henry's righteous sense of justice. He had given Derrick plenty of time to settle back in and be a part of the school again. He occasionally said hello to Derrick as he passed him, just to annoy him. He had to admit Derrick had behaved well, with the old bully swagger and attitude just about gone. But, to Henry, Derrick was unforgiven, and the abuse he and other kids endured for years could never be forgotten.

On his way to the bus, he met George walking his way.

"Well. Six gone. What do you think?"

"Yeah," George replied uncertainly. "I assume you had something to do with it."

"Pretty much."

George chuckled and shook his head.

"No one knows how you're doing it."

"What's right is right," Henry answered.

"Well, there are a few people around here who don't like you. So watch your back."

"I've had plenty of practice doing that."

"Look, uh, probably stay away from Caleb for a while. He's kind of upset."

"Likewise. I'm just trying to get him to stand up for himself. That's how it's done around here now."

"He has the right to do what he wants," George said succinctly.

"Fine. I'm done with him anyway."

"If that's the way you want to be."

"It's not me, George. It's the whole world. You're one of the lucky ones. You never had to deal with it."

"I've had to deal with things, Henry."

"What, losing a lacrosse game?"

George chuckled. "Asshole."

"That's the way things are now, George," Henry said.

"Whatever," George replied.

George walked off into the crowd and Henry decided he had to let George go as well.

Childhood's over.

Henry searched for Adam and finally found him talking with a few kids. He waited for that to break up and followed Adam to his locker.

"Hey."

"Thanks, Wilton."

"What?"

"You got Peterson to call me in, didn't you?"

"I did."

"Not cool, buddy."

"Look, you weren't going to do it. So it was the only way. Nothing's going to happen to you."

"Sure about that?"

"The Office isn't going to say anything, and neither am I. Did you actually tell them who they were?"

"In a roundabout way."

"There you go. Because of you, those kids are gone. Thanks."

Henry left Adam and went to his locker. He pushed his pack inside.

You're doing good. You're scared but you have to keep up your strength. You're not done yet.

He passed the Vultures, Pam included. The sight of them talking quietly, innocently, unpunished, provoked him, especially with Carla lying in a hospital bed. This time, he had to say something.

"Hey," he said. "You heard about Carla?"

"You mean suicide girl?" Meaghan said.

"What do you mean?"

"The rumor is she tried to hang herself," Laurie said.

Robin smiled. "And apparently she screwed it up."

"I don't know," Henry said. "But I'm going to visit her tomorrow. You wanna meet me there? She'd love to see you."

"Why would we do that?" Pam asked.

"I don't know. I thought you were friends."

"Friends," Laurie said. "How are we her friends? We hardly know her."

"What's it to you, Wilty?" Robin asked as she pulled a few things from her locker.

"It's Wilton. Well, you seem to talk to her a lot. Or is it you make fun of her a lot?"

Robin slammed her locker door shut.

"Go away, Wilty."

"Don't call me Wilty, Madam President."

"Why would we care about Amazon?" Meaghan asked.

"Well, if she's not around, who else you going to bully?"

Robin glared, her eyes black and hard. Pure evil, Henry thought.

"Get out, Wilty," Laurie said, putting a few things into her large blue shoulder bag. "No one wants you here."

"Yeah, right back atcha, Vultures."

"Wilton, you've caused enough problems around here," Pam said. "Don't mess with us."

"But who you going to pick on now? Who you going to assault?"

"Let's go," Robin said.

"We're going to prove it, you know. We're going prove you cyberbullied her."

"You're crazy, Wilty."

They walked away, laughing amongst themselves as though nothing or no one could touch them, as well. Queen bullies. Henry wasn't sure if he could bring them down.

At home after school, Henry hopped onto his bed, whistling out residual anxiety. He let all the issues go for the evening, feeling safe and sound in his room. The cat jumped up next to him. She nuzzled his chin, smelling it as if searching. He allowed himself some precious moments to doze for a while.

At dinner, Henry and his parents sat chewing away silently. Henry had nothing to say, so he didn't venture anything.

"How did school go today?" his father asked.

"Pretty well, actually," Henry replied. "Rather calm after those kids got booted. I think things are getting better."

"You remember your father and I are going away this weekend. We'll be back Sunday afternoon," his mother added.

"Have fun."

"And if there are any problems, call Uncle Bill. You have all the phone numbers in the drawer."

"Okay. I'll make sure to clean up after the party."

"No parties," his father remarked, quite seriously.

Henry snorted, which burgeoned into steady laughter that he couldn't stop. Tears ran down his cheeks. He had to stop eating.

"What is so funny?" his father said, aggravated.

"Nothing. You wouldn't understand. That was funny, though. I needed a good laugh." He wiped his eyes. "Well, I'm going to the hospital tomorrow anyway to visit someone."

"Who?" his mother asked, surprised.

"A classmate."

"What's wrong with her?"

"I think she tried to kill herself."

"Oh, my God," she said. "That's horrible. Is she going to be alright?"

"I don't know. That's what I'm going to find out."

"Does anyone know why she did it?" his father asked.

"Oh, she's been abused and assaulted a lot in school, and other things are going on, I hear."

His father shook his head sympathetically.

"Well, I hope she'll be fine," his mother added. "It's awful how many kids are doing that today."

Henry nodded. "That is true."

She glanced at Henry. "Have you ever thought about...suicide?" she asked tepidly.

"Uh-huh."

"You have?" she asked.

"Of course."

"Why?" she asked, perturbed.

"Why do you think? All the humiliation wears you down. And I got no help. So after a while..."

"We're here to help you," she remarked.

"You've tried lately. Unfortunately, it didn't change much."

"But you're doing things the wrong way," his father added. "Just listen to us and you'll be fine."

"I'm not doing anything wrong. But you have to be tougher with the school."

"I still say you need to see someone, talk to someone who can help. You have me scared now. The school suggested a counselor a while ago. I can set you up to see her."

"Relax. I'm not going to do anything. Things are going better at school. I've turned things around there and I'm happier."

"Well, I want you to promise me you'll talk with us if you feel depressed. It's always good to talk about it."

"You're correct," Henry said, mainly to placate her. "I will."

In the morning, with the parents gone, Henry had breakfast and headed for the hospital by bus. He nervously wondered what Carla would look like. Walking past the busy nurse's station, patients and doctors, smelling the strong odor of antiseptic, he found Carla's room. She shared it with another girl, who talked with a woman seated next to her. They both glanced at Henry as he passed and he wondered if she had attempted suicide.

On the other side of the white curtain lay Carla, slumped and asleep in a sitting position in her bed, an intravenous needle pinned to her arm, thin oxygen tubes in her nose. Henry looked out the window to a partial view of the city skyline. She was alone, which didn't surprise him. Thin and haggard, her cheekbones protruded. Thick bandaging covered her throat, partly stained from a brownish leakage, and then, behind the bandage, Henry made out a bluish-black line embossed in her skin. She slowly opened her eyes.

"Hi," he said softly. Carla's eyes widened. Henry couldn't tell what that meant. "Thought I'd come to see you."

Carla tried to move but she flinched in pain.

He smiled. "How you doing? But I guess you can't talk."

Carla's face scrunched up as if she were going to cry. She raised her hand and dropped it. Henry sat on the edge of her bed and contemplated her a minute.

"So," he sighed. "You did try to. You didn't have to, Carla. We could have made our lives better together. We could have gotten rid of them together. There was no reason to do this. No reason to do this at all."

Carla closed her eyes, and her lips trembled as if holding back crying that would likely be painful.

"Instead, they win and we end up here. And we're stronger than that." He glanced out the window. "The Vultures know you're here. They walk down the hall easy and enjoying life, and we're here. I was trying to get you to understand that. Things could have gotten better for you. But, in the end, no one really cares about kids like us. The whole fucking world doesn't care. We're throw-away kids. Abused in school, in church, or anyplace else. Throw-away kids. Dispensable. And we have to live with the scars, while they walk free."

He looked down at Carla.

"But I'm changing that, Carla. I've already started. I got a lot of kids expelled. The Vultures are next and then the adults. I'm gonna get them all, and I'm never gonna stop."

Henry took Carla's limp hand. She tried to pull it away, but Henry grasped it in both of his own, squeezing it softly.

"Whether you like it or not, you have friends in school who like you as you are. So hurry up and get better. I want you better. We have a lot to do."

She pulled her hand away, tears running down the bridge of her nose and onto the pillow.

"Hello."

A woman stood holding a large coffee cup.

"Hello. I'm, uh, Henry. I'm a classmate of Carla's."

"Oh, really," she said, a smile breaking out on her face. "Good."

She had the same nose, eyes and height as Carla.

"I'm Martha." They shook hands. "Thank you for coming. She hasn't had any visitors."

Henry returned a sad grimace.

"She, uh, getting better?"

"She's trying. It will be a long recovery. Are you in her classes?"

"Yes, I'm in a few. I'm sorry this happened."

"It's been a shock," she said, sitting on the bed. "But we'll get through it." She rubbed Carla's leg. "The surgery went fine. But it will be a while before she speaks well."

Henry sadly watched the two of them.

She looked up at Henry. "Something wrong?"

"Can I talk to you outside?"

"I suppose."

Carla moved her hands in what Henry thought was a protest.

"Honey, relax," she said taking Carla's hands. "You can't get upset. I'll be right back."

"Bye, Carla," Henry said. "Get well. I'll see you soon."

Martha followed Henry into the hallway.

"Yes, Henry?"

"Do you know why she did this?"

"We don't know," she said.

"I do," Henry said hesitantly.

C'mon. You know what's best.

"She was harassed and assaulted, by some of the girls at school. I think it finally got to her."

Martha looked at Henry a moment, as if sizing him up.

"I see."

"She may have been bullied because the girls think she's gay."

Henry had a twinge of regret saying that when surprise spread across Martha's face. She attempted to say something but the words wouldn't come.

"Well, kids harassed her about it and the teachers did nothing. They're criminals in that school."

"Excuse me?"

"They're all bullies. Vice Principal Peterson. Principal Ruzzo. The teachers. They knew what she was going through, what I was going through, and they did nothing. You didn't know either."

She looked at him, speechless.

"I figured as much," Henry said brazenly.

Martha raised her eyebrows defensively. "If she's not going to talk to me, how am I supposed to know?"

Henry nodded. "You ask."

Her sadly befuddled expression made him feel sorry for her.

"Have you checked her phone or her computer for any nasty messages or texts?"

"Not lately," she murmured.

"She's been cyberbullied. Check for them. If you find any sent during a school day, we can get the kids who did it to her."

"Okay, I will check on that."

"I stopped receiving texts and e-mails a few years ago because they were pretty bad. Calling me worthless and if I die no one would care and blah, blah, blah. There's a lot of bad stuff going on in that school. It's a school of hate. All schools are."

"I never realized," Martha said, softly. "Well, thank you for bringing this to my attention, Henry."

"If you do find something, bring it to Principal Ruzzo. Well, I better go. I'm really sorry about Carla. Goodbye."

"Goodbye, Henry."

Outside the hospital, Henry waited in the chilly breeze at the bus stop. He was happy Carla was alive but believed she wasn't coming back.

I'm gonna get you all for that.

At home while doing homework, he found himself drifting off, desperate for the revenge he so believed in.

"No. Stop. You got work to do here. You're way behind. Tests start Monday."

With grim determination in every step, Henry arrived at school feeling strong, believing more in himself. He scanned the halls with authority, free from most worry.

You can trash your frickin' rules.

But exams were now his most intractable problem. Henry, again, had asked all the questions he could and studied to the point of nausea, all irrelevant if he couldn't recall it at crunch time. And all the other issues he had dealt with prevented any improvement. But he noticed the weight of worry between bullies and exams had begun to shift. He liked that exam worry became his main concern, not kids and conflicts and what to do about them.

"That's the way it should be," he muttered to himself, hovering over a textbook in the library. "I've wasted enough of my life on those idiots."

Then, in math class, he waited nervously for the first exam.

Okay, this is it. You can do it. Just relax. No, don't say just relax. That doesn't work. Breathe. Nice and easy. Take it slow.

As he waited, he forced his heart rate down and kept his brain in math mode. Davis walked in, asked for any last questions and then handed out the test. With the exam now lying in front of him, his heart beat inexorably faster.

Oh, c'mon. Stay with it. Keep it together.

He eased himself into the first two pages, but the last three pages bogged him down as time ticked away to the point where he threw Hail-Mary answers just to complete most of them. He fought through the test but came out angry and unsure. He believed he had messed up too many problems.

In history, Johnson handed out his version of Henry's futility. His mind went stone cold, enraging him again.

You're so fucking weak doing this. You got nothing. You can't do shit with this. Oh, forget it.

Then, he gave up and let it go—the tension in his stomach, the pressure in his chest.

Why not? You spend more energy fighting it.

He stared at the exam. Water filled his eyes to the rims and he blinked it back. He then pictured himself walking out the room, the school, walking away, relaxed and free—face in the sunshine like never before.

If you can't control it, then forget it. You can't keep going like this, anyway. It's killing you. Let's see how well you do without the nerves. You have to find out.

He closed his eyes and let his head fall forward, his chin nearly on his breastbone. He could fall asleep right there he was so tired. The room was quiet, as if he were alone at the reservoir lounging at his favorite spot. When he finally opened his eyes, seeing the first question on the exam, an essay, he realized he could answer that one pretty well. And he did. But when he turned to the more exacting multiple choice, he found again that he didn't know as much as he thought. His studying still was not good enough, his fear of the wrong choice muddled his mind, and the wrong choices piled up.

Wow. This is just insane.

The next class, as he started his English exam, he realized the nerves helped him to focus and concentrate. Now, totally relaxed and uncaring, he drifted. But he kept to it, enjoying the relaxation, all the way through chemistry, where he wrote down what he definitely knew and guessed on the rest.

He walked into the hallway. *Well, at least you're coming out dry and sane. But you're not doing much better. Maybe worse.*

With exams done, Henry returned to school the next week a little happier; he actually liked Mondays now. He grinned at the Vultures in math class, winked, and sat down. He heard Carla's name in a conversation as he sat few rows away from them. But he didn't want to think about her now. He started talking to two middlings, Ginny and Roberto, both good math students, about the homework problems.

"Wilty."

He ignored the voice and continued his conversation.

Then in a sing-song voice, "Wilty."

Henry rolled his eyes as he looked at Ginny and Roberto, who both smiled at him.

Then a sterner voice, "Wilty."

Henry sighed.

"What?"

"Have you seen your girlfriend, lately?" Robin asked.

"What girlfriend?"

"Amazon," Meaghan said.

Laurie chuckled. Robin curled up a condescending smile.

"Yeah, I saw her Saturday in the hospital. You were right. She tried to kill herself. She doesn't look too good. There's a purple mark around her throat where the rope was."

The class went silent.

"I don't think she'll be back. Her mother's gonna check her phone and computer for any bad texts or e-mails. If there are any from you during school, she'll take it to the Office." He smiled. "The noose is tightening, girls. It's only a matter of time."

"We never did that," Robin said.

"Baloney. You did. And we'll prove it."

He gave them a broad, close-lipped smile as the other kids glanced at the three girls. Meaghan's smile dissolved. She glanced at Laurie, as though looking to her for help. She peered around the room at kids looking at her. Henry turned back to his books.

Laurie got up and put one hand on the back of Henry's chair and the other hand on his desk. She leaned in.

"You think you have something on us? You think you're a big man? You're not. You're a little twerp. You always have been and you always will be. So leave us alone."

Henry looked into Laurie's dark brown eyes, her light brown, wavy hair hanging down. Pure hatred and menace, he thought.

Gee. This girl actually is crazy.

"You know, you're kinda cute when you're mad," Henry replied with a toothy smile.

Laurie straightened up, her face crinkling with disgust. Henry laughed out loud as she sat down. Robin stared back under her thin, black eyebrows, looking like she could commit murder.

Mrs. Fields finally arrived.

"Hey, Mrs. Fields, did you know the Vultures cyberbullied Carla and she attempted suicide?"

Robin sprang up. "We never did anything like that," she exclaimed.

"I saw you two do it," Henry said to Laurie and Meaghan. "In the library that day, you typed something and Carla's phone rang. I bet she still has that text and her mother will find it."

"Alright, calm down, everybody," Mrs. Fields said. "Henry, these are serious accusations that you should take to the Office. They are not meant for the classroom."

"I already have. Other girls are coming forward now. They saw what you did to Carla in the locker room. They're going to the Office."

Meaghan, her mouth open, her face suddenly drawn and agitated, got up and walked out. Robin instantly eyed Henry, who looked back at Robin, faking a yawn. He flicked his eyebrows at her.

"Oh, this is ridiculous," Robin said and stormed out.

Laurie peered around her, everyone staring.

"What are you waiting for, bully?" Henry said.

Laurie's stubbornness did not hold. She headed for the door.

"There she goes, everybody. The reason Carla almost died."

"That's enough, Henry," Fields insisted. "No more. That's the last time I'll say it."

"You're right. Let's get to work. I have lots of questions for you," he said as he rummaged through his pack.

Fields passed the exams back, sooner than expected. Henry saw a B minus. He looked over all the little mistakes he didn't know he had made at the time and boiled inside.

The Vultures never returned to class.

On his way to the Office that afternoon, he passed Mrs. Roach standing at her door.

"Afternoon," he said pleasantly.

Roach said nothing. *I don't think she likes me.*

With Mary absent, Henry went straight in to see Peterson.

"Okay," Henry said as he plopped into the chair. "How did it go?"

Peterson expectedly frowned at his boldness. Henry enjoyed how she struggled to stay in command.

"Well? Did you get those girls to come in? Sharonda? Chloe?"

She sighed. "Yes, we did."

"And?"

"We will call in Laurie, Robin and Meaghan and talk to them."

"And expel them."

"Well, we have to talk to them first to find out what they actually did. Then we'll decide what to do," she said.

He stood up. "They bullied Carla almost to death, and she wasn't the only one. I saw Carla on Saturday, by the way. Have you?"

Peterson looked down at some papers. "Not as yet."

"I bet if Robin was in the hospital, you'd be there in a second."

She sighed. "Anything else, Henry?"

"Call Carla's mother. There may be texts on Carla's phone from the Vultures."

"We'll look into it," she said.

"That is correct."

While he knew they would do something about the Vultures, he could not believe Peterson or Ruzzo would allow him to push them much longer. And even with fewer enemies now to encounter as he made his way across the hostile landscape, he remained vigilant for any assault that could likely happen at any moment.

Upstairs later, Meaghan walked alone through the hall and Henry wondered why. She was rarely without her friends. She clutched her things to her chest tightly, keeping her gaze down.

"There goes the cyberbully, everyone," Henry called out as he pointed. "Hey, Meaghan."

Meaghan's mouth shut tight and her chin wrinkled as if she were about to cry. Henry pushed out a laugh.

"Wilton," Bronner said, walking up to him. "Stop that."

"Stop what?"

"Don't do that. Don't do that to anyone."

"How come you never told the bullies to stop doing that stuff to me?"

"Well, we're stopping that kind of behavior."

"Oh, and you're starting with me? The all-time victim? What did you do after Derrick hit me in the head with that book? Look what just happened to Caleb. Where's Carla now?"

"Keep your voice down."

"The only reason you're doing this is because I started complaining about it. And the fact that you are all trying to stop it now clearly shows that the abuse happened, you saw it and did nothing. And any teacher who sees it and does nothing, doesn't deserve to be a teacher. Not in my school."

Bronner stood silent, his mouth clamped shut, face crimson against Henry's rage.

"That makes you an enabler, Mr. Bronner. An enabler." (He always liked that word). "Typical bully teacher." Henry turned theatrically. "Another too-late hero, coming in to save the day after all the damage is done."

"That's enough," Bronner demanded.

"Bully adults don't last long in my school. Their careers, that is."

He pushed through onlookers, some of whom had their phones up, recording the outrage. Bronner did not stop him.

Henry's intensity exhausted him again. Around the corner, he leaned his shoulder against the wall and kneaded his forehead, almost feeling faint from his anger. He wondered if all the strain on his heart would make it give out. "I want this to end ."

"Uh, you alright?" Christy asked with a bemused smile.

"I don't know." He again was pleasantly surprised that Christy took the time to ask.

Does she like me?

"Good going, Wilton," Andrew said in passing.

Henry couldn't tell if Andrew meant that or was just being sarcastic. He pushed himself off the wall.

"You really are losing it, aren't you?" Christy asked.

He smiled tiredly. "Maybe. Do my eyes look angry?"

"Somewhat."

"What did Bronner do?"

"He told us to break it up and he walked."

"He was taking credit for making things better. I'm not letting them get away with it. I'm the one who did that. He's just covering his ass."

They walked on silently for a moment, which made Henry nervous. Even though she was queen middling, she was still hot. What to say next? Something clever and funny. He searched, but the pressure gave him brain freeze.

Don't. Don't even try. You're about as clever as a lamp post.

"So anytime you see a girl being harassed, go up and stop it. I could use your help, everyone's help. Why don't we, uh, get together and talk about it?"

Christy grinned. "I have to go, Henry."

"Hey, ya know, I'm always having a problem with math. No pun intended. You're pretty good at it. I was wondering if you could help me out?"

"So you want some tutoring."

"I guess, yeah. I need to get my grades up."

"I'll think about it." She smiled, pathetically, Henry thought. "I'll let you know."

He watched her walk away.

Well, she didn't say no.

Upstairs, he passed Sharonda but did not want to speak with her.

"Henry," she called. "You got your wish. Peterson called us in about Carla."

"Thanks for doing that."

"We didn't have much choice."

"I know. But think of the good you did."

"Did you hear Carla's mother was in the Office?"

"No, I didn't," he answered. "That's, that's good. Hopefully, she had something."

Sharonda closed her locker and picked up her soccer bag.

"So long." She made off as though she wanted nothing further to say.

Well, that's the way it's going to be.

The word finally came down the next morning—the Vultures had been summoned. By late morning, each Vulture had been escorted to her locker and then back to the Office, likely to await a parent. Henry heard they had put up a fuss. Robin protested, completely denying the accusations against her. But she didn't cry. Laurie also denied doing anything wrong, and she swore her parents would sue the school. But Meaghan bawled and apologized over and over, pleading that she wouldn't do anything like that again.

Henry laughed out loud in the hallway.

"Oh, I wish I had seen it. I always miss the good stuff."

At lunch, Henry nodded to Pam with a wide smile. Pam and her girls sat silently and looked like they were all lost and didn't know what to do. He thought Pam would become the new vulture queen.

"So typical," Henry said to one classmate. "When they're finally caught, they turn to jelly and *cwy*."

Derrick, Trevor and two of their puppies sat at another table.

Henry nodded at them. "Hey guys. How ya doin'? You next?"

"Shut up, Wilton," Trevor said.

"Make me. Nah, I don't think you will."

Henry relaxed and strode through the day feeling good.

Ahh. Now this is nice.

He studied that evening with more energy and in the morning he arrived to peer around the kingdom that might be his. The building in front of him didn't seem as menacing as before.

"Well, you knew it was never the building."

Henry gazed up at the glass façade for ghostly images of a teacher or vice-principal, but none were there. He walked a straight path through the hall, as if kids had a sense he was coming and made slight adjustments to avoid his way. His vision encompassed the total hallway scene, and there were some kids eyeing him. He loved the attention, and a corner of his mouth turned up in a self-satisfied, but still vengeful, smile.

C'mon. Don't lose focus. Being nice is being weak.

He made a point of entering the classrooms near last so all the kids would look at him as he triumphantly took his seat, with, of course, an indifferent manner. He'd finally turn to his classmates and nod.

Exams came back, but he didn't worry about it. It is what it is, he thought. You are what you are. He averaged all his exams to a B minus. He clamped his mouth sadly.

Oh, well. But you're only starting with this new strategy, so see how you do next time. It won't get any better if you give up.

Over the next several days, he wondered what school would be like going forward. What would change? Who would change? And was he considered a lion or pariah? A squealer?

In the cafeteria, no one bothered him as he sat alone. He relaxed, concentrated on his eating, checked his phone and read over a paper he was writing for a class, enjoying not having to socialize. Derrick sat with some bully friends, laughing at something someone said, seemingly enjoying life. Henry stared at him and finally caught Derrick's eye.

Henry gave him a slight smile and a foreboding nod. Derrick looked back at him blankly but with the same menacing, dark eyes.

You have to get rid of him.

He also noticed Christy sitting with some of the football players. She talked with Wyatt rather closely, making Henry wonder what was going on. Henry didn't think Wyatt was her type. She was smart and cool and Wyatt was not, in Henry's mind. He would have to watch that.

In his classes, he remained quiet. But he was pleasantly surprised that more kids asked more questions, critical and analytical ones, putting teachers, like Davis, on the spot more often, pressing them to explain things better. Henry enjoyed that and the idea that maybe he had some positive influence on his classmates. If I'm no longer around, he thought, they can carry on.

Between classes, he went up to Mrs. Roach. He gave her the wide smile that he knew irritated her.

"Well, what do you think about your favorite girls getting expelled?" He shook his head slowly. "Terrible, isn't it? Just, just terrible."

She frowned at him. "Go to class, please."

"You knew Carla was having a bad time. You knew what they were doing to her and you didn't stop it. Because you don't like what Carla might be. We don't need teachers to spread prejudice around a school."

He gave her a haughty smile as he ambled away. Roach shot forward and stabbed her forefinger at him.

"You mind your own business, young man," she exclaimed. "Who do you think you are? You don't know what you're talking about. Just keep your mouth shut and do what you're told."

She startled Henry, but he stood his ground.

"Wow. You're so out of touch, you can't see beyond your own nose. And I feel sorry for you. And every kid who comes in contact with you. But not for long." He started to walk away, then stopped. "Oh, remember those two girls who called me an idiot after the assembly? Remember? You said you were going to speak to them. Did you?"

Roach would not answer.

"I didn't think so. You hypocrite."

He left her staring. Downstairs, he raised his eyebrows at that encounter. *That was good, but they're coming for you.*

In his next class, Henry eased himself down from Roach's outburst, then straightened himself up.

Pay attention. If you have to be in this place, then get your ass down to business.

At the end of the day, Henry boarded the bus, nodding to a few of the kids sitting near him and then stared out the window.

"Hi, Wilty."

Jeremy dropped onto the seat and bumped Henry's shoulder. Joe sat down in the seat in front of them.

Shit.

"Well, look who's here?" Henry said with a forced jovial tone.

"Thought we'd come to see you, Wilty," Joe said.

"Well, thanks, guys." He gave Jeremy a little tap on the leg. "Good seeing you, too." Jeremy sat silent. "So what's happenin'? You two lookin' good. Getting expelled agrees with you."

Joe and Jeremy stared at him, while the other kids watched frowning, expectant.

"Won't this bus take you far out of your way?"

"We'll be fine," Jeremy said softly.

"Gonna get off and walk me home?"

"Yup."

You can't let that happen.

"So, you're finally coming after me. Actually, I kind of expected you sooner. A little slow, aren't ya? Ha. You clowns will never learn. Hey, Mrs. Pierson," Henry yelled to the bus driver. "These two kids here. They don't go to the school anymore. Why are they on the bus?"

Mrs. Pierson looked into her mirror a moment and then walked back.

"What's going on?" she asked.

"These two don't go to the school anymore. Why are they on the bus?"

Mrs. Pierson moved her short, stocky frame forward.

"We do so," Joe said.

"They were expelled last month because they attacked me and other kids, and they blame me for it. So they're here to, ah, pay me a visit, if you know what I mean. All these kids here know it. Also, notice they don't have any backpacks or books with them?"

Mrs. Pierson looked them over.

"Alright, you two, off the bus," she said with a wave of her hand. "Let's go."

Jeremy and Joe didn't move.

"You idiots," Henry said. "You forgot to look the part." He laughed.

"Move it. Now," Pierson said. "I'm not going to tell you again."

"Yeah, come on," Henry added, just to aggravate his old friends. "You're holding up the bus." He clapped. "Let's go. Let's go."

Both boys slowly got up and walked off the bus, Pierson following them.

"Buh-bye," Henry called out.

As the bus pulled away, Jeremy and Joe stood on the curb in front of the school. Henry waved to them gleefully. Then a teacher appeared and confronted them.

Henry sat down satisfied but relieved.

This won't be the last time. Gonna have to start figuring how to protect yourself out here.

As the days moved on, Henry sat alone in the cafeteria or the library, trying to study every moment. A year earlier, sitting alone had made him an easy target. No one picked on him now. His friends didn't approach him either.

Henry comfortably looked over a paper due soon. He yawned, gathered his things and headed for the gym. Ironically, gym class had become a respite for him. Being more relaxed, he concentrated better and played better and enjoyed it. He deliberately let a ball carom off his hands just to hear if he would get a typical degrading remark. Instead, there was a strange silence as he retrieved the ball. Roach certainly said nothing.

Good. Get used to it, people, because this is the way I like it. You had your time, now it's mine. If you don't like it, get the fuck out.

In the locker room, they showered and put on their clothes.

"Hey, Wilton," someone called out.

Henry ignored Trevor.

"Wilton."

"What?"

"Who you gonna get kicked out this week?"

Henry pulled down his shirt and adjusted it.

"Maybe you."

"Maybe we should kick you out," Jose added.

"For what? For making this a better school to come to, even with you in it?"

"Yeah?" Jose said walking toward him. "You pretty much can do what you want."

"Mmmm, yeah, pretty much."

Other boys dressed quietly.

"You're a meek, right?" he said.

"You're a bully, right?"

"I'd rather be a bully than a meek."

"I know. I think you'll make a good one. And as soon as you are, I'll get rid of you."

Henry laughed.

"But you know who isn't a good one anymore?" Henry asked. "Good ol' Derrick here."

"Look at him," Henry said. "A shadow of what he once was." Derrick stood up straight and stared passively at his former victim. "He used to own the school. Now look at him. No more making fun of kids. No more tripping them or pushing them into lockers or nailing them in the back of the head with a book. Just a nice, quiet little boy. Kinda sad to see him like this, though." He smiled. "Just jokin', Derry. Just jokin'."

Henry stepped in front of Derrick and turned his back. "He's a good boy now. Nothin' much left of the old bully." Henry put his hands on his hips with authority. He noticed the other boys moving away in embarrassment, as if they knew it was the truth, or they knew what was coming. Henry glanced around the place as if it was his kingdom and practically felt Derrick's breath on his neck.

"Must be tough, you know? Not being able to do the things you love, be who you really are. You know, do the things that really turn you on."

Get ready.

Henry smiled up at Derrick and gave him a wink. He sauntered back to his clothes, imitating the bully swagger.

A huge weight hit Henry from behind, and an arm throttled him. Forced to his knees, Henry shouted, then gasped when his neck was wrenched. His head was yanked from side to side with a suddenness that was meant to tear muscle and cartilage. He shouted again. Then something hard pressed against his spine as his head was pulled back by his hair. Henry grunted aloud each time he was yanked and his hands slapped the floor in pain.

Henry was willing to allow some injury to get rid of Derrick, but this might be too much, he thought. He felt his neck crack and a warm rush of something flow into his head.

Henry's eyes flitted about, searching for help. He saw some of the boys slip out, while others had their phones up recording it. Trevor and Jose watched with deep frowns and hard eyes, as if this was supposed to happen—proper payback to a squealer who got their friends kicked out.

In this vulnerable position, Henry thought of cracking vertebrae and a life in a wheelchair, so, with a suddenness out of fear, or necessity, he flipped himself over. Derrick lost his balance and Henry pushed him off and kicked him in the chest. He took in gulps of air and coughed and tried to swallow. Derrick flew back on top of him and threw down punches as fast as a jackhammer. Henry avoided them as best as he could, unable to throw any himself, but a few landed on his cheekbone.

"Derrick!"

Roach trotted through the spectators and pulled Derrick off. But Derrick pushed the teacher away, straining to get back to Henry. Roach tried again to grab Derrick, who threw an elbow up that caught Roach in the jaw. Enraged, Roach pulled Derrick to the floor and anchored him there. More boys slipped out.

"Derrick. Stop."

Derrick struggled and even snarled to release himself from Roach's grip. Henry rolled over onto his back, his hands at his badly strained neck.

Ruzzo and two other teachers burst in. He lowered onto one knee to check on Henry, who shrugged stiffly. Ruzzo called the nurse on his phone.

Derrick wrestled some more.

"Need some help here," Roach said.

"Alright," Ruzzo said. "Grab his shoulders and legs and we'll take him outside."

Derrick squirmed wildly. Ruzzo and the other teachers knelt down. Derrick whipped a knee at Ruzzo, who pulled away just in time to miss it. Ruzzo snagged the leg. After a count, they all lifted Derrick like a writhing crocodile and walked him into the hallway.

"I'll kill him! I'll kill you all!" Derrick screamed.

"Shut up," Ruzzo shouted.

The nurse hustled in and knelt down. She examined Henry, asked him if he could breathe, swallow or move okay. Henry whispered that he was fine, but he was in pain. She said he had to go to the hospital, and she carefully installed a neck brace. Asked if he could sit up, Henry tried, but the pain of strained muscles laid him out. With the nurse bracing his head, he finally sat up, groaning deeply. His head drooped limply against the brace.

"I can walk. I can walk."

The ambulance came and Henry was helped into it. He was helped onto a gurney and was strapped in. Kids outside gathered and stared—Henry the star again.

On his way to the hospital, Henry stared silently as the EMTs asked him questions, checked his pupil dilation and blood pressure, and made him comfortable. Only his eyes moved as he lay quietly, an emotionally drained lump. But he had feeling everywhere, so he wasn't too worried.

That's it. You're done. No more.

At the hospital, he watched ceiling lights sail by as he was rolled into a large, brightly-lit examining room. More questions from two doctors, and he muttered answers. X-rays showed no cracks or breaks.

No more.

Henry's mother picked him up. On the ride home, she said nothing. He had never seen her so quiet, obviously upset, and he noticed tears fill her eyes. At home, he gingerly got out of the car, pulling himself up carefully and bracing against anything near him. He grimaced with every step. His mother, still silent with frowning concern, waited patiently as Henry slowly got himself into the house.

Better get your ass upstairs.

He climbed the stairs to his room, gripping the banister for help. He groaned as he sat down on the bed. His eyelids closed and opened slowly. He felt a dull throbbing in his throat and spine.

The cat eventually jumped up and sniffed at the brace.

"That was... almost the end, cat. Oh, this is gonna... suck."

His father came home, went upstairs, looked Henry over and shook his head. He told him how unnerved his mother was.

"Alright, look, man to man," Henry began, his speaking restricted by the brace. "This is the last of it. He was the bully I had to get rid of. There will be no more fights after this."

His father sat down on the bed. "I wish I could believe that."

"Well, you can. You think I want to go through this again? Now you can get a lawyer. Sue the school and Derrick's parents to pay the hospital bills."

His father sighed. "Ruzzo said you goaded this kid into attacking you."

"It doesn't matter what you say, you don't assault someone. That's the rule I have to live by, and so does everybody else. All he had to do was walk away, but he didn't. Sue the bastards. It's the only way they're going to learn."

His father let out a heavy sigh. "Well, this kid is expelled. Ruzzo assured me nothing further will happen."

"He is correct. It's done. There's no other kid to have a problem with. Sue them. You can't let this go. No reason for you to pay the hospital bills."

"I'm thinking about it." He stood up. "I assume you won't be eating."

"No, I can barely move."

Henry lay sleepless all night, finding few comfortable positions. But, with eyes half-open, he breathed calmly knowing the school was cleaner and safer. He had hoped he wouldn't get hurt too much in doing so, but he swore at the beginning that he would sacrifice himself to it. A corner of his mouth rose slightly. Derrick was gone.

"So long, asshole."

Now he dreaded the simple task of just getting up. In the morning, using the banister, doorjambs and the wall to brace himself, he finally made it to the kitchen table. His father had already left for work.

"You really shouldn't go today, Henry," she said. "You're in too much pain."

217

"No," Henry whispered, turning his shoulders in tandem with his head, his mouth only partly opening when he spoke. "I'm...I'm going. I got the pills." He half-chewed a spoonful of cereal. "It's...it's amazing how every move affects the neck muscles. No. Don't sneeze. Don't sneeze." He squeezed his nose.

His mother drove him, silently, to school. Henry was afraid to bring anything up. Again the talk of the hallway, he made his way carefully through the crowd to his locker and then to first class, everyone looking at him. He let his pack drop next to his seat, keeping his head and shoulders in a vertical plane as he sat down.

"How do ya feel?" Trevor asked.

"What do you think?" Henry muttered. "Where's your buddy Derrick?" he asked, showing a weak smile. "He gave a whole new meaning to getting thrown out of school."

He snickered, but, more importantly, other kids did, too, laughing with Henry, not at him, for the first time.

Respect.

"You better hide after school from now on," Trevor said.

Jose shook his head.

"Hope it was worth it."

"Oh, yeah," Henry replied, squeezing his cheeks against his eyes from discomfort. He adjusted the brace. He was the only one in the school wearing one. "Totally."

What did the kids think about him now? he wondered. And, at this point, why care? He got what he had always wanted—the last of the apex predators gone. The other bully kids didn't matter.

Bronner finally walked in.

"You're late," Henry said to him.

Bronner darted a glare at him. "Too bad."

Henry's tough-guy performance lasted only till noon. Exhaustion and nausea took him over. He tried to hold on but ended up calling his mother for a ride home. He cramped up as well and got himself to the bathroom, painfully emitting fluids from both ends.

Over the next few weeks, Henry noticed the hallways became increasingly cheerier, kids laughing more, teachers smiling more, which pleased him. But he maintained a frowning demeanor, easier with the neck brace and persistent aches with every little move. He needed to control his newly-won territory and be vigilant to any abuse from anyone against anyone, especially himself, and then report it to the Office.

Stay tough. You smile, you're weak.

He found it easy to forget the expelled kids, their existence vaporizing in the school air, and with them would go his rage and his fear. He could deal with the remaining, second-rate bullies. They existed, in class and in the halls, but they didn't bother him.

He still reveled in the liberating feeling of not worrying about enemies. Walking the corridors relaxed and just about, but never completely, empty of anxiousness—what a change of life for a former prisoner of the bully gulag.

So this is what the bullies and middlings feel like when they come to school every day. And they've enjoyed this all their lives. I'm in the frickin' tenth grade and I'm just starting.

He believed all the abused kids in the school liked it. He didn't have to ask. He could have asked Caleb, but Caleb didn't stand up to it. Henry was proud he had emerged from the cocoon of his own cowardice and could not abide anyone else who didn't. He tried to save Caleb (from himself) but the kid refused to rise with Henry. So be it, Henry decided. He hoped that cutting friendship with Caleb would teach him the necessity of standing against abuse anywhere. Instead, Caleb would be an unpaying beneficiary of a safer school he could have helped create.

Pondering his achievement so far, Henry realized it had come about easier than he had thought it would. Last summer, it seemed insurmountable, impossible.

You built it up so much, you thought you couldn't do it. Damn fear, fucking, fucking fear. You can't ever be afraid like that again.

Once he stood up to his enemies, badgered them, threatened them with outside forces, he believed everything came together. These adults who put up such an intimidating, menacing front finally wavered under his show of strength.

Still more to do. You're not done yet.

The discontented winter days slowly gave way to spring. Easter Sunday arrived. He removed the neck brace occasionally now, enjoying that freedom. Henry's parents invited his uncle, aunt, and two cousins to join them for sunrise service and later for dinner.

The morning dawned cold but clear on a wide-open field not far from the church, with the sun ascending slowly above the horizon of stiffened trees. After the service, many parishioners lined up to have a word with the pastor. Henry caught Charles standing around with his family. He thought the bully seemed sad, walking slowly, with little energy, the old bright smile and swagger gone.

Henry caught his eye and waved.

"Charles, how's it going?"

Charles frowned and looked away. Henry smiled.

The parents lingered and talked with friends until most parishioners had left the field. He tried to slink away, but Reverend Garcia caught him.

"Henry, how are you?" she asked. "I haven't seen you in a while."

Henry shrugged. "Busy with school, I guess."

"How are you doing with that brace? I heard about your altercation. Healing okay?"

"Every day gets a little better."

"You look tired," she ventured.

"It's been tiring dealing with it."

"I'm sure. I remember we talked about some other issues you had at school," she said, catching her white, gold-embroidered robe in a sudden breeze. "How is that going?"

"Good. I got them to expel some of the kids who caused those issues. So things are going better."

"I see. Was that the best way to handle it?"

"It was the only way. And one of those kids is Charles, right over there."

"Yes, I'm aware," she said. "His parents are quite upset. They asked me to have a word with him."

"Hopefully he's learned his lesson. And that his parents know they raised a bully."

"That may be a little harsh."

"It's true."

"Well, when we're young, we sometimes don't understand our behavior."

"Really, like when he and four other bullies assaulted this kid behind the school?"

"I know. But I believe Charles better understands what he's done, and he's been very apologetic."

"Really. Who did he apologize to?"

"Well," she replied, folding her hands over her robe, "he had to apologize to the boy he attacked."

"What about to me and the other kids he abused?"

"His parents have to make sure that happens."

"Won't hold my breath on that. But as long as he's out of the school, that's the main thing. And I'm sure there will be more issues to come over the next few years. I'll take care of it."

"Hopefully not," she said.

"Oh, there will. That's the way people are. I'm gonna try to get rid of the teachers and the principal, too. They saw what was going on and did nothing about it."

"Are you sure?"

"Well, of course. I've proven it." Henry smiled. "I'm gonna get them fired."

"I see," the pastor replied softly. "One thing I still notice from the last time we talked, Henry, is that you're angry, even bitter. That's difficult to deal with, especially at your age."

Henry couldn't disagree.

"Well, it's not my fault. I'm not the cause of all this. I'm the victim of it."

Henry took a few steps away from her, not wanting to continue an unwelcome conversation.

"But I just want you to understand how strong emotions can be," she added. "You want to be careful how you respond to people and their behavior. Your parents have been concerned."

"Don't blame me for being mad about it."

"Remember anger is one thing, Henry, but bitterness is a sickness of the soul. Once it's planted, it can be difficult to deal with."

"Well, if they're in there, it's not my fault," Henry said, irritated. "I've gone to hell and back in that school. There's no God there."

The pastor appeared to pinch a smile.

"I'm not sure that's true."

"It is true, whether you want to believe it or not."

"Maybe you have been mistreated, but you must understand that your actions are your responsibility. Please be careful."

"It's up to the bullies what happens and then we'll go from there," Henry said. "I tell you what, tell Charles to come over here and beg for my forgiveness. Tell him, 'Charles, go to Henry and humbly beg his forgiveness.'"

The pastor glanced at Charles.

"I don't think he'll do that."

"Let's give it a try. He's right there."

"I'll talk to his parents."

"Right. Well, I have to go. Good-bye."

"Henry, God is with you all the time."

"Well, then he chose me to beat the bullies. Christ couldn't beat his."

"Well, actually He did."

Henry waved. "Have a good day."

"You do the same."

Henry sped off to end the conversation. He headed to the car all tensed up, but relaxed during the ride home.

He found the time at dinner with relatives unusually enjoyable—none of the griping, complaining or squabbling that had afflicted his family for so long. He felt very much at ease and contributed to the humorous babble. He didn't smile, but he liked it—maybe things can get better, he thought. He heard his phone in the kitchen chime indicating a text and waited for the end of the meal before checking it. When he looked at the text, his mouth opened. It was from Sharonda:

Meaghan's dead. No other info.

He stared at the phone a moment.

"Everything alright?" his mother asked while bringing dishes to the sink.

He forced a level tone. "Uh, yes. Everything's fine."

He went back to the table and sat down stiffly, then re-filled his plate with ham and potato.

Henry did not want to go to school and face another day of more bad news. Some girls openly cried. Henry tried to ignore it all and kept to himself, hard and unconcerned. But in the hallway, Jose passed him and said, "Happy now, Wilton?" Henry didn't answer. When he finished his lunch, he returned his tray, passing and ignoring the table where his friends sat.

"Asshole."

Sounded like Kam. He stopped.

"What was that?" Henry asked.

No answer.

"I didn't think you'd speak up."

"Alright," Sharonda interjected. "There've been enough problems around here without you all goin' at it."

"Yeah, and I've solved a lot of those problems."

"Like how?" George asked. "Meaghan offing herself?"

"So, she did. How?"

"She cut herself," Kam said, sharply.

"Okay, so what do I have to do with it?" he said.

Henry raised his voice enough so everyone could hear.

"Hey, I don't want to see anyone doing that. But don't blame me. It was her choice. Guess she couldn't handle being expelled or something. Obviously, she had a lot more issues than we knew."

"She did," Becka said. "Everyone knew Meaghan was the weaker one, hanging on to Robin and Laurie. She always had some problems. She couldn't stand on her own."

"I heard her parents came down on her real hard," Chloe said. "Grounded her completely. She had to go to the hospital and apologize to Carla."

"So there ya go. I'm not to blame after all. But we all have to put the blame on somebody."

"No one's blaming you, Henry," George said.

"Then why was I called an asshole?"

No one answered.

"Do you see the big bullies around here anymore? No. Because I got rid of 'em. And all of a sudden—poof—a lot of the problems are gone. There are a lot of kids around here who are very happy those assholes are gone. I'm wondering if you people get that."

"What do you mean, 'you people'?" Chloe said, looking up at him.

"You people who don't get involved. But, you're among millions."

"We did help you," Sharonda said.

"Yeah, but I had to push you. And you became part of the solution. Instead of watching it happen, you stopped it from happening. How do you feel about that? Don't you feel good about yourself?"

Sharonda smiled. "Sure, Henry."

"You don't sound very sure."

"I'm happy I was able to help," Sharonda added.

"How about you, Chloe?"

"Yes, Henry, me too."

He looked at George and Kam. "You helped me out, too. Maybe I had to push you a little, but, in the end, you did it."

He took off his neck brace. "Alright. Hold on."

Henry went to his pack for the No Bullying sign-up sheet. He liked the fact that all his things were still there after leaving them unguarded for a while. Not too long ago, they would have disappeared. He placed the paper on the table and held out the pen for Kam to take.

"Sign it for me."

Kam looked it over.

"Well?" Henry said. "Why not?"

Kam hesitated. Henry held the pen out in front of him.

"You want me sign it over 'Wilton's an idiot'?"

"That's right."

Kam chuckled, took the pen and wrote his name.

After Kam signed, Henry snatched the pen from him and handed it to Sharonda.

"Your turn."

After a moment's hesitation, she scribbled her name under Kam's.

He took the pen and pushed it at Chloe.

"Your turn."

Chloe looked up at Henry. She signed it and dropped the pen. "Happy now?"

"Your turn." George, with a smile, signed his name. Then Becka.

Henry grabbed the pen and the paper and brought them to another table.

"Sign it, please," he said to one of the kids.

The first kid looked at the paper. He glanced up at Henry. "Alright, Wilton."

Henry put the sheet in front of the next kid, who signed it and then the next kid. He went to each table. Then the football players.

"Here you go, guys. Sign it."

Gray looked it over.

"Wilty, we're not signing this stupid thing,"

"Is that because you're a bully?"

"I'm not a bully."

"Prove it, helmet head."

"Don't call me that."

"Don't call me Wilty."

Wyatt took it.

"Oh, let's just sign it. Get the idiot off our backs." He chuckled. "It'll be good PR, anyway."

He did, and the five others did, too. Gray had it last and reluctantly wrote his name. Henry snatched it.

"Didn't know you guys could write."

"Screw you," Gray said.

In a few minutes, the kids at all the tables had signed.

"Thanks," he said to the final table.

He stuffed his pack and stomped off to the Office.

Mary's back was turned as Henry came in, allowing him to sneak past. Peterson, talking on the phone, froze as Henry stomped up to her and placed the sign-up sheet down in front of her.

"There you go."

In the final class of a morbid day, Henry got the idea that his task had neared its end. With about six weeks remaining, the time had come to take the final step. He saw himself tired but strong, trudging up to the top of a rise on enemy land and turning back to see the dust and smoke clearing away to reveal the bodies of bullies strewn over the landscape. In front of him, the land ended at the coastline, the sea sparkling in the sunshine. Two ivory towers stood tall and strong and gleaming, smooth and unscathed. He smiled vengefully.

The little rats are gone. Now for the big ones.

As Henry sat at his desk at home, his elbows propped up and fingers tapping his lips, he mulled over the means to change someone's life. He also thought that forcing enabling teachers and administrators out of their long-time positions could not be taken lightly. But, having been badgered under the rule of monsters who fed greedily on his fear for years, he believed he had every right to bring an end to their days and their crimes, as he saw fit.

He allowed intuition to tell him when to make the final trip to the Office. He wanted to take his time with it, so he could have a normal life for a while and concentrate on school. He was confident and in good spirits, working hard on just relaxing.

After a few weeks, he felt ready.

Alright. You have to do it. Be scared all you want, but tomorrow's it.

As he closed in on the Office the next morning, the same petrifying fear as before took him over. He stopped.

Damn. Will you stop it? He gave himself a minute and breathed. *Now go.*

He walked up to the counter.

"Hi, Mary. I'd like to see Mr. Ruzzo."

He waited only a few minutes to go in.

"What is it, Wilton?" Ruzzo asked tiredly.

Henry sat down.

"Time for our final meeting."

"What?" he asked.

"Our final meeting." He folded his hands on his lap to keep them steady. "We have to talk about your future. Everyone's future, actually."

"I'm sorry?"

"Your resignation. Mrs. Peterson's, too. Can you call her in, please?

"Oh, Wilton, I don't have time for this silliness. We have done what you've asked…"

Henry jumped up and asked Mary to have Peterson come to the principal's office, then sat back down and waited quietly.

"Wilton, I know things haven't…"

Peterson walked in.

"Please close the door," Henry said without turning. He crossed a leg over the other and extended his hands over the arms of the chair authoritatively. "We've come to the end of the road. You both have done a decent job doing what I've asked you to do. We've cleaned up my class. Well, mostly. But now there's just one thing left to do. It's your turn to go. Call the superintendent and tell him you will resign as of the last day of school. You first," he said to Peterson. Henry nodded toward the phone. "Go on."

Ruzzo snorted and shook his head. Peterson stood with her arms folded, her red-painted lips shut tight. Henry's heart thumped.

"Wilton," he said, scratching the back of his neck, "we're not doing that. Now leave."

"I remember you said that if we did what you wanted, we would be alright," Peterson said. "So what are you trying to do?"

"Yeah, well, I thought about that," he said. "The thing is, you are what you are. I've always heard from you adults that you can't change people. You'll always be bullies—"

Peterson slapped her hand on the desk. "I am not a bully."

She forced a moment of silence.

"But you are, Mrs. Peterson," Henry said softly. "I'm sure it's difficult to finally realize what you've always been."

Exasperated, she rubbed her forehead.

"See, if you two stay, things will go right back to the way they were once I'm gone." He shrugged. "Human nature. And I can't allow that."

"Wilton…" Ruzzo began.

228

"But enough talk. Call the superintendent." Henry lifted a hand to inspect his fingernails. "Now."

Not hearing anything, Henry pulled out his weapon.

"We can do this privately, or publicly. I can make my own phone call now, if you like, or you can make yours. You choose."

"Very well," Ruzzo said. He snapped his phone off the desk, tapped in a number, and waited. Peterson glanced at him.

"Joanne, this is David Ruzzo. Hi. Can I speak with Robert? Thank you."

Ruzzo sat back, waiting, watching his fingers slide along the edge of his desk.

"Robert, how are you? Well, not so good here. Um, we have been having an issue with a particular student for a while now. He wants us to resign our positions at the school. Well, he's accusing us of supporting an unsafe environment in school. Obviously, that's rubbish. But we can't convince him how wrong he is."

Good move.

"Let's go over and see him today," Henry blurted out, challenging the principal.

Ruzzo listened a minute longer, turning in his chair to look out the window.

"Okay, I think we can do that. I will let him know as well. Right. I will call you later." He placed the phone down. "Alright. The superintendent is willing to meet with you and your parents. You'll just have to make an appointment."

"What about you?"

"Mrs. Peterson and I will meet with him separately and give him our take on the issue."

"Oh, I see," Henry said, skeptically.

"The opposing parties usually meet separately first," Peterson said, "and then come together if need be."

"I can just imagine what you two are going to tell him." He threw his hands out. "You adults will protect each other.

You always do. But I won't give up. I'll make the appointment. Thank you for your time."

Henry stood off to the side in the foyer. *So they weren't going to come after you. Interesting. Now you have to convince the parents. But you gotta do it. Ya gotta do it.*

In class, Henry listened quietly as Bronner tackled a few difficult problems and decided it was time for this teacher to go as well. After class, Henry waited for Bronner to end his conversation with a student.

"Mr. Bronner."

"Yes?"

"I would like you to resign as of the last day of school. Put in your resignation today, please."

Bronner's eyebrows arched. "What?"

"I told Ruzzo and Peterson to resign, too."

Bronner's head reared back in laughter.

"Wilton, I think you've taken this bully crusade a bit too far. Now, we are addressing your concerns, so go to your next class."

"You saw the abuse and did nothing. You support the strong kid theory that weaklings like me have to suffer humiliation and keep their mouths shut. You did that with Derrick and Donny this year."

"I don't know what you mean."

Henry smiled. "Oh, yeah, you do. I'll call you out as a bully in public."

"I don't think that will do much, Henry."

"So, you don't mind if I do?"

"There's nothing much you can do to us."

"Who's 'us'?"

Bronner froze a moment.

"Who are you talking about?"

"This conversation is over. Go to class."

He picked up his briefcase. Henry followed him into the hallway.

"I'll call you out as a bully in public. Resign now and I won't do it."

Bronner kept walking down the crowded hall but Henry did not pursue.

Later, Henry demanded the same of Davis, which led to the same conversation, and then the Roaches, and finally Johnson, who also laughed it off.

Asking for resignations from those people felt surreal to Henry, charging into the unknown again, and then waiting for the consequences.

For the next few days, kids joked and outright laughed about Henry's brave demands for resignation. Henry tensed as he watched the effect on the school in general and the other teachers specifically.

In the cafeteria, he glanced around and realized that sitting alone after what he had done would make him a target of jokes and ridicule, so he stepped out and went to the library. He got a sandwich from a vending machine and settled down in the library to study.

But worry needled him. He was still in enemy territory, coming closer to the end but with adult enemies all around. On the other hand, he thought, what could they do to him? He was too unsure.

Christy had agreed to tutor Henry and they met in the library. As they started on math, Henry talked about calling out those teachers, an easy conversation that amused her, hopefully making points with her, but he couldn't tell. They sat rather close together. He liked that nearness, the slight scent of her perfume, the bare knee of her crossed leg. She knew her functions well, and Henry did get something out of it. But he didn't admit that much in order to ensure another session. And he wondered about her and Wyatt, although he hadn't seen them together very often.

Later at home, he dropped his pack on his bedroom floor and sat tiredly on his bed, rubbing his face, massaging a healing neck. He delved into history before supper. He had his history text open and began typing some notes into his computer when his father's stern voice broke his thoughts.

He bounced down the stairs.

"Yes?" Henry said sharply.

Henry's mother sat on the couch as his father stood nearby with his arms crossed.

"Sit down."

"I'll stand. What is it?"

"We got a call from Principal Ruzzo today. He said you're telling them and some of the teachers to resign?"

Henry hid his surprise. "Correct."

"Why?"

"Because they're bullies."

"Henry," his mother said. "Several kids were expelled. I think you've made your point."

Henry chuckled.

"This is funny?" his father blurted. "You threaten people with their jobs? You won't succeed at that."

"Then what are you worried about?"

"Your behavior," his father said. "You can't go around doing these things."

"Sure, I can. These people saw what happened for years and did nothing to stop it. They have to go. I have zero tolerance for teachers like that. But we have to go see the superintendent to get it done."

"We're not going to see the superintendent about anything."

"I'll make the appointment and we'll go convince him to fire these people."

"There's no need to do that."

"Then I'll go myself.

"No, you won't."

"Well, you can't stop me. Anyone can meet him. Ruzzo and Peterson are meeting with him, too."

"Henry," his mother continued, "I'm sure the principal and vice principal will do a better job in the future."

"Which means you agree they weren't doing a good job before?"

She hesitated. "Well, I suppose not," she answered softly.

"Can you guarantee me that everything will not go right back to normal after I graduate?"

His parents hesitated.

"Well? Can you?" He raised his eyebrows.

"Of course we can't," his father replied. "But you'll be gone, so it won't matter."

"Hmm. So, so you're saying it's possible the abuse can come back after I'm gone. Ergo, Ruzzo and Peterson are the wrong people to run the school."

"I'm not saying that."

"They are. They're criminals. They can't see beyond their own bully noses. Kids like me are nothing to them. They have to go."

"They are not criminals," his mother said with a slight chuckle. "They made mistakes."

"Well, listen to this. Finally, an adult admitting to adult mistakes. Aren't we coming along. Thanks to me, of course."

"Look," his father said. "I admit we may not have supported you as much as we should have. But this means getting adults fired. Let's give them a chance, Henry, to see what they can do."

"I have every right to talk to the superintendent. Just one little meeting. Is that too much to ask?"

His father thought a moment.

"Alright, fine," he replied quietly. "Nothing will come of it, but go ahead and make the appointment."

"I'll do it in the morning," his mother said.

"Thank you. I'll be right back."

Henry went upstairs and returned with one of his diaries.

"Read this."

Upstairs, Henry let out a heavy sigh and put his head in his hands, musing over Ruzzo calling the house. Good offensive, he thought.

"But what are you gonna do now?" He yawned deeply and wished he could sleep for a year.

After homework, he lay in bed and thought about a lot of things coming to a head.

"Ruzzo and Peterson hurt themselves by going to the superintendent."

He eased his mind by thinking about Christy, the one bright spot in his life. He closed his eyes and sighed, wanting to think of something nice and good. He thought she might like him and a spike of anxiety hit him thinking about asking her out.

"Well, you got to ask a girl out sometime. May as well be now."

As Henry drifted toward sleep, he imagined being with her. A nice dream, for once. They stood in her bedroom in her vacant house. She smiled coyly. He stepped closer and pushed her hair back, and slowly pressed his lips against hers. She pressed back for the longest time. He pulled away slightly and lifted her sweater up. She raised her arms. Her hair fell around her shoulders as he dropped the sweater to the floor. He kissed her again and moved his hands around her back, expertly unhooked her bra and pulled it away. Her face turned crimson. He put his fingertips on her shoulders and moved them down her luminous skin over her chest to each of her petite breasts. He lifted them and felt her erect nipples and pinched them between his fingers, making her flinch pleasurably. Her lips appeared swollen, desiring something. And he crushed them with a passion he barely understood.

He opened his eyes. His heart trotted along differently than when he was angry or scared. Each beat was strong, not sharp or unpleasant, but softer and fuller, as if showing him this is how it should be.

"You're gonna make it happen."

He rolled over and fell asleep.

Henry hummed through the hall the next day. He attempted normalcy amid the new chaos he had created, ignoring stares and snide remarks and still asked his pointed questions. After one class, Mr. Berry asked him to stay behind.

"Mrs. Hernandez talked to you a while back?" he asked when the classroom emptied.

Henry nodded. "Correct."

"Well, we're still talking about how we can help with the problems around here. Unfortunately, there's a lot of disagreement on what to do. But, we all agree that telling teachers to resign was not very bright."

"Why? It has to happen. They have to go."

"I understand. But now you're making things more complicated. You want those teachers to resign? Then we all have to resign because we were all a part of it. We all saw it happening."

"What, so you all resign or you all don't?"

"Appears that way."

"Well, I just told the worst of them to leave."

"But I was a part of it, too, Henry. And Mrs. Hernandez. At least that's what they'll say."

"Okay."

"So, you see, Henry, it's not all that simple."

"So what happens?"

"I know the teachers are going to be more reluctant to do anything because of what you did. And some even feel the problem isn't that bad."

"Of course they do. I'm meeting with the superintendent with my parents."

"You are?"

"Yes. I'm gonna try to convince him to fire Ruzzo and Peterson. I have a diary of all the assaults on me and other kids going back years, and I could get some kids to write down what happened to them so I can show him at the meeting. I just thought of that. That's a good idea. But it would really be great if you and Mrs. Hernandez could talk to him, too."

"I'll discuss it with her and let you know."

"Seriously, I need you two to do this. I need at least a few teachers to step up and let them know what's going on. That will be huge. Do you have anything, uh, written down about the bullying you've seen?"

"I have passed in several forms. I assume they're logged in somewhere."

"They've probably been deleted."

"I don't think they would do that."

"Can you find out?"

"I suppose."

"I'm tired of doing this alone. You two have given me some confidence."

"Well, I think you've helped a lot of kids here. Don't quit. And," Berry sighed, lifting his briefcase, "hopefully, we can somehow help you. But you're going to need a lot more evidence than that diary of yours, if you want the principal and vice principal gone."

Henry smiled. "You yourself will be more evidence."

"Time for class. Let's go."

Berry's suggestion of evidence made Henry wonder that night.

"Well, what are you going to do? You have your diaries." He lifted his head. "Hmm, wait a minute."

He stomped over to his desk. "I know."

He settled at his computer and worked up a form for kids to fill out recounting any of their own incidents of harassment or assault and addressed it directly to the superintendent.

"You want evidence? I'll give you frickin' evidence. This will back up my diary. Oh, yeah, this is good."

He sifted through the diaries, read over the tales of abuse and chose three from freshman year and the rest from the past several months. Then he had to convince his fellow meeks to do the same.

Okay. Time to schmooz.

He started the next week and sat with a handful of them. Each kid was represented by an assault or two in his diary, and Henry asked them to confirm that each attack had occurred. But no one was willing to help, because, Henry thought, they wanted to forget about it. Henry told them the importance of stepping up and that only admin would see their statements, but he knew they worried about retaliation. Henry remained passively persistent, not pushing them too hard, trying to get them to change a school, a world, that despised them. The problem, Henry realized, was that he despised them, too, as kids who refuse to help.

After several days of talk and convincing them that he had some control over the outcome, Bradley and Freedman agreed to fill out his form. Better than none at all, he thought. Henry left blank forms with the other kids and asked them to fill them out if they changed their minds. He became ambitious and approached more kids for their support. They also refused. But one day a kid who initially wanted nothing to do with it surprised Henry by giving him a filled-out form, saying he had always supported Henry and liked what he had done. That encouraged Henry to go after the others, telling them three had agreed to do it. He finally cajoled two more kids to write their stories. Five statements would not be enough, but they were better than nothing since his appointment with the superintendent had arrived.

He visited Ruzzo.

"Alright, I'm going over to see the superintendent today. Do I get a pass?"

"When you come back you can get one."

"Did you go see him?"

"Yes, we did."

Henry smiled. "What did you tell him?"

"I can't say. But, state your case and see what happens."

"Oh, a lot's going to happen," Henry said with a glare. "Did you two go to Meaghan's funeral? Or her wake?"

"Yes."

"I assumed you would, considering she's one of yours."

"What do you mean?"

"Bullies. A bully killing herself. It's usually one of mine. Cemeteries are full of my people."

"Enough, Wilton."

"Did you go see Carla in the hospital?"

Ruzzo dropped his head silently.

"Just to let you know, a couple of teachers came up to me and told me there's a group of them that agree with what I'm doing and are going to try to help me. Looks like I have allies among you adults after all."

"Who are these teachers?" Ruzzo asked.

"Like I'm gonna tell you. The enemy of us all."

"Suit yourself, Wilton," Ruzzo said tiredly.

"And five kids wrote about being assaulted in this school. I'm going to bring those to the meeting. Evidence."

Ruzzo looked inquiringly at Henry.

"Well, it's time to go, uh, to make my case."

He went outside to await his parents, holding on to a folder containing copies of the statements and one of his diaries.

What the heck are you doing? You're going to the superintendent. What are you going to say to him?

After a minute, he finally noticed the sunny, warm spring afternoon. Some students ambled about; others sat on benches either in a group or alone, mostly engrossed in their phones.

He snickered to himself. *They don't have a clue.*

He heard Christy laugh. She waved to him.

"Hi," she said.

"Hi," he said, venturing over to them. "What's happening?"

"The usual," Christy said.

"Ah, spring is here. Finally," Henry said,

"Yes, it's nice out here," Christy agreed.

Her friend, Mandy, sat next to her, pressing buttons on her phone.

"Why were you standing over there?" Christy asked.

"I'm waiting for my parents. We're going to the superintendent's office."

"Why?"

"Oh, because I need to convince the superintendent to fire Ruzzo and Peterson."

"Wow. Why?"

"Because they're bullies."

"Oh, here we go," Mandy said, not looking up.

"Yeah, right, Mandy. There they are," Henry gestured. "See you in the library later?"

"Okay."

"I'll be back. At least, I hope."

In the superintendent's office, Henry accepted the anxiousness that seeped into his gut as they waited to be called in.

Well, what are you going to do? Stick to the strong points. Stand your ground.

Finally, they were told to go in. Sitting behind his desk with glasses settled half-way down his nose, the gray-haired superintendent looked up as he held some papers.

"Mister Superintendent," Henry said, boldly walking up and extending his hand.

The superintendent pulled his head back slightly, dropped the papers and removed his glasses. Henry kept his hand airborne until the superintendent slowly stood up to shake hands. He was tall, thin and smartly dressed, which, to Henry, made him appear more like a politician than an educator.

"Good meeting you," Henry declared, smiling.

"Good meeting you," the superintendent replied in a forced manner.

Henry then sat right down in front of the desk. His parents also shook hands and took their seats as well.

"So, how can I help you, Henry?" he asked.

Henry began to feel overwhelmed by the situation.

"Well, uh, I want Principal Ruzzo, Vice Principal Peterson, and some of the teachers at my school to resign."

"I see. Can you explain why?" he asked.

Henry cocked his head in confusion.

"I'm sorry, don't you know? Haven't they been keeping you up on the happenings in the school? You've heard of all the kids being expelled, right?"

He nodded. "Of course."

"They let bullying and assaults go on in the school. And a lot of that happened to me. I had to force them to put an end to it. Because of me, the school's better. But they are bullies, too. They can't see the world in any other way." Henry shook his head. "No. No doubt about it. The only way is that they resign or be fired. We can't have adult bullies running schools anymore. Those days are over."

The super's face tightened.

Wow, dude. Keep it goin'.

He leaned forward, resting his arms on the desk.

"I see. Well, uh, Henry, I appreciate you coming here and expressing your concerns about this. There is no one more committed to stopping this kind of behavior than me. However, Mrs. Peterson and Mr. Ruzzo are very experienced, and the fact that they took your comments and feelings seriously and removed those students from the school, I think, shows their commitment to a safe environment for everyone."

"That's not the point," Henry said, raising his voice.

The super sat back.

"Henry," his mother admonished.

"What is the point?" the super asked.

"They wouldn't have done it if I hadn't forced them to."

"I understand what you're saying. But it doesn't appear like they're going to resign."

"Then you will have to remove them." Henry's tone suddenly sharpened. "If you don't, I will assume you support them and what they've done, and that will make you a bully, too."

"That's enough, Henry," his father said.

240

The super looked at Henry's parents in surprise and chuckled.

"Well, Henry, this is very unorthodox. I can't speak to you about terminating anyone."

Henry gave quick, impatient shakes of his head.

"Look, I'm not going to argue about this. I'm trying to keep this private for you. But if nothing happens, I will go public. Police, lawsuits, media, whatever it takes. I'll go out there and I will blast this all over the place."

"Henry, stop," his father demanded. "We didn't come here for you to be on your soapbox."

"Something has to be done and done now," Henry insisted, hotly.

"Alright, alright," the super said, rising. "Obviously, there is more going on here than I'm aware of."

"And why's that? All the abuse going on in that school. In your whole school system? In every school system?"

He glared at the superintendent, who looked back at him with what Henry could see as only helpless confusion.

"Henry," his mother demanded, "apologize to the superintendent now."

"The only one who deserves an apology is me. It's even too late for that. I hope you make the right decision," he said to the superintendent, and handed over his folder. "Here is some information you might find interesting. Letters from kids who were assaulted and one of my diaries. Thank you for seeing me. I'll be waiting at the car."

Outside, Henry leaned against the car with arms folded. *This will get interesting.*

He turned his face to the sun and breathed in deeply, liking what he had done in there—short and sweet, not wanting another lengthy debate. He moved his head around in a circle rhythmically, which relaxed him and made him want to sleep. His neck felt good.

His parents appeared at the car after about twenty minutes.

241

He wanted to know what they had talked about but decided to stay quiet.

"The superintendent is going to talk to the school board," his father said as he drove out of the parking lot. "We may have to meet with them."

"The school board?" Henry shook his head. "Passing the buck on to someone else and someone else after that. Typical adults. Just can't make a decision. It'll be a waste of time."

"Well, that's what might happen," his father said firmly.

Henry lifted his shoulders and kept them in a long shrug. "It will just hold off the inevitable. The evidence against them is clear. But they'll protect each other anyway."

"The superintendent said it's too serious not to meet with the board," his mother added.

"Well, we'll see how that goes."

His father moved in his seat, his face red, agitated.

Henry walked into math class casually.

"Wilton," Davis said, "where have you been?"

"Over the superintendent's office," Henry answered, placing a pass on the desk. "We discussed important matters about this school." He nodded to the blackboard. "Please continue."

Davis stared a moment and went back to the lecture.

Concern? Henry wondered.

Henry clung to the idea of evidence and wanted more of it, canvassing kids from his journal to get more written accounts. He dropped in at a table where some of past victims sat.

"Okay, here are some more forms. This is great, guys. This will help a lot. Imagine Ruzzo and Peterson gone?"

"I'm wondering if that will make a difference," Bradley said.

"Oh, it will, trust me. What about Donny and Joe and Todd gone? Does that help?"

"Yes," Freedman said flatly.

Henry smiled. "They were on you all the time. More evidence, guys, will help me out. Help us out."

Gray passed the table. "What's going on, guys?" he said, stopping behind Freedman.

"What's this?" Jose asked, picking up one of the blank forms.

"None of your business, that's what," Henry tried to grab it, but Jose pulled it away.

"Give it back."

"Relax, Wilty," Gray said, squeezing Freedman's shoulders. Freedman's face twitched, and Henry saw that Freedman could not stop him.

"Get your hands off him," Henry said.

Gray darted a menacing glare at Henry, who stood up.

"Now!"

Gray lifted his hands. "Hey, okay, Wilty. Don't get your skirt all tangled."

"Put it down," he said. Jose complied. "Now get outta here."

"What's the problem here?" asked Miss Petrovsky.

"They're harassing us. Gray's putting his hands all over him and he's picking up things that don't belong to him. Tell them to get away from us."

"Okay, Wilton. Keep your voice down," she said.

"We just came over to say hi and Wilton loses it again," Gray said. "I've had enough of this guy." He and Jose walked away grinning to each other.

"Please tell them not to bother us again."

"Okay, I will," she said.

Petrovsky walked over to Gray's table and said a few words to them.

Henry and his friends watched her.

"Did...did she actually go over there and do it?" Henry asked, surprised.

"Appears like it," Bradley said. "She's got guts."

Henry watched her. "Interesting."

"She's new, trying to show she's tough," Freedman said.

"We'll see how long that lasts," Bradley added.

Henry managed to get six more statements by the school board meeting at the end of the month. As a joke, he brought a form to Trevor and asked him to write down the times he had bullied kids, telling him he would take it to the school board. Trevor crumpled it up.

The night of the school board meeting arrived. Henry told his parents he would meet them there after going to the library to work on another report. His father said no to that, but Henry insisted, since he was already downtown.

He rode the bus to the library to seek out a bit of peace and quiet. After looking over some books for his history paper without taking notes, he closed his eyes to calm his increasing anxiety as the time neared. He eventually nodded off.

"Excuse me," someone said in a whisper.

Henry sat up.

"There's no sleeping," the library employee said.

Henry cleared his throat. "Sorry."

He rubbed his eyes and sighed deeply. He peered up at the clock. The time for the meeting neared. He jogged down the street and up the steps of an imposingly gray building. The wide lobby was empty except for two security officers standing and talking in their white-shirted uniforms.

He puffed out anxiousness as he opened a large wooden door. He entered a rectangle of a room, much wider than deep, with a high ceiling laced with girders and pipes all painted white. The board members, four women and three men, including the superintendent, sat along an arcing dais of polished wood decorated by light blue panels all along its front. A few spoke to each other while others looked down at something they were reading or checked their phones. Muted voices murmured among the sparse audience.

Ruzzo and Peterson sat at a separate table to the right, in front of the rows of seats. Two people, a man and a woman, sat nearby in the front row next to them—spouses, Henry surmised. Mr. and Mrs. Roach, Davis, Johnson and Bronner sat together to his right, as if in unity. Henry chuckled at that. But Berry and Hernandez were not there.

He smirked. "Of course."

Stay calm. You got this. You're the boss, not them.

"Alright, this meeting will come to order," said the woman whose nameplate marked her as the chair of the board.

Everyone quieted.

"We are here to discuss an issue concerning a tenth-grade student and his request for the removal of teachers and administrators from the school," she began. "Because this concerns a student and because of the particular nature of this business, we will be in executive session."

She turned a page.

"Is the student and his parents here tonight?" she asked of the audience.

Henry's father raised his hand and stood up.

"I'm John Wilton. This is my wife, Elaine. My son has not arrived yet."

"Yes, he has," Henry said aloud, waving his hand.

The board members stared out at him, and people in the seats turned and looked.

Henry smiled at everyone as he paraded down the middle aisle. He grinned wide and waved to the teachers.

"Please have a seat," the chairwoman said. "Let's proceed. Mr. Superintendent will speak."

The superintendent adjusted a microphone in front of him.

"Thank you," he said. He quickly cleared his throat. "We have here rather an unusual situation. This student has demanded that the principal and vice-principal and even some of the teachers resign as of the final day of the school year. He has also threatened to expose them publicly as enablers of abusive behavior in the school, according to Principal Ruzzo and Vice Principal Peterson. But both say his contentious and uncooperative behavior in school has led to an atmosphere of tension and insecurity."

Henry rolled his eyes. He had sat down in the front row a few seats from his frowning mother, to whom he gave a wide smile.

"Abusive behavior?" asked one board member.

"This student believes Mr. Ruzzo and Mrs. Peterson have allowed bullying to occur in the school."

"And have they?" the same board member asked.

"They have assured me that they have not. I've known them for years, as some of you have. They have never displayed anything but the best in their conduct and treatment of students, and in encouraging civility and respect among them."

Henry laughed out loud. Everyone looked at him.

"Quiet," his father said, while his mother gave him a stern glare.

"Sorry," Henry said to the chairwoman.

"Needless to say," the super continued, "we wanted to bring this to your attention and see what we can do about it. Apparently, there will be comments made on both sides of this issue."

The chairwoman lifted some pages and perused them.

"I have your report here and have read through it and, um, I do find all this very concerning as well. We discussed it before this meeting. According to the report, there have been previous verbal threats by this student against Mr. Ruzzo, Mrs. Peterson and certain teachers, such as telling them he will quote 'destroy their reputations and careers'." Henry smiled. "The student's behavior has worried, even frightened, teachers and students. He has been designated a habitually disruptive student by the school and has shown no willingness to correct his behavior. And, of course, in these days of school tragedies, we do not in any way condone such behavior because we just don't know what any student is capable of doing. On the other hand, the student has made accusations that administrators and teachers enabled, even allowed, abusive incidents to occur unchecked at the school for years. So, we agree, as a board, that this issue should be addressed and resolved, especially considering the student will continue into the eleventh grade."

The chairwoman, who sat with elbows out, presenting slightly wide shoulders and long brown hair, moved some papers aside. Other board members sat quietly, a few with glasses perched on their noses as they peered down in front of them, a few others leaning on their elbows and looking around.

"Well, this report basically explains the school's position on this issue. So now, why don't we hear from the student? If there is anything you'd like to say? Please sit up there and speak into the microphone."

Henry gazed around the audience, who stared back at him as if challenging him to "explain" himself. That lit a spark of fear in his chest, but it also angered him.

Alright, screw these people. Go slow and easy.

He sat down at a table. He dropped his head back and thought a moment as everyone waited.

"You know, I'm not going to go into a long, drawn-out discussion about this. I've already done that enough with the principal and vice-principal, teachers, kids. I'm done with that. All my life, I've always been a kid who sits quietly and minds his own business. I never made fun of other kids. I never hurt anyone. But I've been hurt. A lot. And, this year, I just wanted all this bad stuff to stop. And I don't see why it can't. But these teachers and the principal have done nothing to help with that. A lot of kids like me, you know, we don't fight back and we're easy to pick on. So, finally, I decided to step up and...and stop it. That's something unusual in my school, standing up and protesting being bullied, which I have every right to do. Then, of course, they make me the problem." He pointed at Peterson and Ruzzo. "They've got that school working their way. The strong kids can do and say whatever they want and the weak kids have to quietly take it. That is exactly Principal Ruzzo's philosophy of life. But when I decided I didn't like that anymore, and started to do something about it, I'm the bad kid, the disruptive student, the HDS. How dare I? Ha. Yeah, there's no choice now. They are the bullies, allowing bullies to do what they want. I changed all that. I forced them to stop the abuse." He threw his arms out. "And here we are. But, see, once I graduate and leave, everything will go right back to the way it was if they stay in that school. I can't have that. So, I'm asking that they be, well, fired and replaced by people who can make the school safe for everyone." He picked up his folder. "And I have something for you. May I approach the bench?" he said jokingly.

He stepped up and handed the folder to the chairwoman.

"Inside there, you will see a diary of the many, uh, altercations and assaults that have happened to me and other kids going back to the seventh grade. I have the original diary. The principal and vice-principal and the superintendent have one copy, too, which they still have. There are statements from many kids about the assaults on them, some that will back up what I wrote in my journal. On the first page, you can see the names of teachers that I want permanently removed from the school. There are also the names of two teachers that came forward to let me know they support me. I was hoping they would be here tonight. Please contact them. You also see the names of kids who've been expelled. I assume you've heard about that?"

The chairwoman frowned. "Of course," she said as she examined the paper and diary. "Let me ask you a few questions, Henry. Do you honestly think they are all bullies?"

"Of course."

She looked over at Ruzzo and Peterson, into the audience, then back to Henry.

"Well, we don't know if bullying is actually occurring here," she said. "That's what we have to determine. They are basically accusing you of bullying them."

Henry smiled. "Of course. That's what they do. Turn it into our fault."

"What do you mean 'our'?" one board member asked.

"Kids bullied like me. Just glance through the notebook. Start at the end for the assaults that just happened and what I had to do to protect myself."

The chairwoman took a moment and read a few pages. She looked up at Henry.

"Why would you keep such a journal?" she asked as she passed it to the next member.

Henry leaned forward. "By the eighth grade, I had a feeling that all the, uh, advice you adults told weaklings like me to deal with bullies didn't work. And I was right. But I also realized that I wouldn't be believed if I wanted to report it. Writing it down helped me deal with it."

"Why didn't you report these incidents?" one member asked.

"I did a few times, in junior high. But it didn't do much good. So I kept quiet. Mostly," he sighed aloud, "just too scared to. We're taught to keep our mouths shut or we'll get attacked for narcing. Only a small number of kids ever tell on their bullies. So, I continued to be a victim, all the way to today. I'm the one who got those kids expelled. If I hadn't forced those two to do it," he said, gesturing to Peterson and Ruzzo, "those kids would still be in that school doing what they do best. I've made that school better and safer because of it. Now I'm wondering if you'll victimize me, too."

"Why would we do that?" one member asked.

"I guess that depends on what you decide. Read it." He pointed to the diary being read by a board member. He pushed his forefinger again out toward Ruzzo and Peterson. "They see my behavior as a threat to the status quo, the bully world that I ended. And they can't handle it. And they refused to treat me fairly. I'm wondering if you'll do better."

"That's what we aim to do," the chairwoman said quickly, as though trying to end the conversation. "Thank you for coming in, Henry, and talking about this. We appreciate it. If you could step out now so that we and your parents can discuss the matter."

Henry's eyes widened. "Why do I have to step out?"

"We have to determine what we should do."

Henry gave a quick shake of his head. "Ha, no, let me clarify here. I've already told you what you're going to do. There is no discussion here. They will be removed."

"Henry, that's enough," his father said.

Another board member darted forward.

"But you have presented us with legal and employment issues. There will have to be a lot of discussion before any action takes place."

"Really? What action took place to help me and other kids who were being abused?" He pointed at him. "In your school."

He sat back as he stared at Henry, then he glanced at the board member next to him.

"We understand, Henry," the chairwoman replied. "But doing what you ask doesn't happen overnight. There's a lot to be determined."

"Well, I guess you're right. The abuse that happened to me happened over many years."

"But, we have to be fair," added another board member. "They have brought charges against you and you them. Now this board has to determine who's right. If you're right, we will take action."

"Oh, really? And how do I know you'll do that?"

"Henry," his father called out, standing up, "leave the room."

Henry ignored him.

"We also have to determine your state of mind in order to decide whether you can continue in our schools without being a threat," another board member suggested.

"How am I the threat when I'm the one who's always threatened? Every day in a school overseen by those two monsters."

"We don't allow name-calling here," the chairwoman said.

"You all went through school," Henry began. "You know what happens. You know when kids get assaulted, they don't say a word because of retaliation. And as long as no one complains, you adults take full advantage of it and let yourselves believe the great lie that nothing's wrong. So we suffer in silence while you go back into your cozy little offices because you're really busy with all your important work on your desks. These people over here, the principal, vice-principal and those teachers, they saw what went down every day and ignored it, as long as no one complained. Well, I've complained, and, hey, look where we are?"

"Do you honestly believe all that?" a board member asked. "That they know about this behavior and deliberately allow it to happen?"

"Exactly. In every school, everywhere, looks like since forever. There's something about this bullying thing that makes you adults run in the other direction. But now I scare you all. Because I'm breaking down that perfect little set-up you've had since, like, forever. They are criminals, aiding and abetting bullying and assaults in your school. So, I have every right to take action, one way or another. And I will if you don't do exactly what I need you to do."

His father stood up. "Henry, go outside now and leave the rest to us."

He turned back to the board, raising his voice. "The only threat I am is against the bully status quo of this whole stinking world. And then, when I suddenly do the threatening, I'm considered unbalanced while the bullies who've been abusing for years," Henry shrugged, "they're just normal kids joking around, and poor little Henry just can't take it. What's wrong with that picture?" His shout echoed and silenced the room.

Henry seethed. "You wonder…you question if bullying is going on in this school. Why haven't you ever asked? None of you ever did. Why? Because nobody complained. Well, I guess I'm the whistleblower. And now I'm on trial."

"You're not on trial here, Henry," the chairwoman said.

Henry stepped away from the microphone and stood in the middle of the room, moving his hand along the back of his neck. He raised his voice. "You know, you're right. I'm not. You know who is? You. All of you. What you do here is on trial. The future of this school system is on trial. How we treat each other is on trial."

The board stared back, as though processing it all, which Henry enjoyed. He was pleasantly surprised that he felt good. He accepted displaying his rage. In full control.

Alright. Keep it going. You're doing well.

"How many kids have killed themselves, or tried to, because of this? I know someone who tried, with a rope, and someone who tried and succeeded. Ironically, she was a bully. Or maybe you didn't hear about that?"

The chairwoman sighed. "Of course we did," she said softly. "We are all saddened by it."

"Are you. Do you know why Carla put a rope around her neck?"

No one answered.

"I didn't think so. Call her mother and she will talk to you. More evidence against them," he said, poking his thumb out.

The board members glanced at Ruzzo and Peterson.

"This is about you, Henry," one board member said, "and how we can help you."

"You will help me, and yourselves, by meeting those demands."

The chair shook her head. "I can't guarantee that."

"And I can't guarantee I won't blast to the world what has happened here. When I go out there and tell this city what you've done."

"We don't think you should do that, Henry," the chairwoman said.

"Why not? You haven't done anything wrong, have you?"

Henry settled himself.

"After what you all did to me? I will turn this town into ground zero for bullying. I will go on a public campaign that

252

will never, ever end. By the time I'm done, people will be moving out of this town instead of moving in."

"You would do that to your hometown?" one board member asked.

"Sure. What has my hometown done for me? Look at me. *Look* at me! What do you see?" He glanced around the room. "You adults. You're the ones who walked away. You avoided this. You ignored this. You were supposed to protect us. We *trusted* you. We had *faith* in you. And you betrayed us, and threw us to the wolves every day." He sneered at them. "Now, you will do exactly what we tell you." He swung his body around. "All of you. We will no longer ignore you. We will not avoid you." He threw his fist into the air. "We will confront you. We will retaliate. We will do to you what you do to us. We will no longer go over here, up there, around here, down there, to cower around some corner, while you bullies go straight down the hallway, down the sidewalk as easy as you please, laughing it up and enjoying life and we hide until it's safe to come out. Heck, last year even our own governor said he had to go a half-mile out of his way to avoid bullies. Those days are *over*."

His voice resounded around the room until it faded, leaving a disturbing silence. Henry remained stock still, his exhilaration pulsing in his body. His father stood still with his arms folded, slightly shaking his head.

"So welcome to my world."

"You don't have to raise your voice," the chairwoman said. "All these issues you bring up will be addressed quite seriously. This board owes it to you and everyone to conduct a fair investigation."

"And what makes me think you adults won't protect each other and nothing will change? After what I've been through in their school, how can I trust you?"

The room went silent. Henry continued in a softer voice.

"Enough," he said, breathing out steadily. "You see my terms there. Principal Ruzzo and Vice Principal Peterson and those teachers will be removed from the school. They are a danger to all kids who go there. If you decide not to remove them, you will agree to a full police investigation of the assaults at the school that will be made public. You see the names of some kids who were expelled. I thought about them. They will be allowed to come back to school only after six months of psychiatric therapy, the kind everyone wanted me to get. I figure they're just kids who were never told to stop. Maybe they can be saved. Maybe not. And my final term is an official apology from the board to me and all the kids on those statements and in my diary for the horrible way we've been treated." He shrugged. "That's it. Simple."

A moment of silence passed.

"We will take all this into consideration," the chairwoman said tiredly. "Is there anything else?"

"If you do not follow my instructions," Henry lifted his phone, "I will go public."

"We're not afraid of that," said a board member.

"You should be. You won't like what I'll say." He raised his hands. "Hey, all I ever wanted in my whole life was peace. To be left alone. To get along. But they didn't. This isn't my fault we're here. It's theirs, and yours, because you should have known."

Henry glared at the board.

"And I'm the HDS?" Henry laughed. "Fine with me. It's an honor."

He walked up the center aisle, stopping at the top.

"Do the right thing. And I'll expect your decision by the next board meeting." He gazed around at everyone and smiled. "Thank you for your time. Have a good night."

He pushed open the door and raised his eyebrows. *Wow. Good job.*

"Excuse me." A young woman walked up to him. "You just came out of that meeting. Are you the student they're talking about?"

"What?"

"Something about school bullying?"

"Who wants to know?"

"I'm a reporter for the Daily Sun."

She handed Henry her card.

Henry looked over at the doors he just walked through.

"It's a closed meeting."

"I'm aware. But if you ever want to talk about it, you can reach me there."

He looked at her card and then at her.

"Maybe I will."

Henry saw her eyes twitch at his tone and then he walked out of the building.

He stopped at the top of the steps, drew in a deep inhale of the warm evening air and turned back to the room he came out of, wishing he was a fly on the wall to hear what they were saying. What would they do? he wondered. What could they do? He knew it didn't matter. He had told them everything one last time, and that is all.

Henry decided to walk to the bus stop. He looked around as he strolled along the wide sidewalk, enjoying the city noises and the lights and an early warm night. He buoyantly passed bus stops, enjoying himself, until he got tired and finally sat down to await a bus with a handful of other disparate persons. As he peered around at people and cars passing by, he believed he had the city in the palm of his hand. He could destroy it at any time. Tell the world about the bullies and what they had done to him.

When he got home, he passed his parents in the den watching TV. They didn't call for him. He didn't want to talk to them either, so he went upstairs. He brushed his teeth, got into bed, turned off the light, and stared solemnly into darkness.

The next night at dinner, he finally heard what happened after he left the meeting. His mother said he had made quite an impression. The board members questioned Ruzzo and Peterson about Henry's accusations and said they would also talk with all the teachers.

His father brusquely criticized his son's behavior, but Henry noticed a diminished conviction in his voice, which sounded more tired than usual. His mother said she now understood a little better what he was going through. Henry shook his head. *Really? You mean, as if what I've told you the past year didn't clue you in?*

For the last few weeks of school, Henry let life settle into a regular routine of study by night and classes by day. There was nothing more to do. He eased through the halls, humming away, not looking for enemies, even though he felt impelled to by mental habit. He stared hard at the blackboard, trying to understand, questioning the teachers, arguing and cajoling, as other students now did. He found it strange being taught by the same teachers he had just told to resign, even though many kids had made a joke of it—just crazy Wilton acting up again was Henry's take on that. He shrugged it off. He knew their careers would be over soon. They already were, as far as he was concerned.

He even allowed an occasional smile. The anxiety and fear of assault faded, but not when it came to exams. There was something about that terrible challenge he still could not grasp. He had come to realize the problem ran too deep, that it was something more than just the exams that he couldn't quite understand. But he continued his yoga-style meditation anyway—closing eyes, breathing quietly. This total relaxation routine at test time hadn't changed his grade average yet, but he liked it a lot better. So he turned his steadfast mind to doing the hated work in front of him, trying to figure it all out.

"C'mon. Gotta get this right," was his mantra during those last days.

Finals week arrived, and just thinking about them raised his usual tension. Out in the halls, he had gone from agony to ecstasy, but, in class, not so much. He had dug deep for weeks in search of the answer to improve test scores, so he sat slumped on his bed Sunday night before the first exam.

He looked down at the cat, curled up sleeping.

"I guess I'm never going to be bright and brilliant, cat. Not for me. But, I'm…I'm worn out. I feel like I'm eighty years old." He nodded. "I'm like you now," he said, lying down next to his pet, running his fingers across her fur. "You don't care about anything, so why should I? I guess in the end, you are what you are. I'll be you. Be the cat."

So Henry continued his I-don't-care strategy. In front of the first test, he lounged in his chair, rested his face in his hand and yawned as though it meant nothing. In the end, he felt he didn't do that well on each exam, but at least he had kept his sanity. He just needed that one test to prove his smarts. It didn't come. Yet, his newly relaxed approach gave him some odd confidence, and he believed he was on the right path.

Trust yourself. You have to trust yourself. When you listen to yourself, you're happy. When you listen to anyone else, not so much. And that's too bad.

Striding down the hallway on the last day of school, he weaved through the throng of animated kids he knew he had saved from villains. He peeked into the Office. Ruzzo was filling his briefcase.

Go on.

"Well, good luck to you."

Ruzzo chuckled. "I'll see you in September, Wilton."

"I don't think so. My case was a bit strong."

"Not that strong."

"Brought down by a meek. That must really bug you. You do see the irony."

Ruzzo shook his head. His calm and assured manner aggravated Henry.

"I had to become someone I'm not because of you."

"That was your choice."

"I had no choice," Henry answered. "But, good always beats evil in the end."

Ruzzo chuckled. "The only evil is in your mind."

"So long, David."

Henry left and saw Peterson upstairs talking to Mrs. Roach. He didn't want to bother with either one and went to his last class with Mr. Johnson.

"What's the matter, Henry?" Sharonda asked. "You're all red again."

"You gonna pass out?" George said.

"No. Just more arguing with Ruzzo."

"Thought that was over," Kam asked.

"It is now. Thank God."

"Any word from the school board?" Chloe asked.

"Probably a couple of weeks."

"What's going to happen if they don't see things your way?" Kam asked.

"Everything will happen. You'll see this all over the news and I'll be on camera."

"You sure 'bout this?"

"It's the only way, Sharonda."

After class ended, Henry smiled broadly at Johnson, who stood stiffly at his desk.

"Well, goodbye, Mr. Johnson. Good luck to you."

"Not going anywhere, Wilton," Johnson said.

"Don't think so. You'll be looking for another job."

Johnson glared. "That's enough."

"We'll soon find out."

Henry gave Johnson a victorious smile.

Well, even if they aren't gone, I definitely got them worried.

Caleb passed Henry in the hallway. He noticed Caleb glancing at him, but he stared straight ahead as he made one last trip to his locker.

"Hey, it's the bully boy," Trevor called out.

Trevor stood around with Jose and Pam.

Henry smiled. "Yeah? I'm the boy and you're the bully."

"He's the meek," Pam said.

Henry's face flushed. Pam's bold remark showed him that the Vultures were still flying.

"I'd rather be a meek than a bully."

"I'd rather be a bully than a meek," Jose replied.

Henry expected a lot of laughter, but that didn't happen. Just an uncomfortable silence.

Jose stared frowning at Henry.

"Bully boy here has saved us all. Thank the Lord for you, Wilton."

"That's right. You should be thankful."

Henry pulled everything out of his locker and, instead of slamming the locker door as he had so often done, he gave it a respectable push. He glanced down the emptying hallway—for ages the stage of assault and humiliation. He wondered if even he would return. But he felt satisfied that he had accomplished what no teacher, principal or vice-principal had ever done—he made the hallways safe for everyone.

As he headed for the stairs, Wyatt and Christy walked his way. They walked close together, more than just friends, confirming to Henry what he feared.

Henry hid his disappointment. He thought Christy was better than that. He never thought she would stoop so low as to date the high school quarterback.

"Well, hi, you two," Henry said, smiling. They stopped. Christy slipped her hand through Wyatt's arm.

"Have a good summer."

Wyatt smirked. "Yeah, you too, Wilton."

"So, stay in shape, bro," Henry said. "Big season coming up. You, ah, want to take good care of that arm. Yeah. The fate of the school is riding on it. You definitely don't want anything to happen to it. You know, like do the wrong thing, say the wrong thing. So, be careful." Henry gave Wyatt a glare of warning. "Be very careful."

He held Wyatt's gaze a moment as he placed his hand on the quarterback's muscular shoulder, gave it a little squeeze and left them standing there as he bounced down the stairs and out into the summer sunshine.

"Guess tutoring's over," he snickered.

Henry wasn't surprised. *Girls love the power.*

259

He boarded one of the waiting buses, peering around at the usual kids he bused with and nodding to them. Arriving at home, he walked into a quiet house, ate some crackers and then slowly climbed the stairs to his room. His pack dropped with a thud and he fell prostrate onto the bed, one eye staring out the window at the bright green leaves fluttering in the breeze.

The cat jumped onto the bed, silently walked up to Henry's somber face and nuzzled it a moment. Then she sat down and began licking her paws.

Henry eventually looked at her and considered his pet a while.

"You know, you're the only one I really like to talk to."

He then closed his eyes and slept.

The next morning, Henry threw the sheet off and sat on the edge of the bed, rubbing his face. He had slept deeply. Morning light filtered through the curtains. He went to the bathroom, got dressed, and then made breakfast.

After chores, he filled his pack with food, water, something to read, jumped on his bike and rode to the reservoir outside the city. He pedaled along a hiking trail, the sun lighting up the domed ceiling of green leaves, nobody around. He stopped the bike and listened to the quiet, closing his eyes, breathing in the mossy scent and exhaling with great ease.

"Yes, this is good."

He noticed two deer amid the trees, watching him. They lowered their noses to nuzzle the ground and pulled their heads up to eye him again. He smiled because he well understood their wariness, having been one of them for so long. A few minutes later, he arrived at his favorite sitting spot that gave a wide view of the calm blue expanse in front of him. He lay down with ease and allowed himself to doze and to calm his young body ravaged for years by fear and anxiety. He simply decided never to think about those two things again. What's done is done, and justice had prevailed. He felt alive and well taking in the beauty around him.

"Ahh, now this is the way life should be. No worry. Not afraid of anything. Not pissed off all the time." He stretched like his cat. "Free at last. Ha. Maybe I can become a middling, too. Nah. You can't be useless."

Then he allowed himself to doze off for a while.

"Hello, Wilty."

Henry awoke. Jeremy, Donny and Todd stood in front of him.

"What…what the hell are you doing here?"

"We followed you, moron," Todd said.

"You thought you were getting away with it?" Donny said. "C'mon. Let's throw him over."

They ran at him. Henry jumped to escape, but they grabbed him too tightly and dragged him to the cliff edge.

"Hey." Henry fought and kicked. He couldn't stop being thrown over the cliff and dashed on the rocks below.

"Bye, Wilty."

Henry flew into air, and the rocks came up fast. He bolted up.

"Enough. Will you stop? For God's sake." He sighed. "Knock off the stupid dreams. It's over. Alright? You're done with it."

He looked around, but he was alone, with just a slight breeze. He lay back down and tried to visualize himself drifting out on the open water.

Over the next month, Henry kept busy, happy and at ease, taking advantage of his last summer with no job. He walked the house humming nonsensical tunes, saying Mamma Mia and Bro to his father and other crazy names to his parents. His mother smiled at him, but eventually his father told him to stop.

The next school board meeting arrived and Henry heard nothing, which didn't surprise him. However, he heard from his parents about some squabbling going on among the board members and with Ruzzo and Peterson, each of whom had to meet privately with the board to discuss the issues. Henry smiled, picturing Ruzzo and Peterson being harassed and aggravated, likely worried, and their kids must know by now what was going on. But, they were still principal and vice-principal and the others were still teachers, and Henry wanted everything decided now.

That left Henry the decision whether to call the reporter who had approached him after the board meeting. He imagined sitting down with her in his living room and recounting the horrors of his school life. Then he had the idea of going to the school board's website to find the chairwoman's public e-mail. He found it and sent her a message expressing his disappointment and what he now had to do.

In about twenty minutes, the chairwoman responded, apologizing for the lack of a resolution to the problem, but they were working toward it and needed more time. She asked Henry not to publicize anything, especially naming names that could lead to legal issues. That would only aggravate a situation the board was attempting to negotiate. Give us more time, she concluded, so that an equitable conclusion could be reached.

Henry typed back that he understood her position but that he had to stick to his plan or no one would respect his words or promises; that he'd be more than happy to sacrifice his family for the cause; and he couldn't fully trust her to get Peterson, Ruzzo and the teachers removed. He needed to set an example for everyone who enables bullying in their schools. He added that he would hold off going public with his complaints, though, if those people were removed within the week.

The chairwoman again stated she would work hard to have an answer soon.

"I will call the reporter at the end of the week," Henry responded.

He smirked. *Typical. They want mercy. Did I get any? Be tough. Never forget.*

That evening, his father confronted him at dinner about going public.

"Henry, the chairwoman of the school board called me. She said you're going to contact some newspaper reporter? I don't want you doing that. Give the school board some time. They'll have an answer soon."

"Just putting pressure on them," he replied.

"If you start calling out names in public, that could cause us problems."

"Relax," Henry said. "They're not going to do anything because it's all true and they know it."

"You don't know what you're talking about," his father barked.

Henry smiled and continued eating.

"Henry," his mother beseeched one more time, "don't do anything yet."

Her tone didn't work with him anymore.

"Everything will be fine. Nothing's gonna happen to us. Why don't we talk about things that matter? Like, look at me. I'm smiling. I feel good. Don't you see how happy I am?" He pushed up both corners of his mouth with his fingers. "See? I'm enjoying this stupid life for once. I was afraid and I'm not afraid anymore. I feel like my life is going somewhere. Going in the right direction. But have you noticed? No."

"I don't think your life is going in the right direction," his father replied. "Look what you're doing?"

"Just like I said. You don't notice, so your opinion doesn't matter. When I listen to myself about what I should do, I'm happier. When I listen to all of you, I'm not. Simple."

His father sighed and placed his elbow on the table and his face in his hand. His mother looked down at her plate.

"You don't care. You never have. You've never asked me once, not once, if I'm happy or what I like or what I want. You had to see how miserable I was. And if you didn't, that's worse. It took the school board meeting for you to understand anything about my life. All you care about is what *you* want." He narrowed his eyes. "You know what

263

I've noticed, though? When I was miserable, everyone was happy. Everyone walking around enjoying life, and I wasn't. But now that I'm happy, everyone's miserable. Ha." He smiled broadly at his silent parents. "Well, too bad. Get used to it." He finished his meal unpleasantly. "I have two more years in this place. Right after I graduate, I'm packing up and getting out and never coming back."

"What's that going to accomplish?" his mother asked.

"I don't know. But getting out of this town will be the first step in the right direction."

His mother picked at her food.

"You'll find, Henry, that people are the same everywhere."

"I guess I'll see." He rose from the table and gave a slight bow. "Very good dinner as usual, Mother. Good night."

He cleaned off his plate, put it in the dishwasher, and went upstairs.

I hate this house.

Within a few days, he hadn't heard from the chairwoman. He decided to e-mail again. She responded that a resolution was possible soon so hold off doing anything that could compromise their work. He didn't reply and waited each day out rather nervously.

Henry spent his days actually studying. With just two years left for him to lift his grades to get into a decent college, he had to do anything he could to make that happen. So he gathered all his tests and analyzed them and gritted his teeth at his mindless mistakes.

He shook his head. *How can I beat something I don't even know I'm doing? God, this whole thing's crazy. How did I get like this?*

He decided to take several math and science tests online, to practice, to do anything.

With silence from the school board, Henry lost confidence. Sitting on his bed cross-legged, he breathed rhythmically and closed his eyes, angry that the depression

264

he thought was gone for good hung over him like a hulking demon.

He rocked himself back and forth. *It's been over a month. What're you going to do?*

"Let it go, buddy. Let it go."

Henry and his parents heard nothing from the chairwoman. Impatient, angry, Henry e-mailed her that he would give her until nine o'clock for a solution or he would call the reporter. Still no response.

"Alright, you made your choice," he said out loud. He looked at the reporter's card but hesitated, thinking over such a big step. He punched in her number

A little past nine, his mother called for him. He told her he'd be right down. He turned to the door. Curiosity pulled him downstairs.

"Yes?"

"We just got a call from the chairwoman of the school board," his mother said.

Henry looked at his father. "And?"

"Principal Ruzzo and Vice-Principal Peterson have agreed to resign."

Henry's eyes became fixed as he stood speechless. Then he slowly nodded.

"Good," he said softly, like someone who found something hard to believe. "Finally did the right thing."

"Maybe, maybe not," his father said. "But it's done. You got what you wanted."

"You don't look very happy."

"I don't really know what to think."

"What about the teachers?"

"She said it would be difficult to remove them," his father said with a sigh. "It may not happen. The two teachers who supported you did speak to the board, and one of them ended up resigning, too. You'll have to be satisfied with what you got."

"Well, I'll take care of the others."

"No, you won't. Enough is enough, Henry."

"Whatever. Hopefully, everyone learns a lesson."

"And what would that be?" his mother asked.

He dropped his head. "Forget it. It's done."

In his room, he sat down at his desk with his phone in front of him, wondering if he should call the reporter anyway. They should have known, he thought. Instead, they sat in their comfortable little seats, never asking, never wondering. Until he came. He circled his finger slowly over the smooth surface of the call button. Just one push would do it. It would be so simple, and fitting.

"Well, they did what you wanted, so forget it."

Then he sat back in joyous realization. He raised his eyes to the ceiling and chuckled and reveled in his victory. The ivory towers had collapsed into a mushroom cloud of dust and debris, and, as the air cleared, he stood victorious on the gleaming shore, staring out over the endless sea. He shot his arms up.

"I did it! Ha, ha. I did it! They're gone." He punched the air. "Yes. Yes. Yes."

He breathed in and out deeply, luxuriously. He dropped his arms onto his head and rocked himself side to side in complete relaxation. He still found it hard to believe.

Finally, he shut off his computer, jumped on his bed, picked up his phone and played some games.

Henry believed his victory to be complete. Life was good. But that burning sensation in his mind still irritated him, and he could not understand what it was. He had ignored it for weeks, able to tolerate it with everything else going on. But now, he was alone with it.

What is this thing?

He held his head in his hands, as though trying to squeeze it out. "It's not going away," he said. "Leave it. You're happy. It will go away now that you're happy. There's nothing to worry about now. That's good. Good."

He brightened a moment. *Don't let it take you down.*

"Stop being stupid. You can beat this. You can beat anything now."

As the summer went on, he had his bad days and his good ones. He knew to keep active, running at the park, yard work, sitting at the reservoir, hiking, practice tests, which he felt were beginning to help. He looked at September without the dread of past years.

He came in sweaty from mowing the lawn, grabbed some water and checked his phone. He had a text from Kam, happy that he was remembered by someone, even though he hadn't sent one himself.

"Oh, shit."

Caleb's dead. He shot himself.
No one knows why.

Henry stared at it. He could not take his eyes off it. He pressed his fingers against his forehead. "No." Then he shouted, "For Christ sake!" He threw his phone across the counter.

He knew he couldn't suppress the shock this time. He went out to the porch and sat down. He could not think or feel or even cry and stayed that way for a long time. He placed his forehead in the palm of his hand.

"Damn it, Caleb. What the hell."

Eventually, he went upstairs and lay down.

Over the next week, melancholy took Henry over. He had a nagging guilt. He shook his body to rid the awful sensation pulling him in and down. His mother and father were just as saddened about Caleb and kept after Henry to talk about it. Henry told them that he hadn't spoken much to Caleb in the last few months of school, hadn't seen him since, and didn't know if anything was particularly wrong. He felt good that he could separate himself from it.

"C'mon. It's not your fault."

He had dinner but didn't feel any better. As he played his games, he kept thinking about Caleb and his family. His head felt heavier in the morning. Later, he received a text from George, telling him that Caleb left behind three of Henry's forms filled out, recounting assaults and abuse, and that his parents would bring them to the school board. Henry shook his head and sighed.

He got himself some breakfast and finished his mother's chore of painting the backyard shed. He kept busy, in desperation to keep away the depression that hovered like a dark cloud, the same one following him all his life. He well knew he couldn't be rid of it as tears rolled down his cheeks and each brush stroke delayed the inevitable. He stayed out of his bedroom, afraid to lie down.

"For God's sake." He slammed the brush into the grass. "Get away from me," he shouted. "Leave me alone. I'm happy now. Nothing's gonna stop that."

Sharonda texted:

> Missed you at the funeral.
> A lot of kids and teachers were there.
> His father was pretty strong but
> his mother and sister were a wreck.

Henry didn't get out of bed the next morning. He watched the sun's slits and rectangles move across the room all day until they vanished. He rubbed his wet eyes as the weight of depression pressed down on his brain.

Nor did he get up the next morning. His mother knocked on the door before she went off to work. He mumbled that he was fine just to appease her. He lay numbly, staring, letting his eyes close to fall asleep, then waking up and staring at nothing. He felt nothing, too listless even to think.

His breathing weakened as if he had no energy for it. By late afternoon, he hadn't eaten anything and only had a few gulps of water when he went to the bathroom. His mother came into the house, and after a minute, knocked on Henry's door.

"Henry," she said, "have you been up today?"

He mustered enough strength to answer. "Yes."

"Well, dinner will be ready soon."

"I'm not hungry."

She tried the doorknob. "Henry, unlock the door."

"I'm sleeping."

"What is wrong?"

"Nothing."

"Doesn't seem like it."

Henry said nothing more. His mother finally gave up and went downstairs. After his father gave him the same routine, Henry finally relented. He pulled himself out of bed, got dressed, and walked downstairs with heavy footfalls. Sitting down at the table, he picked up his fork and stared down at the food.

"Henry, you're in a letdown from the school year and Caleb dying," his father ventured. "It's understandable. It will be difficult, but you'll get through it."

"It's so horrible what Caleb did," his mother said, grasping Henry's hand. "The best thing for you to do is keep yourself busy."

His mouth hung open. He peered half-way up.

"I'm not hungry," he murmured and got up.

"Don't leave the table," his father said. "Sit and eat."

"I can't."

Henry trudged upstairs and locked the door. He lay down and pulled the sheet up to his chin. Staring into the oncoming darkness, he wondered how long he could go without food.

The next morning, his father knocked hard and fast on his door and tried the doorknob."Henry, get up."

"I'm fine." Even though his stomach felt differently.

"I left a list of things for you to do on the table. Get out of bed and you'll feel better."

His father stood there a moment. Downstairs, he said something to Henry's mother and left the house.

His mother beseeched him as well, and Henry gave her the same answers. Throughout the day, sadness turned to hopelessness, pushing Henry into the mattress. He didn't fight it. No longer any point to that, he believed. His fighting was done. But after a while, with his back aching, he decided to do something. He played some games on his phone, only to quickly lose interest and lay back down.

He portrayed a better demeanor to his parents to get them off his back the next day. He would do a few things around the house while they were at work, then slump in a chair and stare at the carpet, without a thought, feeling completely spent. He carried on like that for several days until one morning, he woke up and felt fine. The morning appeared brighter to him and his head felt lighter and clearer. He sat up on the edge of the bed as though he had come out of a long illness overnight.

He had a new energy and used it to complete some chores and then run down to the park. He glided around the track, boosted by a stronger stamina after almost two months of running. His heart pumped hard and fast, and he felt good and strong. He wiped sweat off his brow and onto his cheeks as he galloped down the lane, envisioning a big crowd in the stands cheering him on. He started thinking about what he had done over the past year. His vengeful smile returned as he reveled in his glorious victory. Ruzzo and Peterson gone—out of work, out of school forever. That put more speed into his legs.

Let 'em suffer. Feel the pain. Anyone else want to be a bully? You deal with me. You deal with me.

And there would be more, he knew. There had to be— just look at the world. He enjoyed the thought of putting teachers on warning. He would watch them every minute, just waiting to take them down.

I will get you all.

Henry now ran his hardest as gleeful rage filled his veins, fueling his limbs. *Now you're happy.* His eyes widened and his heart thumped as his lips pressed hard against a world he loathed; a world that left him open to a destruction he barely survived. Now, he must live with the shame of those years of weakness and take everyone on to prove the strength he always had, and would keep going and going to prove himself over and over until everyone is…

He suddenly pulled off the track and came to a stop, gasping for air, bent over. He fell to his knees, sweat dripping onto the football grass.

"I can't…" he whispered. "I can't do this anymore"

He clenched the grass.

"This…isn't the way…it's supposed to be."

He rolled onto his back and stared up into the blueness, his chest heaving. The searing sun beat down on him.

"It should be gone. After all I did."

His rage was not gone, and he realized that was the thing burning in his mind. It was firmly in control, still powerful, along with an unquenchable thirst for vengeance.

"You shouldn't feel this way. You're happy now." His eyes flitted about, frightened. "I'm happy!" he shouted, trying to convince himself and the empty stands around him.

He grabbed his head and pressed, as if trying again to squeeze out the pain. "It won't go away."

Henry tapped his head with his fists, trying to grasp the reality of who he really was. He lay still. "I hate…I hate everything."

If defeating the enemy would not make him happier, he wondered, then what would? He knew he had done the right thing, so what was the problem?

He groaned slightly, pressed his fingers to his forehead and closed his eyes hard in psychic pain. His breathing slowed, and he glanced around fretfully with a sense of doom. He tried desperately to understand, but couldn't.

"That was your way out. That's what kept you alive."

For a long time Henry stared into the empty bluenesss, thoughtless, feeling nothing. He finally sat up, drooping forward as if he had little energy left. He rubbed sweat down his face as a cool breeze rushed around him. He lifted his face to the sky and laughed. "Wow. All you did was put off the inevitable. You were going to die all along."

He slowly stood up and looked around him.

"Well, Caleb, I wish things were different. But, I'll be joining you soon. Because I'm not gonna live like this anymore."

He left the track and, as if he had a burden on his back, made his way across the field to the corner opening in the fence for the long walk home.

When he got there, he showered so he would be found clean. Downstairs, he filled a glass of water and sat on the porch for a long time. He dropped his head back and closed his eyes, inhaling the humid summer warmth and the lush greenery he had always loved in his backyard. He remembered how much fun he had there when younger, at one time the center gathering place for all the neighborhood kids. A lot of fun for a while. But as they all grew older, a few moved away, others split off into other groups and some just got inexplicably mean. From there, Henry became more isolated.

He stood up, glanced around the backyard, and said goodbye to it.

"I guess we still lose, Caleb. I wish you could have felt the power. It was good."

As he stepped into the kitchen, he felt rage beating against the walls of his brain, slavering to get out. There was only one way to end it. He opened the cabinet doors under the sink and pulled out a white trash bag. He cut the bag in half and stuffed the rest of it into the wastebasket. He went down to the basement for rope.

Upstairs in the bathroom, he pulled a bottle of pills out of the cabinet, took his water and then sat down on his bed, placing the glass on his night table. He opened the bottle, dropped a pill into his hand, stared at it, then pushed it into his mouth and took water. He instantly coughed. Then he swallowed another, then another.

His head dropped, and the anguish of another young life lost welled up inside. He tapped his palm against his forehead and sobbed.

Do it. Do it. You want peace.

He stared at the pills in his hand as if he were dreaming it — He swallowed three more at once. He coughed a few times, and kept pushing them down his throat, each pill a nail in his future coffin, lying in his church, the reverend sermonizing, and lowered into a cold rectangle in the ground.

He had thought about death all his life and now it was real. He still had a chance, he knew, to save himself: Cause himself to vomit, call his parents, get himself to the hospital. But he just sat and stared. What could save him now, anyway? he thought. What was left? A person he detested? A hater? A destroyer?

"No. No way. Not a chance."

Henry raised his chin with the pride of strength enough to break his bondage, but not enough to overcome his disdain for the world and everyone in it.

"This was always going to happen. You never had a chance." He chuckled to himself.

He lay back on the bed for quite a while, not thinking, then sniffling a few sobs, just waiting. His parents would discover him there, just as many parents had done before them—finding their child lying in a pool of blood, lost in permanent slumber, or hanging lifeless in a closet. But he believed he had the right to choose. He had earned that right.

Minutes passed like hours and the pills began their work. A queasy pain slowly grew in his stomach and sleep slithered in like a deadly snake.

There's still time. You can reverse it. You can.

But he let it go. His eyes closed and he had no fear. Tears rolled out from the corners of his eyes, and he experienced the deepest relaxation of his life.

So this is how it feels.

The cat jumped up beside him and licked a tear. His eyelids weighed heavier now. He took the bag and placed it over his head and pulled it down to his shoulders, wound the rope around his neck and pulled it tight. He settled back onto the pillow, the crinkling of the bag loud in his ears, and viewed nothing but warped white plastic as he breathed in the last of the oxygen. He placed his hand on the cat's warm fur and held his eyelids open.

"I was the good kid."

His eyelids dropped. A few minutes later, he became unconscious, and, after that, he lay still, not a breath. The plastic was tight to his skin, a white death mask, a concave shape in his opened mouth as if gasping for one last breath. Finally, the peace that death brings. And there was no coming back. That's the thing about death. There is *no— coming—back.*

But he couldn't do it. He had played it out in his mind and glanced at the pillow where his plastic-covered head should be. As tears filled the rims of his eyes, he chucked the bottle across the room. It smacked against the wall, with the pills flying across the carpet. He grabbed the plastic bag, crumpled it up and threw it into the air.

He wanted that peace, that rest. He wanted it always but now realized it would never come.

"What am I going to do now? What?" He began to sob. "You damn people." He jumped up. "*Look at me!*" He coughed from gagging anguish and fell to his knees. "Look what you've done."

He knew all the shouting he could muster would not change the fact that he didn't have the guts.

"Why can't I do this?"

He fell into relentless sobbing on the floor. Caught between life and death, he rocked himself back and forth. His fingers curled.

"I'm so angry I can't stand it. I want to tear myself apart but I can't. I want to die but I can't. How…how can they let this happen to me? They don't even know what they've done."

He struggled to breathe.

"I can't take this. I can't fight anymore. I'm just too tired."

He sat hunched in his cowardice. Still the coward. But not Carla or Meaghan or Caleb.

He understood now the pain that pushed them and thousands of other kids to do it. Their own anguish so intense that ending life became easy. He visualized Carla tightening the rope and kicking away the chair, feeling her neck stretch and her breathing cut off. And Meaghan, pulling the tip of a blade up her soft young skin and watching the thin red line bulge with warm blood, streaming down her hand to her fingertips and onto the floor—likely watching the puddle grow larger as life slowly drained from her. And Caleb pulling the trigger. Did he just pick up the gun and do it or did he sit and agonize over it? Henry admired the courage of all those who made the awful choice. The courage he did not have.

He rolled onto his back and closed his eyes, hoping for a death that would never come. The three pills he did take began their work and he slipped into sleep.

He awoke and raised himself up slowly, stiffened by an awkward position. He had slumbered so deeply, he had to take a moment to recognize where he was. He yawned gapingly, rubbed his eyes and looked around him. He lifted himself onto the bed next to his pet that looked up at him carelessly. The day appeared different but pleasant—quiet and breathless. Hours had passed. But the same problem within persisted—his precarious balance between life and death.

"Well, now what?" he asked in tired words. "Can't live. Can't die." Through the window, the green leaves hung still against a deep blue sky. He smirked at the outside world. "You don't want me to come out there. You know what I'll do and you're not ready for it. You never will be."

He dropped his forehead on his arms.

"They don't care about you. They never will."

A breeze crept into the room, pushing the curtains out a bit. Warm and inviting, it enveloped Henry's defeated body. The breeze slowly grew until it became a wind. The two curtains billowed out. Henry raised his head and wondered at its strangeness, because the leaves outside barely moved. The curtains flapped out toward Henry, as if beckoning him. He got some feeling about it and he reached out and took one and held it. He looked out the window. The wind slowly abated until it was gone.

The fabric between his fingers felt soft yet resilient and it seemed to him something welcoming, which lifted him up with a strength he needed desperately. He walked to the window and turned his back to it, to the world. He laid the curtain across his body and glanced around his sunlit room. He struggled to understand why he could not die by his own hand—maybe it was his pride, being defeated, defeating himself. Was there some moral fortitude that stopped him, he wondered, or just too afraid of death to go there? He didn't know why exactly, but the will to stay alive over-powered death. Maybe just too much left to do in life to end it? Other kids had made another choice. They left themselves no chance to get things right. And there will be many more missed chances to come, as the epidemic of teenage suicide persists.

"Alright, c'mon. Look how far you've come. All you've done. Maybe…maybe you can find a way."

Henry finally let himself feel the pride of his new-found strength, rejecting the meek victimization bred in him by his bully captors. He decided he would no longer play the savior, for there never was one anyway. All he could do was save himself. He had achieved retribution and it exhausted him. He had his fill of it for now and wanted to rest. As he peered around his room, he was as relaxed as he could be, although tinged with a clinging sadness. He wanted to be rid of that someday, and wondered if what he had done over the past many months started him on that path, and toward a very uncertain future. More battles? Of course. He accepted that he was only at the beginning, and that he would fight the rest of his life against the demons that surrounded him, and those that grew within. Rising from the depths, he accepted the new person he had become—bolder, harder, one with the courage he always had to confront those who victimized him and who nearly crushed him with his own youthful innocence. Henry had to live in a world he could never love, so he had to make a decision as he stood there. The time had come to think differently, relate in new ways, and that will take a new attitude, and a long time—months, even years. He wondered how he could do that, if he could do that, to be rid of the sickness in his soul and live in a world that betrayed him, to accept and forgive the abuse and make peace with it, with them. There are bad people in the world and there always will be. It was the understanding of those people and his relationships with them that had to drive the change in his attitude, and to define that future. But, to have any peace at all, that change couldn't come only from him. It had to come from everyone, everywhere. And he thought about all of this, as he turned to look out into the world where he must go.

Printed in the USA
CPSIA information can be obtained
at www.ICGtesting.com
LVHW010847250923
759135LV00032B/1015/J

9 781638 680215